THE PALE SHADOW OF SCIENCE
…AND THE LURID GLARE OF THE COMET

Brian Aldiss, OBE, is a fiction and science fiction writer, poet, playwright, critic, memoirist and artist. He was born in Norfolk in 1925. After leaving the army, Aldiss worked as a bookseller, which provided the setting for his first book, *The Brightfount Diaries* (1955). His first published science fiction work was the story 'Criminal Record', which appeared in *Science Fantasy* in 1954. Since then he has written nearly 100 books and over 300 short stories, many of which are being reissued as part of The Brian Aldiss Collection.

Several of Aldiss's books have been adapted for the cinema; his story 'Supertoys Last All Summer Long' was adapted and released as the film *AI* in 2001. Besides his own writing, Brian has edited numerous anthologies of science fiction and fantasy stories, as well as the magazine *SF Horizons*.

Aldiss is a vice-president of the International H. G. Wells Society and in 2000 was given the Damon Knight Memorial Grand Master Award by the Science Fiction Writers of America. Aldiss was awarded the OBE for services to literature in 2005.

Other essays from The Brian Aldiss Collection:

This World and Nearer Ones
The Detached Retina

BRIAN ALDISS

The Pale Shadow of Science

... And the Lurid Glare of the Comet

The Friday Project
An imprint of HarperCollinsPublishers
77–85 Fulham Palace Road,
Hammersmith, London W6 8JB

www.harpercollins.co.uk

This paperback edition 2013
1

The Pale Shadow of Science first published in Great Britain by
Serconia Press, 1985
... And the Lurid Glare of the Comet first published in Great Britain
by Serconia Press, 1986

Copyright © Brian Aldiss 1985

Brian Aldiss asserts the moral right to
be identified as the author of this work

A catalogue record for this book is
available from the British Library

ISBN: 978-0-00-748232-0

CONTENTS

Contents

THE PALE SHADOW OF SCIENCE

Introductory Note

This book preserves a few of the many articles and reviews I have written over the last few years. My passport describes me as 'Writer and Critic,' because a fair proportion of my writing has always been non-fiction. Non-fiction has a role to play in an author's life. It is to fiction what target practice is to a soldier: it keeps his eye in in preparation for the real thing.

For the record, these are the various places where the pieces originally appeared.

'Preparation for What?' in *The Fiction Magazine*, 1983; 'Long Cut to Burma' (as 'Drawn Towards Burma') in *The Fiction Magazine*, 1982, here revised; 'Old Bessie' first told at a Halloween party in Chris Priest's house in Harrow, October 1984.

'Science Fiction's Mother Figure' (as 'Mary Wollstonecraft Shelley') in *Science Fiction Writers*, edited by E.F. Bleiler, Simon & Schuster, 1981; 'The Immanent Will Returns' (as 'Olaf Stapledon') in the *Times Literary Supplement*, 1983; 'The Downward Journey' in *Extrapolation*, 1984; 'A Whole New Can of Worms' originated in a speech delivered at the City Lit on 9 January 1982, later published in *Foundation*, 1982; 'Peep' formed the Introduction to James Blish's *Quincunx of Time*, published by Avon Books, 1983; 'A Transatlantic Harrison, Yippee!' was printed in the programme book for Novacon 12, held in Birmingham, England in 1982.

'The Atheist's Tragedy Revisited' is a new piece. 'The Pale Shadow of Science' was delivered as a talk to the British Association for the Advancement of Science during their annual meeting at Norwich, 11 September 1984, and an abridged edition was published in *The Guardian* newspaper, 13 September 1984; 'A Monster for All Seasons' in *Science Fiction Dialogues*, edited by Gary Wolfe, Academy Press, 1982; 'Helliconia: How and Why' has not yet been published anywhere.

My thanks go to the committee of Norwescon 8, to all my friends attending that illustrious event, and in particular to Jerry Kaufman, Donald G. Keller, and Serconia Press.

4

This volume is divided into three sections, autobiographical, followed by articles on individual writers, and articles on more general aspects of science fiction.

This section is the most fun. Here are a few of the experiences which went to shape me as a writer. An American audience will surely find them very strange, especially when they come to the piece about the haunted house in which my family once lived.

These pieces have been published here and there in England. They are an approach towards an autobiography which I intend one day to write ... once I have set a few more pressing novels down on paper.

Preparation for What?

There should have been a law against the preparatory school I went to. Later, there was a law, and places like St Paul's Court no longer exist. In the thirties, there must have been many of them dotting the country, little plague spots of pretention and ignorance.

I was sent there at the age of eight.

'Be brave,' my mother said. It was easier to be brave the first term than succeeding terms, when one knew what one was in for.

At the best of times, St Paul's managed twenty pupils, twelve of whom were boarders. It was the headmaster's resolve to turn us into gentlemen: that much was clearly stated in the brochure. Of course we all turned into scoundrels. The parents were mainly tradesmen in a modest way of business who wanted their sons to grow up to despise them.

My father was irked to discover, after a year or two, that he was the only parent who was paying the full fees demanded in the brochure. I kept this revelation secret, knowing that the boys – whose sense could not be entirely beaten out of them – would despise him if they found out.

St Paul's was a large brick building which stood out starkly against the flat Norfolk coastline. Beach and sea lay just outside the back gate. The house was surrounded with sharp shingle, as if it had been caught by a high tide. To one side lay a large games field. In one corner of this field, behind a line of old apple trees, boarders were allowed to keep little gardens. One thing at least I learned to love at St Paul's: gardening. It was almost a necessity.

The food was abominable. Meat was delivered in a van by Roy's of Wroxham. To us little exiles, the van was a messenger from a happier world, for Wroxham was where one went to get boats to sail on the Broads. But the headmaster ordered the cheapest cuts, and our opinion of Roy's became low as a result.

Most of the cooking was done by the headmaster himself. His name was Mr Fangby. He was a smoothly porcine man with a thin nose and thinning hair swept and stuck back over a domelike head. I never really disliked him for much of the time, though it is hard to say why. His wife looked after their child and, when meals were over, Mr Fangby could be seen doing the washing-up and dolorously drying the dishes on an old baby's napkin.

Breakfast was the worst meal. The rule at St Paul's was that plates had to be cleared. It was that rule, rather than the cooking, which made it possible to claim that the food was edible. The porridge was an impossible paste. One other boy and I often remained after the others had gone, getting the paste down spoonful by spoonful, with occasional bolts to the lavatory to vomit.

I took some tiny sweets back with me the next term. By concealing one in my mouth before we filed into the dining room, I used its flavour to camouflage the taste of the porridge. This ruse worked well for some weeks. But our enemy, the bootboy, who helped Fangby with breakfast, detected the sweet; I was in trouble, and my tuck was confiscated.

We were always hungry. Fangby was a lazy man, and the worst news of all was when he felt too lazy to take lessons. Then he would enter the dining room at breakfast time, all smiles, and announce a day's holiday for good work. The news spelt starvation and boredom.

Out in the field we had to go. We were not allowed back into

7

the house all day. Sometimes it would be eight o'clock or even later before either Fangby or his only master, Noland, came to tell us to get inside quietly and go to our dormitory.

During those long days, we would be visited twice, either by the hated bootboy or by Mrs Fangby. At lunch time, they would bring out a big toffee tin containing meat and lettuce sandwiches. At tea time, they would bring a tray with mugs of tea and perhaps buns. That was our day's food. The meat in the sandwiches was inedible.

We cultivated our gardens, although we had never heard of Voltaire's advice. It was possible in spring to take our pocket-money to a small shop just down the road from the school. Since the Victorian Age lingered in Norfolk until World War II, the shop was run by a lady in black called Miss Abigail. From Miss Abigail, penny packets of Carter's seeds could be bought.

We tilled our strips and sowed them before the spring holidays. When we returned for the summer term, there among the weeds would be thin lines of lettuce, carrot, radish, and spring onion. These lines we tended with care. They were our food. We used them to eke out the meagre rations provided. And we ate, or at least bit into, the green apples on the trees.

The unripe apples provided useful ammunition, along with stones, in our wars against the local lads. The local lads hated us, and made the life of the dozen prisoners of St Paul's as hazardous as they could. They would creep along the footpath which ran behind the field, to launch a stone barrage as we pottered about our garden strips. We fought back. We aimed to kill. When one of us was hit, we hushed it up and made excuses for any visible gashes.

Sunday was the day when the local lads triumphed, when our humiliation was greatest. For the fool Fangby, impelled to destruction by some folk-myth of decent schools which he had never seen, made his boarders dress in Sunday best. This meant black pinstripe trousers, black jackets, ties, and Eton collars. Eton collars are wide and stiff, permitting the wearer about as much freedom and comfort as an ox gets from a yoke. In this loathed outfit, and with the addition of straw boaters, the twelve of us were made to march in crocodile five miles to Mundesley Church for the morning service.

What a raree-show for the local lads. In their hobnails, cords, collarless shirts and braces, they would turn up to laugh and trip or kick us as we passed. It was a relief to arrive at the church.

Our hero for a few weeks was Legge. As we were passing the village pond, he managed to skim his boater into the middle of the duckweed. To get it out, we broke ranks and all became desirably muddied almost to the knee. In that state, we became less of a free advertisement for Mr Fangby's menagerie.

I liked church. I had fallen in love with the local policeman's daughter. We smiled at each other across the intervening pews. In her smile was forgiveness for the whole world of Eton collars.

In that church, gazing at the beautiful stained glass windows, I experienced the first of my eternal moments. Everyone was singing, and the policeman's daughter was at the outer end of the pew on the opposite side of the aisle, so that we could exchange looks. Carried away by everything, I was filled with an oceanic feeling of happiness. 'I will remember this moment all my life,' I said to myself. And I have.

The picture of that moment returns easily. I can see the organ, the timbered roof, the choir, the stained glass. The view is an elevated one. The eternal part of me which took the snapshot was floating about twenty feet above my head.

The vicar's name was Winterton. He had two sons, who came to St Paul's at reduced rates. They were badly bullied at first. We chased them round and round the field and eventually buried them head first in a huge pile of grass clippings. Next term, they returned with avenging fury. Their father had been talking to them. Both were small. But they set upon us with sticks and terrified us. From then on, they drove us round the field at whim.

While the garden was one consolation, the library was another.

Library was the name of the bookshelves behind the door of our classroom – it was more than a classroom, being the room in which we were trapped when we were not in the dormitory or exiled to the field. The misery of being back in that room for another term was stifled by being able to pick out *The Captives of the Sea* (or was it *The Prisoners of the Sea*?) and commence a re-reading. The story was sub-Dumas. I read it at the start of every term I was at St Paul's.

Learning to be a gentleman is not something I recommend unless one has a natural bent for it. It included standing in an embarrassed line and singing such catches as 'My Dame Hath a Lame Tame Crane' and soppy songs like 'The Ash Grove,' 'Fare Thee Well for I Must Leave Thee,' 'The Golden Vanity,' 'Cherry Ripe,' and 'The Keel Row,' the words of which we copied into exercise books.

The gentlemanly arts also included football and cricket. Football was all right. Cricket was less satisfactory. With a maximum of twenty players, we could at best play with no more than ten a side. Despite which our parents had to provide us with full cricketing gear – white ducks and shirts, sweaters, caps, cricket boots. The worst ordeal of all was when Fangby decided that a St Paul's team should play a local lads' eleven.

To make it an event, lemonade was provided before play and between innings. We had to take the glasses round to the local lads. How they leered! Our ages ranged from seven to eleven or twelve, theirs from twelve to seventeen. They towered above us. They wore any old dress. The lad from the garage came in his overalls.

The match was a complete disaster. We sneered because they did not take up proper batting positions, whereas we, in our turn at the wicket, came up properly and asked for 'Middle-and-leg.' They batted first, and knocked us all round the field. But we had two good bowlers in Tom and Roger. Since the local lads were carelessly confident, they were vulnerable, and we got them all out for seventy-nine.

After a further round of humiliating lemonades, we went in to bat. The local lads closed in round us like a wall, smirking. The garage lad in his overalls took the bowling and was devastatingly violent. Nothing, of course, compared with the publican's son who bowled from the other end. They made mincemeat of us. We were all out, wounded, for nine. But at least we were properly dressed.

One form of sport I took as an Extra. That Extra got me away from the school grounds once a week. It was generous of my father to pay for the Extra. Perhaps he felt for me in that captivity. At all events, every Monday I was allowed to walk unescorted down the road to a gentleman called Mr Field, who taught me riding.

Mr Field was a cheerful red-faced man. I liked him better than his horses. Nevertheless, as the lessons progressed, even the horses became less stupid. Then we would trot down Archibald Road on the spectacular beach which curved all the way round to Happisburgh and beyond, with never a soul on it. There we would gallop along in the foam, with the sun dazzling and the wind roaring in the ears. On, on, with a world uncluttered – indeed, about to dissolve into speed and light.

Unfortunately, the riding lessons did not last many terms. They stopped and no reasons were given. Maybe it was something I said.

One voluntary sport we endured was swimming. We learnt in geography lessons about the vernal equinox; it was, in Mr Fangby's mind, the day on which swimming in the North Sea commenced. The North Sea throughout most of its career is a grey untrustworthy mass of chilled fluid, in which such alien entities as seaweed, shrimps, and jelly fish somehow contrive to make a living. It is not the natural element for boys of tender age – unless, of course, they are destined to become gentlemen.

On good days, the waves of the North Sea at Bacton, as they cast themselves in desperation on the shore, are not particularly large. But to a child of eight, not long accustomed to thinking of himself as a being apart from his teddy-bear, they are enormous. As you approach them, together with a dozen other blue-limbed disconsolates, they appear to open their mouths, display their sandy throats, and prepare to devour you.

If we did not enter this man-devouring medium with an affectation of eagerness, we were pushed or thrown in. This was not a job for Mr Fangby – whose porpoise-like form had an unporpoise-like aversion to water – but for the assistant master, Mr Noland. The logic of the operation was simple: one swam to avoid a watery grave. Those who pretended to drown were punished.

Despite the regime of starvation and ordeal-by-ocean, I do not recall anyone being ill at St Paul's. There was none of this namby-pamby Jane Eyre stuff of dying of consumption. That would have been frowned upon.

Winters were harder to get through than summers. The greatest deprivation was loss of toys. Bullying and fighting remained as recreation, but I developed alternatives of my own.

One was the making of mazes. Throughout my three years' incarceration at St Paul's, my mazes became bigger and more elaborate. To be caught in one of them was to wander for hours in a tedium of bafflement. Yet they were popular, possibly because that tedium, volunteered upon, was preferable to the larger tedium which contained us.

I also made books. These were mainly notebooks with shiny red covers, bought from Miss Abigail for three-ha'pence. I stuck pictures in them, or wrote stories about enormous square machines which took people to the Moon, to their profit. A treasured microscope was permitted at school, since it was 'scientific'; happy hours were spent poring down its tube, sketching things twitching in a drop of pond water or wild-life moving on someone's hair. These sketches went into books.

A rival to the popularity of the microscope by day was the kaleidoscope by night. I smuggled a small pocket kaleidoscope back to St Paul's, and a torch. Homesickness was worst at night. It could be conquered by snuggling down into the bed and shining the torch up the kaleidoscope. Hours were spent over long winter nights, watching the tumbling patterns of colour. The pattern never repeated, one's eye never wearied.

We also traded cigarette cards. More esoteric were the adhesive pictures to be collected from penny bars of Nestlé's milk chocolate. These were divided into various categories, such as birds (a bit boring), machines (good), famous explorers (okay, especially Mungo Park, because of his funny name), and prehistoric monsters (best of all). Another point of interest was that Nestlé's – presumably in the cause of a rapidly disintegrating world peace – printed the text in English and Esperanto.

Several of us were interested in the idea of Esperanto. Latin was boring, because dead, but Esperanto was of the present, an invented language. For a penny, one could buy a special Nestlé's album in which to stick the pictures. There was more Esperanto. We set ourselves to learn it. Progress was rapid on some fronts, since the Esperanto for Brontosaurus is Brontosauro.

A child's world in the thirties was not knee-deep in dinosaurs, as is the world of the enviable child today. How can any child be miserable when Hanna-Barbera throws the beasts at you in full animation almost every week-day and twice on Sundays? Time was when you had to hunt to turn up a dinosaur in black-and-white. I slowly acquired works of reference. Particularly valued was *A Treasury of Knowledge*, which my father had from the *Daily Mail* by clipping out coupons.

I began to feel I knew something. It was an illusion, but a strong one, and during my later days at St Paul's I gave lectures on Prehistoric Monsters for one penny per attendee. Nobody ever stumped up, as far as I remember, but at least the charge stood as a kind of guarantee of everyone's seriousness. My pupils took notes and had to draw a diplodocus every week (side view only – nobody had seen a diplodocus from the front in those days, not even Nestlé's).

Dramatic distractions were few. The best was when brave Tom, our head boy, decided he had had enough of the insufferable bootboy. One dull Saturday afternoon, when we were kicking our heels in the classroom, the bootboy was invited up, and Tom told him to fight if he was not a coward. It was done in the best traditions of English boys' school stories. Tom and the bootboy took off their jackets, rolled up their sleeves, brandished their fists, and set to.

It was a desperate conflict. The bootboy was much bigger and thicker than Tom. But Tom had made up his mind. They slammed at each other furiously. The fight carried through to the landing, and then to the narrow, winding stair. With a final flurry of blows, Tom knocked the bootboy down the last few steps. He fell backwards to the floor, his mouth bloodied, and lay looking up at us. Tom flung his jacket down at him. He grabbed it and slunk away.

The weeks of our incarceration passed, Hitler grew bolder. Echoes of that larger world reached our backwater. We had a German-Jewish boy whom we called Killy-Kranky. He was lively and comic and popular because he taught us German swear-words and insults. 'Du bist eine alte Kamel!' was, we were assured, a terribly rude thing to say. We treasured the knowledge; I at least have never forgotten it, my first sentence in German.

Poor Killy-Kranky! His parents disappeared. He had to stay on at school in the holidays. One day in the summer holiday, my father drove our family past St Paul's. There, in a corner of the immense field, stood Killy-Kranky, gazing out across the wire fence at liberty.

'Look, there's Killy-Kranky!' I exclaimed. 'Can I go and speak to him, Dad?'

'What do you want to say to him?' my father asked, contemptuously. Of course it was one of those adult questions which cannot be answered. We sped on our way.

After the beginning of one summer term, an Italian drove up St Paul's shingle-strewn drive in a big car. He was tall, bronzed, elegant, well dressed. He came with Mr Fangby to speak to us in the classroom. We stuttered or were silent. He spoke excellent

English and smelt of perfume. With him was his little son, aged five. The son was going to stay with us while his father went back to Italy, to resolve a few problems.

I still remember seeing that man embrace his son in the drive, squatting on his heels to do so. He gave him a child's paper – probably *Chatterbox* – and kissed him fondly. Then he drove away.

We were so cruel to that boy. He wore a little blouse, with braces under it. This was cause for endless amusement. We teased him about it, about everything. We ran away with his *Chatterbox*, which he tried always to keep clutched to him, a symbol of his father. We excelled in being unpleasant. We made his life a misery. We made his every day a torment.

Why did we do it? Our triumph over the child was the most awful thing about St Paul's. Years later, as an adult, I was wracked with guilt about our treatment of that Italian-Jewish child whose name eludes me. Why had we no compassion? Was it because we recognized in his father a civility superior to ours? Was it the barbarity of the Anglo-Saxon way of life? Or was it something more basic, more cruel, in human behaviour?

The child's only refuge was Legge, the other outcast among us. Legge's popularity after the duckpond incident had not lasted. Tom had fought and beaten him, too. Unlike the bootboy, Legge could not escape, except to the upper branches of the apple trees. There he took the Italian boy, hauling him up like a gorilla with young. There they sat. Waiting for end of term and a release from misery.

Next term, the Italian boy did not reappear. My remorse did not develop till some years later, when I started to comprehend the world from an adult viewpoint. Compassion springs from a position of some security.

The assistant master, Mr Noland, was sacked. He went out and got drunk one night. Next morning, he refused to leave his bed. Fangby sent Tom to Noland's room to command him to come down. The answer was a rude one. So Noland left at the end of the week. There were those who hung out of the window and cried openly as he drove off in his backfiring blue car. Those who had almost drowned at his hands experienced a certain relief.

It is easy to believe now that St Paul's was more unbearable for adults – perhaps even for Fangby – than for its principal victims, the boys. Perhaps the rule applies to all prisons.

To cheer us up, Fangby took us out. He drove us over to Wroxham, where the bad meat came from, where there was a cinema. I still remember the excitement of being out that night, of speed, of seeing the willows flash by and vanish forever from the blaze of the headlights.

We went to see a film version of *Lorna Doone*, the boring novel of which we had read. The film was better. John Ridd fought Carver Doone, and Carver Doone fell back into an Exmoor bog and sank slowly down, down into the bog. It compelled our imaginations for a long while.

Legge was caught in his own personal bog. He did something which Fangby found unforgiveable. What it could have been still escapes conjecture. Was he caught smoking? I do not remember that any of us had cigarettes in a world where even ice cream was forbidden. Was he caught masturbating, or even in bed with another boy? With the Italian boy? It seems unlikely. We knew nothing about sex. We were still at an age when we were uninterested in our own or other penises. When Roger returned at the beginning of one term to say he had been in bed with his sister and she had told him that cocks went into the wee-wee hole and produced children, we were shocked by such coarseness, and gave him six with his own cricket bat.

Whatever it was Legge had done, he was treated like an absolute pariah. He was removed to a bare room in the attics and his clothes were taken away. The rest of us moved in silence and fear.

Then he was brought down among us to the classroom. Fangby announced that his crime was so great that it could not be mentioned. It meant that he was to be beaten and expelled. A similar fate would befall us if we did the same thing.

Legge was deathly white. He was told to drop his pyjama trousers and bend down. Fangby then proceeded to thrash him with a cricket stump. He laid on twelve strokes, putting all his porpoise-like strength behind them. One of our number fainted, another ran out crying and was dragged back, another was sick all over the floor and was made to mop it up later. Then Legge was helped away. We never saw him again.

Before that incident, I had not minded Fangby. There was at times a sort of cringing friendliness about the man, as if he might be afraid of us, or at least had some sympathy for our predicament. Now we all hated him. He had utterly estranged himself from us.

It was clear that to become gentlemen we had to undergo the same sort of treatment as Dr Moreau dished out to the Beast People on his celebrated Island. Fear and force make gentlemen. It is the Law.

Long Cut to Burma

War shapes individuals and nations like no other experience. As my boyhood slipped away, Europe, with a terrifying inevitability, sank toward Hitler's war. When I was thirteen, we started digging air raid shelters at school. But at the age of eighteen, I was drawn into the war against Japan, and despatched to the East: to India, the great whirlpool that sucked men into action in Burma.

Things get out of control in wartime and, in 1944, I found myself spending sixteen days on an Indian train. A detachment of eleven of us entrained at Mhow station. We crammed into a compartment with a little bone notice above the door: TO SEAT EIGHT INDIANS.

We were loaded down with kit and rations. We crammed in somehow, in the best of spirits as troops always are when on the move. Mhow station, beset by monkeys and banyan trees, smelt powerfully of cooking, frangipani, animal droppings, and hot steam engines. Soon the station fell back into the night.

We pulled the windows down to enjoy the warm breeze. We rolled our sleeves down. We applied acidic anti-mosquito cream to face and hands. All night we sat among our kitbags and rifles, talking and joking. In charge of us was a genial Yorkshireman, Ted Monks – fresh from England like the rest of us. He was a foreman bricklayer in Civvy Street.

Indian towns came flashing out of the night like Catherine wheels. A nostril full of pungency, a glimpse of eyeballs human and animal, and we would be tearing through, on, on, with the challenge of Burma somewhere at the end of the line. By dawn we fell asleep over our kitbags, huddled against one another or dozing on the luggage racks.

The Mhow quartermaster had issued us with rations for what was intended to be merely a five-day journey. No air transport in those days, you note. By the time we emptied a tin full of stale hard tack, we had a useful pail. In this pail – whenever the train stopped for inscrutable reasons of its own – we collected hot water from the engine with which to brew ourselves tea.

India was endless. The railway lines were endless. Sometimes the train pulled into a siding, where we waited in heat and silence for an hour or two for an express to thunder by.

Days passed. We ran out of food and money. The great lands, the bringers of famine and plenty, rolled past. Flat, achingly flat, always inhabited. Out on the glazed plains, frail carts moved, figures laboured. Always the bent back. No matter what befell elsewhere, those figures – men and women – were committed to their labours without remission. While I stared out of the window, talk in the compartment was of home, always of home, the work and fun, the buggers at the factory, the knee-tremblers after dark behind the pub, the years of unemployment and disillusion in the Welsh mines. All this was news to me at eighteen, and had almost the same impact as the landscape. I felt so ashamed of my middle-class background that never once in all my army years did I mention that I had been to public school.

Our detachment was at the mercy of the RTOs along the route. RTOs were Railways Transport Officers; they sat at various points along the system of routes the British had forged, like spiders in a big metal web. Occasionally, they would call us off the train; occasionally, we could wrest from them either fresh supplies or a meagre travel allowance.

The RTO at Allahabad, a great steel town, allowed us to sleep on the platform of his magnificent station. Next day at dawn, we were put on a milk train heading East. Every day, Burma – a word synonymous with death – drew nearer.

We visited Benares and, untutored as we were, had only contempt for the pilgrims washing in the filthy waters of the Ganges. Then the train was carrying us across the infinities of the Ganges plain. Again the labouring figures of people and animals, committed every day to struggle beneath the sun.

The line ran straight ahead until it faded into sizzling heat. Our train stopped unexpectedly at a wayside halt. On the platform stood a corporal, immaculate in his KD, rigidly to attention. The Indian passengers leaning from the window or hanging on the outside of the coaches took some interest in him. He was bellowing at the top of his voice.

'Reinforcement detachment from Mhow heading for 36 British Division, disembark from train immediately. Bring your kit. At the double. Fall in.'

'Christ, that's us,' said Ted Monks. 'We're not getting off here, are we? Where the hell's this? This is nowhere.'

We de-trained and fell in with our kit and our sack of bread and bully beef. We stood to attention. The train pulled away. It disappeared into the distance, down the straight line, across the great plain.

Without explanations, we were 'fell in' outside the halt in a column of twos. On orders from the corporal, we began to march. A dusty track stretched away from the railway line at right angles to it. We progressed along it, sweating in silence.

After an hour's march, we reached a transit camp. It was arbitrarily established, and could just as well have been next to the railway line. There was no shade. We paraded in the sun to be addressed by a sergeant, who told us we were there to get properly washed and dhobied; we would be given a meal and would proceed with our journey in the morning. We were fell out.

As Monks said, we had arrived at nowhere. Wild dogs and jackals ran through our bashas during the night (I was thrilled – something that did not happen at home). Kite hawks – the hated kite hawks – dived down and scooped food out of the mess tins of anyone unwary enough to cross an open space with his meal. Beyond the perimeters of the camp was flat desolation. The camp was the British world.

One member of the camp staff was a man I recognized. He had been on the same troopship, the *Otranto*, which had brought our posting to India. I remembered him from among thousands of other troops aboard because he walked about in a distinctly civilian way (i.e. stoop-shouldered) singing a snatch of song over and over again.

Take thou this rose,
This little thing…

There he was, bathed in Indian sunlight, clutching a piece of paper going about some negligible errand. I got close to him. He was singing to himself. It was the same song. I dubbed him the Take-thou-this-rose-wallah. When we got talking, I learnt that he prided himself on this snip of a posting he had secured, office orderly at the Transit Camp; it meant that he would not have to go to Burma. I was convinced that anywhere was better than that nowhere camp.

A year or so later, it happened that I saw the Take-thou-this-rose-wallah again. He was alone in a crowd. To my delight, he was still singing the same unfinished lines of song to himself. War had no power to alter whatever was on the Take-thou-this-rose-wallah's mind.

We returned to our journey with a sack full of fresh provisions. The train was shunted into a siding at Jamalpore, where monkeys swarmed down, climbed throught the open windows of our carriage and stole two loaves of bread from our sack.

Furious shouts. I jumped up and out of the window and on to the top of the train in no time. Six large rhesus monkeys regarded me with disapproval, before making off with their loot. I followed, jumping from carriage to carriage. The monkeys carrying the loaves began lagging behind. I had almost caught one when we came to some branches overhanging the line. The six of them leaped up and disappeared gibbering into the crown of a giant tree. We'd lost our bread.

We were met at Sealdah Station when we arrived in Calcutta. A truck carried us to a transit camp buried somewhere in the greasy outskirts of the city. They say that Calcutta is a memorial to the unquenchable human spirit of survival. One's first impression is that one has – as one was expecting to do all one's life – arrived in Hell, that here is human desperation on a gigantic scale, and that the slums and hinterlands of the Infernal Regions are spreading until they encompass all India. A black water buffalo was calving on an iron bridge over a railway line. Her body lay on the pavement, her legs in the road. All the traffic, including our trucks, ran over her hooves. I looked down as we passed. A calf was emerging from among pulped flesh.

Our camp lay under a railway embankment, surrounded by ferocious slums. Seven Dials in Henry Fielding's time would have looked the same if you had put it under the grill. The tents which comprised the camp were survivors from the first world war. Everything was indescribably filthy, and flies buzzed everywhere.

It was a refuge for deserters. East of Calcutta, the war machine drew everyone into Burma and the fighting. You either jumped off here or were drawn on. Deserters had no chance of escaping to England or to any neutral country. Their best bet was to hang about in this filthy camp, for years if need be. Some of the N.C.O.s also had deserted, a fiddle was working whereby everyone still managed to draw army pay on which to venture into town once a week, to whore and booze.

One of our detachment nervously asked if we would not stand 'a better chance' if we joined the ranks of the deserters.

'I'd rather die in the bloody jungle than rot here,' said Monks, with his usual solid sense.

After two days, we reported to Howrah station, in order to continue our journey to Dibrugarh and 36 Div. The RTO at Howrah mysteriously took two of our number away, for posting elsewhere. No explanations were given. Nine of us were left, with damaged morale.

The line from Howrah northwards had come under American administration. American troops were on the train, noisy, casual, well-dressed. They had attached a canteen, which they called the caboose. Every fifty miles or so, the train would stop in the middle of nowhere, and anyone who wanted could collect a mug of coffee from the caboose. We were hospitably invited to do the same. The coffee was excellent. But we simply could not understand the Yanks and their boyish excitement at going to war. One of them, however, presented me with a copy of *Astounding Science Fiction*, which he had finished reading.

Our excitement increased as we neared Dibrugarh. What a welcome we would get! The railway ran along the south bank of the wide Bramaputra. After many changes of train and mysterious delays, we reached Tinsukia, the railhead. No one was there to meet us. The RTOs had erred.

We waited on the station, kit drawn up round us. Dusk thickened on the plain. In the distance, clear, aloof, still in sunlight, stood the majestic range of the Himalayas, with Tibet beyond. Their snow-crowned heights slowly turned pink with sunset.

A three-tonner rolled up. We climbed aboard and went bumping into the dark. The driver was mad and did his best to run down any dogs which crossed the road. He succeeded twice. All round us was miserable secondary growth, slum jungle.

We arrived at the Dibrugarh camp at three in the morning. A banner over a wooden sentry post announced that we had made contact at last with the British 36th Division. They were about to go into action north-eastwards, towards the River Salween, to strengthen Vinegar Joe Stilwell's Burma Road to Chungking, the wartime Chinese capital.

A corporal was woken. He had no knowledge of us. There was nowhere for us. They did not need reinforcements. We would have to sleep in the mess, on the mess tables, and someone would sort out the balls-up in the morning. No, there was no grub. Not at four in the morning, mate. What did we think they were, a bloody hotel?

The cooks woke us at six. We sat around on our kitbags for some while.

The camp was run on a piratical basis by a captain and two senior NCOs. They were extremely nasty. We stood in the sun and were dressed down by one NCO. for being there at all. Meanwhile, the captain was hatching a simple plot.

Our proper allowance of kit was, as I recall, 95 lbs. It included smart tropical dress uniform. The captain announced that, as we were now in an active service zone, our kit must be reduced to 60 lbs. We had ten minutes to get down to regulation weight.

Our dress uniforms and dress hats went. Books went. I was left with only a World Classics Palgrave's *Golden Treasury* and the copy of *Astounding Science Fiction*. Life in the army was full of abandoned things; we adopted an Urdu word for it, 'pegdo.' Our pegdoed kit, books, uniforms, musical instruments, had to be piled up at the door of the quartermaster's stores.

We were informed that a truck would come immediately and we would be shipped back to the RTO at Howrah. I took action I could hardly believe myself to be doing; without telling the others, I stepped into the captain's tent, saluted, and volunteered to go to Chungking.

'Who are you to volunteer? You're fresh out from England, haven't even got your knees brown.'

'I passed first class as a 19 and 22 set operator, sir. And can work a line instrument.'

'I didn't ask you that. I asked you what category you were. Are you A1?'

'No, sir, I'm A2, sir. But that's only because of my specs. I can see perfectly well with them on. I've had commando training, sir.'

'A2s are no use to us. This is a real fighting division. Get out. Dismiss.'

My old dream of getting to China had triumphed over a sensible concern to stay with my mates. I read every word I could find on Chungking, the muddy, isolated much-bombed capital of Chiang Kai-shek. I longed for its Chinese squalor. Throughout my time in the East, I kept volunteering for China; Hong Kong was the nearest I got.

Before the three-tonner bumped us out of the compound, we had the mortification of seeing the captain and his thugs descend on our pegdoed treasures and begin to divvy them up.

Back to Tinsukia. There, hanging about the sidings waiting for a train, Monks and I were accosted by an ancient Indian and a small boy. The old man would sing to us, good British songs, sir, for only one rupee. As it happened, we had only two rupees in small change between us. We gave him half a rupee and he began to sing, accompanied by the small boy on a flute, a garbled version of 'Tipperary.'

It's a long long the Tipperarip,
It's a way ago.
It's a long long the Tipperarip,
To the Swedish, ah no.
Go try to pick a lilly fair
Well let's scare …

Monks and I stood among the maze of lines and roared with laughter. We pressed more money on the old boy, forcing him to sing his song again. His words grew wilder. He was overjoyed by his success, bewildered by his reception. He went on singing until we had given him our last anna and his metre ran out. Long after, three years later in Sumatra, Monks and I could make each other laugh just by singing in a creaking nasal voice, 'It's a long long the Tipperarip.'

We never got back to Calcutta. At Gauhati, on the Bramaputra, we were caught by another RTO, and directed to the 2nd British Division. This entailed getting a train of a different gauge, heading eastwards. This time, there was no escaping our fate. We were heading for Dimapur, Kohima, and the Jap-infested fastnesses of Burma.

At Dimapur, we de-trained. We were not expected. We checked into a fearsome camp, and one or two of us were immediately collared for fatigues.

This consisted of climbing into the cargo hold of a Dakota aircraft and sitting among the stores, hanging on grimly as the plane took off, to fly low over the hills of Nagaland and drop supplies to British and Indian troops. When a flying type with a clipboard shouted 'Now,' our job was to boot supplies put of the open door of the aircraft as it banked over the target. Such was my first experience of flying.

The next morning, a lorry arrived at the camp and the nine of us climbed in. We were driven eighty miles along the famous Dimapur Road. The road climbed steadily, twisting and turning to follow the convolutions of the mountainside. Sunlight and shade swung about our heads. Parts of the road were still being built or rebuilt. Over the sheer drop, we could see in the valley below burnt out carcasses of trucks which had been carelessly driven.

We reached Milestone 81 rather pale and shaky, and were assigned officially to the British 2nd Division. Our sixteen-day journey was over. A journey into war lay ahead.

Old Bessie

This is a true story, and a ghost story. Yet I don't believe it myself.

What is a true story? It is a tale whose lies you cannot detect.

What is a ghost story? It is this – and with it comes entangled much of my life.

Earlier this year, I had the responsibility for carrying out the last wishes of my grandfather's second wife. That is to say, of my step-grandmother whom I called (for simplicity and other reasons) my Aunt. She died in the spring, almost fifty years after my grandfather, at the age of ninety-five.

My Aunt Dorothy was the reason – or one of them, for life is never that simple – why our family broke up in a spectacular way. My grandfather was a strong-willed, self-made man, to whom his descendants owe a great debt. When he took a young second wife at the age of seventy, everyone was scandalized. In those days, in a country town in the mid-thirties, such a step was regarded as little short of treasonable. Particularly by a family which stood to lose financially by the union.

As a child, and as an adult, I loved my Aunt. She was among the best people I ever knew. I was glad to honour her wish to be laid to rest beside my grandfather's bones, although to do that entailed a journey half across England to the dark dull heart of Norfolk.

Few people attended the funeral service. I spoke a short encomium over the grave. Then our little party climbed back into the cars to head for the only presentable hotel, where I was standing everyone lunch. I had reached that time in life, that position in the family, where it was taken for granted I would provide. How different from when I had lived as a boy in this miserable little town, when I was neglected and allowed to run wild.

On the way to the hotel, my wife dropped me by the council offices. The rest of the party went on their way while I went to pay the gravediggers' fees.

Afterwards, on a whim, I walked to see the house where we had lived before we left the town in disgrace. The house stood down St Withburga Lane and was in fact called Withburga House. It faced across to the churchyard and to the church with its square tower.

There was the house still, much altered, covered with a thick stucco, and half the size I remembered it. It was now the HQ of the Brecklands District Council, or some such absurd name. The house and I confronted each other, to see how we had fared over forty years. Its fate was no worse than mine. We both survived, in our fashion.

To be truthful, I had never liked the house. I had been frightened there, at a tender age. This was where my lifelong habit of insomnia began, in the bedroom overlooking the old graves.

Our garage had been knocked down to allow for a small yard at the side. I walked round and looked over the high wooden gate into our old walled garden.

It was just as it had been, that summer we left. The terrace by the house, the old wash-room, converted into a summerhouse, the central flowerbed planted with annuals, the rustic work, the heavy laburnum at the far end, the lawn. Everything maintained.

My father made that garden. When we bought Withburga, it had been in a state of decay. Restoration had been needed inside, while the garden, a wilderness, had had to be restarted from scratch. My father had thrown himself into the work with his usual energy, digging, sowing, planting, and mixing concrete for paving and to support rustic pergolas. Staring over the gate, back into the past, I could imagine him still at work there, doing the sort of thing he liked best.

The front door of the house had been blocked off. One entered by the side, where once there had been no door. All was quiet. I wandered down a bare corridor. It was chill, unwelcoming. I saw that our old rooms had been partitioned into cubicles. Here was the kitchen, a kitchen no more. Here was our breakfast room, where the sun once filtered in on to the tablecloth, the china, the bowl of stewed apple. Here my sister's dolls house had stood, one memorable Christmas ... now there were instead three little rooms, each with a chair and a pencil on a string.

At the far end of the corridor was one of those hatches which has a button-bell outside it, against which a notice says 'Push for Attention'; when the bell is pushed, it calls forth a girl who opens the hatch and says 'Yes?' With a sense of unreality, I pushed the bell. The hatch opened, and a girl said yes.

'I used to live here,' I said. 'You are sitting in my dining room.'

She looked at me in some anguish. I was dressed in a black suit, with a black tie, and a black overcoat to protect me from the East wind.

'I'll get Mrs Skinner,' she said.

There were three other women in our dining room, but Mrs Skinner entered from an adjoining room and bid me good-afternoon. She was a handsome woman in her mid-thirties, well-dressed with an elegant figure. She seemed to belong in that little menage no more than I did.

I told her of our family connection with the offices. She was interested. So were the other women. They stopped their work and sat with hands on laps, listening as I talked to Mrs Skinner through the hatch. Both of us craned our necks in order to see the other properly.

'Our lounge was on the other side of the old front door,' I said.

'That is now my office – or part of it is,' said the elegant Mrs Skinner, I thought with more reserve than she had shown so far.

'Have you ever heard anything strange in there?' I asked.

The women all looked at one another. An older woman at the back of the office, who did her hair in a bun, said, with a nervous laugh, 'Oh, we've all heard strange things in this place. Some of the girls will tell you it's haunted.'

'It is haunted,' said the girl at the hatch.

'It is haunted,' I agreed.

So I related the story of Old Bessie.

Withburga had been the home of a spinster, Bessie Someone, who had lived there in increasing decrepitude with an aged companion. My mother, given to good works, used to go to see Bessie regularly, taking her a cake, a trifle, or one of her fine steak-and-kidney puddings, wrapped in a cloth. Bessie died eventually. My father bought the house from Bessie's executors.

Our builders moved in. They ripped out a back staircase and put in a new bathroom. They re-roofed the house. They pulled out all the rotting sashcord windows and installed metal ones in their stead. They repainted and redecorated. Then we took up residence, my parents, my sister and I. My sister would then have been four or five, and I eight or nine.

Almost at once, we started hearing the sounds. It was a winter's evening. I sat with my parents in the living room, in the room that was to become – at least in part – the elegant Mrs Skinner's. My sister was asleep in the bedroom above, in the room where old Bessie had died.

We heard footsteps overhead. In the centre of the living-room ceiling was a light whose china shade was supported by three chains. The footsteps were perfectly distinct. As they passed the centre of the room, the chains rattled on the lamp.

All three of us, motionless, followed the trail of the steps with our eyes, as they progressed to the bedroom window. There was a pause. Then the sound – the unmistakeable sound – of a sashcord frame being thrown up, squealing in its runners as it went.

'There's someone up there,' said my father. He snatched the poker and ran upstairs. Thrilled, I snatched the fire-tongs and followed close behind.

There was no one in the bedroom, except for my sister fast asleep in her bed. The metal-frame window remained closed. My father investigated the walk-in linen cupboard – how I was to fear that cupboard later – and found nothing. Eventually, we returned downstairs.

'It must have been old Bessie,' said my mother.

And we laughed. We had a ghost. And it had a name. Old Bessie.

'We never did anything but good for Old Bessie,' said my mother. 'So she won't harm us.'

Well, it is true that Bessie did us no harm. But she was ever active. Most ghosts are content to live on their reputations, or reappear once a year. Not Bessie. She was always about the house. Cats would not stay with us.

The focus of the trouble was always that room with the linen cupboard, where Bessie had died, where my sister slept. I occupied the other front bedroom across the landing, while my parents slept at the rear of the house, overlooking the garden. In a very short while, my sister was bursting out on the landing in the middle of the night, screaming and crying. A lady carrying a lamp had come out of the linen cupboard, or from behind the wardrobe, to stand over her bed. So my sister always told us. A fierce lady with a lamp.

An ideal solution was discovered to this dilemma. My sister and I should change bedrooms. After all, I was by this time at boarding school, and did not sleep at home most of the year.

So I inherited the room with the linen cupboard. When you opened the linen cupboard door, drawers and lockers confronted you on two sides. On the third side was a window without a curtain, leaving the place vulnerable to the night. I always fell asleep with my gaze directed towards that ominous cupboard.

Did Bessie visit me? She did. I cannot remember whether she frightened me. I do know that I understood that here was ideal subject matter for school where, in the little dormitory, I made the nights terrible as I told them the story of Old Bessie. Boys hid their heads under the blankets in fright.

Living with Old Bessie became increasingly difficult. We told nobody in town about her. She was a disgrace, nudging us like a bad conscience.

When she started to visit us downstairs, it all got too much.

One October evening, at about four o'clock, when the dusk begins to fall with peculiar intensity in Withburga Lane, when farmers go mad from melancholy and shoot their dogs and their wives, my mother was alone in the house. My sister and I were at school. My father had not yet returned home.

Mother was in the kitchen at the rear of the house, baking one of her famous cherry cakes, when she heard someone walking about the bathroom overhead. Assuming that my father had returned early, and surprised that he had not at least called out to her, she went through to the hall.

As she removed her apron, she looked up the stairwell and spoke his name. 'Bill?'

No response, although she still heard the footsteps. It was dark up there.

'Bill. Is that you? Are you there?'

The footsteps came out on to the upper landing.

'Bill? Who is it? Who's there?'

The footsteps began to descend the stairs.

She stood petrified as they passed by her eyes. Still descending. She could not leave the stairwell. The footsteps came down to hall level. They turned and came towards her.

It was then that she found the power to scream. She dropped her apron and rushed out of the front door into the lane. There she stood, as it grew dark, and waited for half an hour before my father returned. He had to coax her into the house.

'If Bessie's coming downstairs, I'm leaving,' said my mother.

We sold the house. Nobody selling property mentions the fact that it is haunted. Ghosts do not increase the saleable value. We left Withburga, and shortly after that came the family row which exiled us from Norfolk forever.

Mrs Skinner and her ladies listened to the story with intense interest, peering at me through the hatch.

Immediately I had finished, they burst into excited talk. 'There you are, what did I tell you?' 'So Old Bessie's still about then ….'

Each of them had a tale to tell. They had heard spooky noises. One of them had had to come back at night and had been too frozen with fear to go in. Another had heard footsteps which seemed to walk through the cubicles upstairs. The girl at the hatch, not to be outdone, said, 'And when you come in of a morning, there's always – oh, you know, a kind of sinister something … I've never liked working here.'

Mrs Skinner told me that she had come back one evening after the offices were closed to do some work for her boss. She had gone upstairs to his room – the very room where Bessie had died – and was working there when she heard someone downstairs. Thinking it must be her boss, she had called out. No answer. When the steps began to come up the staircase, she grew alarmed and went to see who it was. The footsteps kept coming. She saw no one. She represented herself as a lady not easily upset – and indeed I believed it – but she had been so frightened that she had run downstairs and out into the lane, where she had waited until her boss arrived.

As she finished speaking, Mrs Skinner and I both realized at the same time the congruence between her story and my mother's. We stared at each other.

And as we stared, I saw her expression change from one of a kind of quizzical amusement to one approaching fear. Her lips parted. She could not cease staring through the hatch at me.

Perturbed myself, I said, 'I must disappear … go and join the funeral party.'

I shut the hatch. I stood there alone. The corridor was chill and empty; its hostility closed in upon me.

As I hurried down the corridor into the open, as I left Withburga, as I moved rapidly down the lane, I knew exactly what the exprestion on Mrs Skinner's face implied. She had become, in that instant, certain that she was talking to the ghost itself.

Back at the hotel, our party was ordering its second round of gin-and-tonics.

'Bessie's still in residence,' I told my sister. Even as I said it, a thought occurred to me which I will leave with you. It had been our asssumption that the haunter of Withburga was Old Bessie. But we could have been wrong. The tormented spirit which still wandered in its imprisoned limbo was possibly much older than Bessie – older and more malevolent.

Is this a true story? I don't know. I still cannot bring myself intellectually to believe in ghosts.

This second section consists of articles on major contributors to the SF field whose work I admire greatly.

They run as follows: Mary Shelley, to whom all SF writers owe a debt, Olaf Stapledon, George Orwell, Phillip K. Dick, James Blish, and Harry Harrison.

Science Fiction's Mother Figure

In Anthony Burgess's novel, Beard's Roman Women (1977), there is a passage where Beard, the central character, meets an old girl friend in an airport bar. Both work in what it is fashionable to call 'the media'; they discuss Byron and Shelley, and she says 'I did an overseas radio thing on Mary Shelley. She and her mother are very popular these days. With the forces of women's liberation, that is. It took a woman to make a Frankenstein monster. Evil, cancer, corruption, pollution, the lot. She was the only one of the lot of them who knew about life ....'

Even today, when our diet is the unlikely, Mary Shelley's *Frankenstein* seems extremely far-fetched; how much more so must it have appeared on publication in 1818. Yet Beard's girl friend puts her finger on one of the contradictions which possibly explains the continued fascination of *Frankenstein*, that it seems to know a lot about life, whilst being preoccupied with death.

This preoccupation was undoubtedly an important strand in the character of the author of *Frankenstein*. Marked by the death of her mother in childbirth, she was haunted, at the time of writing *Frankenstein*, by precognitive dreads concerning the future deaths of her husband and children. By embodying some of this psychic material into her complex narrative, she created what many regard as that creature with a life of its own, the first SF novel.

This perception will bear examination later. Meanwhile, it should be pointed out that *Frankenstein* is generically ambivalent, hovering between novel, Gothic, and science fiction, just as its science hovers between alchemy and orthodox science. To my mind, precisely similar factors obtain even today in the most celebrated SF novels. Heinlein's *Stranger in a Strange Land* contains magic; Anne McCaffrey's dragon novels hover between legend, fairy tale, and science fiction. 'Pure' science fiction is chimerical. Its strength lies in its appetite.

Mary Shelley's life (1797–1851) forms an unusual pattern, with all the events crowding into the early part and, indeed, many transactions that would mould her character occurring before she was born. Both her parents played important roles in the intellectual life of the time. Her father, William Godwin, was a philosopher and political theorist, whose most important work is *An Enquiry Concerning the Principles of Political Justice* (1793). Godwin also wrote novels as a popular means of elucidating his thought, the most durable being *Caleb Williams* (1794), which can still be read with interest, even excitement, today. The influence of both these works on Godwin's daughter's writing is marked. Mary's mother, Mary Wollstonecraft Godwin, was a brilliant woman who wrote the world's first feminist tract, *A Vindication of the Rights of Woman* (1792). Mary Wollstonecraft came to the marriage with Godwin bringing with her a small daughter, Fanny, the fruit of her affair with a charming but elusive American, Gilbert Imlay, who deserted his pregnant mistress in the Paris of the Terror.

A portrait of Mary Wollstonecraft by Sir John Opie shows a moody and passionate woman. Distracted by the failure of her love for Imlay, she tried to commit suicide by jumping into the Thames off Putney Bridge. She survived to marry Godwin and bear him a daughter, Mary. After the birth, puerperal fever set in, and she died ten days later.

Godwin remarried. His second wife was a Mrs. Mary Jane Clairmont, and she brought with her two children by her previous marriage, Charles, and Jane, who later preferred to be known as Claire and bore Byron an illegitimate child, Allegra. Fanny and Mary, then four years old, were further upset by the arrival of this new step-mother into their household, and the alienation was no doubt increased when Godwin's new wife bore him a son in 1803. The five children crowded into one house increased Mary's feeling of inner isolation, the refrain of which sounds throughout her novels and short stories. Another constant refrain, that of complex familial relationships, is seen embodied in the five children, no two of whom could muster two parents in common, Charles and Jane excepted.

Mary grew to be an attractive woman.[1] Her reserved manner hid deep feelings baffled by her mother's death and her father's distance – two kinds of coldness, one might say, both of which are embodied in her monster's being in a sense dead and also unloved. When Shelley arrived, he received all her love, and Mary remained faithful to him long after his death, despite his callow unfaithfulness to her. She was also a blue stocking, the product of two intellectuals, and through many years maintained an energetic reading programme, teaching herself several foreign languages. Moreover, she had the good fortune to know in childhood many of the celebrated intellectuals and men of letters of the time, Samuel Taylor Coleridge among them. Trelawny said of Mary that 'her head might be put upon the shoulders of a Philosopher.'

Enter Percy Bysshe Shelley, poet, son of a baronet. An emotional and narcissistic youth, full of admiration for Godwin's revolutionary but now somewhat faded political theories. When nineteen,

---

1 An enjoyable recent biography is Jane Dunn's *Moon in Eclipse: A Life of Mary Shelley*, 1979.

he had married Harriet Westerbrook. He soon fell in love with Mary, and she with him. Before his twenty-second birthday, the pair had eloped to France, taking Jane with them.

Europe! What freedom it must have represented to Mary, after her sixteen circumscribed years, and what close companionship Shelley, handsome and intellectual, must have offered. But these youthful travellers were among the first to enter France after the Napoleonic Wars, and a desolate place they found it, the fields uncultivated, the villages and buildings destroyed. On the way to Switzerland, Shelley wrote to invite Harriet, now pregnant with Shelley's second child, to join the party. Before they reached Lake Lucerne, Mary knew that she also was pregnant.

Catastrophe followed the harum-scarum young lovers. Mary's child, a daughter, was born after they returned to London and their debts; it was premature and died. A second child, William, scarcely fared better. In the summer of 1816, Shelley and Mary went to Switzerland again, taking along William and, inevitably, Claire, as Jane now called herself. On the shores of Lake Geneva, they found accommodation at the Maison Chapuis, next to the Villa Diodati, where the poet Lord Byron was staying. Although Claire threw herself at Byron's head, and managed to encompass the rest of him too, it was a happily creative time for them, with philosophy and learning pursued as well as the more touted facets of the good life. Here, Mary began to write *Frankenstein*. Summer had too short a stay, and the party returned to England to face more trouble.

Mary's self-effacing half-sister, Fanny, committed suicide with an overdose of laudanum at the age of twenty-two, by which time the Shelley menage had moved to the West Country; Claire still followed them, as the monster followed Frankenstein, and was now also pregnant. Then news reached them that Shelley's wife Harriet had drowned herself, not in the Thames, but in the Serpentine. She had been far advanced in pregnancy. Shelley and Mary were married almost immediately.

The date of the marriage was 29 December 1816. Six and a half years later, in July 1822, Shelley was drowned whilst sailing on the Ligurian Sea. By that time, the little boy, William, was dead, as was another child, Clara; Mary had also had a miscarriage, but a further son, Percy Florence, was born. He alone of Mary's progeny survived to manhood. Even Claire's daughter by Byron, the little Allegra, had died.

The rest of Mary's life is curiously empty, lived in the shadow of her first twenty-five years. After Byron died in Greece in 1824, both the great poets were gone – a loss to English letters. Mary remained ever faithful to the memory of her husband. She edited his poems and papers, and earned a living by her pen. She wrote historical novels, such as *Perkin Warbeck* (1830), *Lodore* (1835), which enjoyed some success, short stories, and one novel, *The Last Man* (1826) which, by its powerfully oppressive theme of world catastrophe, is classifiable as science fiction. Percy married. Her cold father, Godwin, died; Shelley's difficult father died. Finally, in 1851, the year of the Great Exhibition, Mary herself died, aged fifty-three.

This painful biography, as confused as any modern one, is worth retelling, for it helps to explain not only why Mary's temperament was not a sanguine one, but where much derives from what we read in her two science fiction novels, *Frankenstein* and *The Last Man*. Both owe a great deal to the literature that preceded them; more is owed to experience. Critics are liable comfortably to ignore the latter to concentrate on the former.

The essence of the story of *Frankenstein* is familiar, if in distorted form, from many film, stage and TV versions, in which Victor Frankenstein compiles a creature from corpses and then endows it with life, after which it runs amok. The novel is long, and more complex than this synopsis suggests. It is a flawed masterpiece of growing reputation, and an increasing body of criticism attests to the attraction of both its excellences and its flaws.

Frankenstein or, *The Modern Prometheus* begins with letters from Captain Walton to his sister. Walton is sailing in Arctic waters when he sees on the ice floes a sledge being driven by an enormous figure. The next day, the crew rescue a man from a similar sledge. It is Victor Frankenstein of Geneva; when he recovers, he tells his tale to Walton, which account makes up the bulk of the book, to be rounded off by Walton again, and to include six chapters which are the creature's own account of its life, especially of its education. If the style of the novel is discursive, Mary Shelley was following methods familiar to readers of Richardson and Sterne; the method became unfashionable but, to readers of eccentric modern novels, may now be increasingly sympathetic and help to account in part for the new-found popularity of the novel.

One of the enduring attractions of the book is that Mary sets most of the drama, not in the seamy London she knew from childhood, but amid spectacular alpine scenery, such as she had visited with Shelley. The monster's puissance gains greatly by this association with the elements, storm, cold, snow, desolation.

Interest has always centred on the monster and its creation (it has no name in the novel, merely being referred to as 'creature,' 'daemon,' or 'monster,' which accounts for the popular misusage by which the name Frankenstein has come to be transferred from the creator to the created – a mistake which occurred first in Mary's lifetime. This is the essential SF core of the narrative: a fascinating experiment that goes wrong: a prescription to be repeated later, many times, in *Amazing Stories* and elsewhere. Frankenstein's is a Faustian dream of unlimited power, but this Faust makes no supernatural pacts; he succeeds only when he throws away the fusty old reference books, outdated by the new science, and gets to work on research in laboratories.

But SF is not only hard science, and related to the first core is a second, also science-fictional, the tale of an experiment in political theory which relates to William Godwin's ideas. Frankenstein is horrified by his creation and abjures responsibility. Yet the monster, despite its ugliness, is gentle and intelligent, and tries to win its way into society. Society repulses it. Hence the monster's cry, 'I am malicious because I am miserable,' a dramatic reversal of received Christian thinking of the time.

The richness of the story's metaphorical content, coupled with the excellence of the prose, has tempted commentators to interpret the novel in various ways. *Frankenstein*'s sub-title, *The Modern Prometheus*, leads us to one level of meaning. Prometheus, according to Aeschylus in his play *Prometheus Bound*, brings fire from Heaven and bestows the gift on mankind; for this, Zeus has him chained to a rock in the Caucasus, where an eagle eats his viscera.[2] Another version of the legend, the one Mary had chiefly in mind, tells of Prometheus fashioning men out of mud and water. Mary seized on this aspect of the legend, whilst Byron and Shelley were writing *Prometheus* and *Prometheus Unbound* respectively. Mary, with an inspired transposition, uses electricity as the divine fire.

By this understanding, with Frankenstein acting god, Frankenstein's monster becomes mankind itself, blundering about the world seeking knowledge and reassurance. The monster's intellectual quest has led David Ketterer to state that 'basically *Frankenstein* is about the problematical nature of knowledge.'[3] Though this interpretation is too radical, it reminds us usefully of the intellectual aspects of the work, and of Mary's understanding of the British philosophers, Locke, Berkeley and Hume.

Leonard Wolf argues that *Frankenstein* should be regarded as 'psychological allegory'.[4] This view is supported by David Ketterer,

---

2 One thinks here of the scene after Shelley's death, when Trelawny caused his corpse to be burnt on the shore, Byron and Leigh Hunt also being present. At the last possible moment, Trelawny ran forward and snatched Shelley's heart from the body.

3 David Ketterer, *Frankenstein's Creation: The Book, The Monster, and Human Reality*, University of Victoria, 1979.

4 Leonard Wolf, *The Annotated Frankenstein*, 1977.

who thinks that therefore the novel cannot be science fiction.[5] Godwin's *Caleb Williams* is also psychological or at least political allegory; it is nevertheless regarded as the first crime novel.* Surely there are many good SF novels which are psychological allegory as well as being science fiction. Algis Budrys's *Who?* is an example. By understanding the origins of 'real' science fiction, we understand something of its function; hence the importance of the question. Not to regard *Frankenstein* but, say, *The Time Machine* or even Gernsback's magazines as the first SF – as many did only a few years ago – is to underestimate the capabilities of the medium; alternatively, to claim that *Gilgamesh* or Homer started it all is to claim so almost anything becomes SF.

Mary Shelley wanted her story to 'speak to the mysterious fears of our (i.e. humankind's) nature' ... Is that not what SF still excellently does?

That the destructive monster stands for one side of Shelley's nature, and the constructive Victor for the other has been convincingly argued by another critic, Christopher Small.[6] Mary's passion for Shelley, rather than blinding her, gave her terrifying insight. In case this idea sounds over-sophisticated, we must recall that Mary herself, in her Introduction to the 1831 edition of her novel, means us to read it as a kind of metaphor when she says 'Invention ... does not consist in creating out of void, but out of chaos; the materials must, in the first place, be afforded: it can give form to dark, shapeless substances, but it cannot bring into being substance itself.'

In referring to *Frankenstein* as a diseased creation myth,[7] I had in mind phrases with sexual connotations in the novel such as 'my workshop of filthy creation,' used by Frankenstein of his

---

5   David Ketterer, '*Frankenstein* in Wolf's Clothing,' *Science Fiction Studies*, No. 18, July 1979.

6   Christopher Small, *Ariel Like a Harpy*, 1972.

7   Brian Aldiss, *Billion Year Spree*, 1973.

3

secret work. Mary's life experience taught her to regard life and death as closely intertwined. The genesis of her terrifying story came to Mary in a dream, in which she says she saw 'the hideous phantasm of a man stretched out, and then, on the working of some powerful engine, show signs of life, and stir with an uneasy half vital motion.' The powerful line suggests both a distorted image of her mother dying, in those final restless moments which often tantalisingly suggest recovery rather than its opposite, and also the stirrings of sexual intercourse, particularly when we recall that 'powerful engine' is a term which serves in pornography as a synonym for penis.

The critic, Ellen Moers, writing on female gothic,[8] disposes of the question of how a young girl like Mary could hit on such a horrifying idea (though the authoress was herself the first to raise it). Most female writers of the eighteenth and nineteenth century were spinsters and virgins, and in any case Victorian taboos operated against writing on childbirth. Mary experienced the fear, guilt, depression and anxiety which often attend childbirth, particularly in situations such as hers, unmarried, her consort a married man with children by another woman, and beset by debt in a foreign place. Only a woman, only Mary Shelley, could have written *Frankenstein*. As Beard's girlfriend says, 'She was the only one of the lot of them who knew about life.'

Moreover, the casual remark made by Beard's girlfriend takes us into a deeper level of meaning which, although sufficiently obvious, has not been remarked upon to my knowledge. *Frankenstein* is autobiographical.

It is commonly accepted that the average first novel relies for its material on personal experience. We do not deny other interpretations – for a metaphor has many interpretations – by stating that Mary sees herself as the monster. This is why we pity it. She too

---

8   Ellen Moers, 'Female Gothic: The Monster's Mother,' *The New York Review*, 21 March 1974, reprinted in *Literary Women*, 1976.

tried to win her way into society. By running away with Shelley, she sought acceptance through love; but the move carried her further from society; she became a wanderer, an exile, like Byron, like Shelley. Her mother's death in childbirth must have caused her to feel that she, like the monster, had been born from the dead; behind the monster's eloquence lies Mary's grief. Part of the continued appeal of the novel is the appeal of the drama of the neglected child.

Upon this structure of one kind of reality, Mary built a further structure, one of the intellect. A madness for knowledge abounds; not only Frankenstein but the monster and Walton also, and the judicial processes throughout the book, are in quest for knowledge of one kind and another. Interestingly, the novel contains few female characters (a departure from the Gothic mode, with its soft, frightened heroines); Victor's espoused remains always a cold and distant figure. The monster, product of guilty knowledge, threatens the world with evil progeny.

The monster is, of course, more interesting than Victor. He has the vitality of evil, like Satan in Milton's *Paradise Lost* before him and Quilp in Dickens's *The Old Curiosity Shop* after him, eloquent villains both. It is the monster that comes first to our minds, as it was the monster that came first to Mary's mind. The monster holds its appeal because it was created by science, or at least pseudo-science, rather than by any pacts with the devil, or by magic, like the golem.

Frankenstein emerges from the Gothic tradition. Gothic still tints science fiction with its hues of suspense and doom. In *Billion Year Spree* I argued that *Frankenstein* was the first real science fiction novel. Here the adjective 'real' serves as an escape clause. The point about discussing where science fiction begins is that it helps our understanding of the nature and function of SF. In France in pre-Revolution days, for instance, several books appeared with Enlightenment scenarios depicting a future where present trends were greatly developed, and where the whole world became a civilized extension of the Tuilleries. The best-known example is Sebastien Mercier's *L'An 2400*, set seven centuries ahead in time; it was translated into several foreign languages. Mercier writes in the utopian tradition; Mary Shelley does not. Here we see a division of function. Jules Verne was influenced by Mercier, and worked with 'actual possibilities of invention and discovery.' H.G. Wells was influenced by *Frankenstein*, and wrote what he called fantasies – the phrase set in quotes is Wells's, who added that he 'did not pretend to deal with possible things.'* One can imagine Mary Shelley saying as much.

As Muriel Spark says, Mary in her thinking seems at least fifty years ahead of her time.[9] She discovered the Irrational, one of the delights and torments of our age. By dressing it in rational garb, and letting it stalk the land, she unwittingly dealt a blow against the tradition to which Mercier was heir. Utopia is no place for the irrational.

Other arguments for the seminal qualities of *Frankenstein* are set out more fully in *Billion Year Spree*, for those interested. In sum, Victor Frankenstein is a modern, consciously rejecting ancient fustian booklore in favour of modern science, kicking out father figures. His creation of life shows him further usurping paternal power, invading what was previously God's province – the role medicine has played since Jenner's smallpox vaccine. Victor and his monster together function as the light and dark side of mankind, in a symbolism that was to become increasingly comprehensible after Mary's death.

---

* A biographer of Mary Shelley, writing in the nineteen-thirties, advances the argument that *Frankenstein* is 'the first of the Scientific Romances that have culminated in our day in the work of Mr. H. G. Wells,' because it erects 'a superstructure of fantasy on a foundation of circumstantial "scientific fact."' Shrewd judgement, although the excellence of the novel is otherwise underestimated. (R. Glynn Grylls: *Mary Shelley, A Biography*, 1938.)

9 Muriel Spark, *Child of Light: A Reassessment of Mary Wollstonecraft Shelley*, 1951.

As befitted an author writing after the Napoleonic Wars, when the Industrial Revolution was well under way, Mary deals, not merely with extrapolated development like Mercier before her, but with unexpected change, like Wells after her. Above all, Frankenstein stands as the figure of the scientist (though the word was not coined when Mary wrote), set apart from the rest of society, unable to control the new forces he has brought into the world. The successor to Prometheus is Pandora. No other writer, except H. G. Wells, presents us with as many innovations as Mary Shelley.

The Last Man was published in 1826, anonymously, as *Frankenstein* had been. Few critics of standing have praised the novel. It meanders. Muriel Spark, however, said of it that it is Mary's 'most interesting, if not her most consummate, work.'

The theme of *The Last Man* was not new, and could hardly be at a time when epidemics were still commonplace. The title was used for an anonymous novel in 1806. Thomas Campbell wrote a poem with the same title; whilst at the Villa Diodati, Byron composed a poem entitled 'Darkness' in which the world is destroyed and two men, the last, die of fright at the sight of each other. In the same year that Mary's novel was published, John Martin painted a water-colour on the subject (later, in 1849, he exhibited a powerful oil with the same title).

The novel is set in the twenty-first century, a period, it seems, of much sentimental rhetoric. Adrian, Earl of Windsor, befriends the wild Lionel Verney. Adrian is the son of the King of England, who abdicated; one of the King's favourites was Verney's father. Adrian is full of fine sentiments, and wins over Verney. Verney has a sister called Perdita who falls in love with Lord Raymond, and eventually commits suicide. Raymond is a peer of genius and beauty who besieges Constantinople. The relationships of these personages, together with a profusion of mothers and sisters, fill the first of the three volumes. Adrian is Mary's portrait of Shelley, the bright rather than the dark side, Perdita is Claire, Raymond

Byron. Verney plays the part of Mary, and eventually becomes the Last Man. Verney, like Frankenstein, is a paradigm of the Outsider.

There is undoubted strength in the second and third books, once the plague has the world in its grip. Society disintegrates on a scale merely hinted at in the unjust world of *Frankenstein*. 'I spread the whole earth out as a map before me. On no one spot of its surface could I put my finger and say, here is safety. In the south, the disease, virulent and immedicable, had nearly annihilated the race of man; storm and inundation, poisonous winds and blights, filled up the measure of suffering. In the north it was worse ....'

Finally, Verney-Mary alone is left, drifting south towards the equator, like a character in a J.G. Ballard novel. So Mary tells us how life was without Shelley; her universe had gone. Through science fiction, she expressed her powerfully inexpressible feelings.

In his brief book on Mary,[10] William Walling makes a point which incidentally relates *The Last Man* still more closely to the science-fictional temper. Remarking that solitude is a common topic of the period and by no means Mary's monopoly, Walling claims that by interweaving the themes of isolation and the end of civilization, she creates a prophetic account of modern industrial society, in which the creative personality becomes more and more alienated.

Tales and Stories by Mary Shelley were collected together by Richard Garnett and published in 1891. They are in the main conventional. Familial and amorous misunderstandings fill the foreground, armies gallop about in the background. The characters are high-born, their speeches high-flown. Tears are scalding, years long, sentiments either villainous or irreproachable, deaths copious and conclusions not unusually full of well-mannered melancholy. The tales are of their time. Here again, the game of detecting autobiographical traces can be played. One story, 'Transformation,' sheds light on *Frankenstein* – but not much.

---

10 William Walling: *Mary Shelley*, 1972.

We have to value Mary Shelley, as we do other authors, for her strongest work, not her weakest; and her best has a strength still not widely enough appreciated.

This collection of stories from scattered journals and keepsake albums indicates Mary's emotional and physical exhaustion. In the course of eight years, between 1814 and 1822, she had borne four children, three of whom died during the period, and had suffered miscarriages. She had travelled hither and thither with her irresponsible husband, who had most probably had an affair with her closest friend, Claire. And she had witnessed suicides and death all round her, culminating in Shelley's death. It was much for a sensitive and intellectual woman to endure. No wonder that Claire Clairmont wrote to her, some years after the fury and shouting died, and said, 'I think in certain things you are the most daring woman I ever knew.'[11]

11 Claire Clairmont, letter, quoted in Julian Marshall's *Life and Letters of Mary Wollstonecraft Shelley*, 1889.

The Immanent Will Returns

'What of the Immanent Will and its designs?' asks Thomas Hardy at the beginning of *The Dynasts*, and proceeds to demonstrate at length how little the Will cares for its creations. He leaves us with a faint hope that the Will can in some way evolve, and that 'the rages of the Ages shall be cancelled,/Consciousness the Will informing,/Till it fashion all things fair.' Thinking the matter over after the First World War, Hardy conceded that this was a little too optimistic: thereby leaving the door open for Olaf Stapledon.

Stapledon sweeps away the human characters in whom Hardy delighted, to give us a threadbare stage upon which humanity is lost in the incomprehensible toils of creation or the soliloquies of the Star Maker. The Star Maker is the Immanent Will wearing another hat.

W. Olaf Stapledon (1886–1950) is a very English kind of writer. He won no great reputation in his lifetime and has accumulated little since; yet he cannot be said to be entirely forgotten, despite his mysterious absence from most of the histories of English Literature.

His work in philosophy – a subject which at one time he taught in the University of Liverpool – has proved impermanent, although *A Modern Theory of Ethics* went through several reprints.

His kind of visionary writing, which attempts to establish an individual mythology, is not unfamiliar. His novel *Odd John* has a subtitle which recalls Blake ('A Story Between Jest and Earnest' – though there's precious little enjoying of the lady in it); his grandiosities recall Doughty's six-volume epic poem, *Dawn in Britain*, with its quixotic resolve to restore Chaucer to modern English. Two other conflicting voices echo strongly through Stapledon's fiction: the Milton of *Paradise Lost* and that great Victorian storm-trooper, Winwood Reade, whose *Martyrdom of Man* attempted to justify the ways of man to a dead god.

We may call H.G. Wells's early scientific romances science fiction with a clear conscience. It is more debatable whether Stapledon's first novel, *Last and First Men* (1930), and *Star Maker* (1937) so qualify. They are Stapledon's attempt to blend fiction and philosophy. Wells's imagination was untainted by metaphysics, though politics finally eclipsed it; but Stapledon read Modern History while up at Balliol from 1905–09, and most of his fictions strive to iron themselves out into the progressions of historicity, complete with time-charts.

These two vast works, best regarded as a unity, are *sui generis*. The preface to *Last and First Men* warns that this 'is not a prophecy; it is a myth, or an essay in myth.' Even sterner is the disclaimer at the portals of *Star Maker*: 'Judged by the standards of the Novel, it is remarkably bad. In fact, it is no novel at all.'

The Novel has proved itself unexpectedly capacious, but the Immanent Will does seem to demand a less convivial stage on which to enact the rages of the ages. The rages which energise the gaunt structures of *Last and First Men* and *Star Maker* are, basically, religious faith versus atheism and the quest for individual fulfillment versus the needs of the community, whether terrestrial or stellar. Modern rages, one might call them.

With their emphasis on spiritual suffering, catastrophe to come, and the surrealist mutations of shape which mankind must undergo in submission to the Creator, those great glacial novels, together spanning the thirties, now appear oddly characteristic of their day.

In many respects, Stapledon himself is markedly of his time. As were many men of his generation, he was torn by religious doubt; he was a non-combatant in the 1914–1918 war, and had some trouble in fitting himself, essentially a Victorian, into post-war society. Along with other intellectuals of his day, he flirted with pacifism and promiscuity. He had strong leanings towards Communism without ever becoming a member of the Party. Like many writers outside the swim of London literary society, he knew few other authors, and was critically disregarded.

It could also be said that the central premise of his work, that mankind is irrelevant to the purposes of the universe, is unpalatable to believer and unbeliever alike. It is precisely for that unpalatability, so variously, so swoopingly, expressed, as if in contradiction to itself, that his admirers honour him.

Last and First Men belongs to that class of book which needs to arrive in a reader's life at the right moment if it is to arrive at all. Then one never forgets it.

I remember my first encounter with it. I was awaiting a typhus inoculation in Assam in 1943, before the British Second Division advanced on Japanese-held Mandalay. The medical officer was housed in a commandeered bungalow outside Kohima which possessed a considerable library. On the shelves stood a book I had never heard of, in two volumes, the first two volumes Allen Lane published in his blue series of Pelican Books (for he had taken Stapledon at his word and issued the work as non-fiction). I was captivated before I was inoculated.

For the last and first time in my life, I deliberately stole a book. I could not bear to be parted from it.

While great things went forward in the world – destruction and victory – Stapledon's voice proved to be what was needed, in marked contrast to the pedestrian chat of soldiers. His daring time-scales in particular corresponded to something felt in the bloodstream.

What filled me then was Stapledon's all-embracing vision of humanity locked within the imperatives of creation, untainted by a Christianity which seemed to have failed. *Star Maker*, written only seven years later, amplifies this vision, elevates it, and marks a great advance in the writer's art. The two billion year long history of the future which is *Last and First Men* is encompassed in one paragraph of the second book. Again, human kind – this time one individual soul – is confronted with the necessity of comprehending the cosmic process of which it is part: a noble and ever-contemporary quest.

Noble or not, Stapledon has been neglected. He had a dislike of Bloomsbury and satirised the coterie in *Last Men in London* – which presumably did for him. If his name is to be preserved, it will be by science fiction readers. Science fiction studies are now so alarmingly advanced in the United States that the first two studies of Stapledon's *oeuvre* are American. First was Patrick McCarthy's *Olaf Stapledon* (Twayne, 1982). Now here comes the energetic, unorthodox Professor Leslie A. Fiedler, with *Olaf Stapledon, A Man Divided* (O.U.P., 1983). His volume appears in a series flatly entitled 'Science Fiction Writers,' edited by Robert Scholes, in which studies of Wells, Heinlein and Asimov have already appeared.

Fiedler has problems. One initial difficulty is that *Last and First Men* evidently did not arrive in his life at the right moment. He was 'infuriated' that it had no story or characters. He finds it improbable that he should be writing on 'so anomalous an author.' Not an encouraging start, not an encouraging attitude.

One's initial misgivings are never allayed. Fiedler briefly covers Stapledon's life (though not the Oxford years, when Stapledon rowed for his college), deems it an uneventful one, like the lives of most writers, and hurries on to investigate the glories and shortcomings of the fiction. The book reaches roughly the same conclusions as would any reasonable man: that *Odd John* is a worthwhile contribution in the Poor Little Superman line, that

Sirius is late gold, and that *Star Maker* is the great triumph, with its 'all but intolerable appeal.' While finding the other writings disappointing, it relates them illuminatingly to one another.

On the whole, more engagement would have been welcome, and a recognition that Stapledon is the first to write about an Immanent Will, or whatever you call It, which stands completely outside the universe He or It has created – a remarkable alienation effect derived from the scientific despairs of the time.

Despite its remote title, *Sirius* is the most approachable of all Stapledon's inventions. Although Fiedler surprisingly finds its theme pornographic, he gives a perceptive account of its Beauty and the Beast theme, in which the super-dog, Sirius, and the human girl, Plaxy, consummate their love. Stapledon essays this unpalatable theme, interspecific sexual relations, with genuine warmth and pathos.

The scientist who develops Sirius's intelligence exclaims, 'I feel as God ought to have felt towards Adam when Adam went wrong – morally responsible.' But this, as Fiedler rightly insists, is a love story, and a doomed one at that. The ordinary clamour of human affairs, the rattle of coffee spoons, the marrying and begetting, lie beyond Stapledon's compass: yet this harried canine life, with its struggle for self-realisation on lonely hillsides, does grow to represent, as Fiedler declares, 'the condition of all creatures, including ourselves.'

It is Stapledon's most famous book, *Last and First Men*, which most troubles Fiedler. The problem with that splendid flight of the imagination is that four opening chapters intervene before take-off. These are the chapters purporting to cover terrestrial history from 1930, when the book was published, until the fall of the First Men (us), five thousand years after the death of Newton. Not only do these chapters get everything wrong (Germans good, Americans bad, Russians nice, Chinese still sporting pigtails in 2298 A.D.); they show racial prejudice, with short shrift given Negroes, Jews, and capitalist Americans.

Only after Stapledon has struggled through this weary catalogue of fake history do we get to the great scientific myth. Should we trust the myth when the fact is so faulty? Charity suggests that Stapledon was, by all the evidence, a pleasant, self-effacing man who preferred to live quietly with his wife, son and daughter in the Wirral. His contacts with the outside world were few; he was glad to dream and cultivate his garden. He got the facts wrong but the dream right. Many contemporary science fiction writers achieve the opposite.

So Fiedler spends some while talking about the long out-of-print American edition of *Last and First Men*, abridged by Basil Davenport, ignoring what we may term the Allen Lane solution. Such is the price we pay for the defects of English scholarship.

British readers will also sense Fiedler's difficulties in coming to terms with Stapledon's Englishness and his English self-deprecation. That Stapledon was a late developer is clear; his early transplantation to Egypt may help account for that. But there was nothing particularly unusual about a Victorian man remaining virgin into his thirties, owing to lack of opportunity and the sexual mores of the time; repression is a theme occurring more than once in Stapledon's works – however odd this may appear to the generation which invented AIDS. Fiedler stresses the homosexual relationships he detects in Stapledon's books, worries about no loves free of 'shameful miscegenation,' and shakes his head in a fuddy-duddy way over Stapledon's 'not-quite-incestuous' marriage to his Australian first cousin, Agnes. He also claims to find in the works a streak of sado-masochism 'verging on the pathological.' Myself, I think it was just a passing Zeitgeist.

Perhaps this pop psychology serves to add a little melodrama to an otherwise humdrum existence, but it distorts the truth. What a reader of Stapledon would really like to know is whence came his intense imaginative gift, which can at once create such effects of distancing in space and time and yet brings us close to multitudinous beings unlike ourselves in almost every way. Could it have been something to do with those restless early years, exiled back and forth between Merseyside and Port Said? The sea voyages would have been odysseys of estrangement for a sensitive child.

The exclusion of events from his life suggests that, like Bertrand Russell, Stapledon felt cursed by loneliness. His novels are short on dialogue and read often like debates with himself. In one remarkable section of Chapter X of *Star Maker*, the journeying human soul, with spirit friends, views the galaxy at an early stage of its existence. The passage is far too long to quote here; it concludes with a view of the fully evolved galaxy:

> The stars themselves gave an irresistable impression of vitality. Strange that the movements of these merely physical things, these mere fire-balls, whirling and travelling according to the geometrical laws of their minutest particles, should seem so vital, so questing. But then the whole galaxy was itself so vital, so like an organism, with its delicate tracery of star-streams, like the streams within a living cell; and its extended wreaths, almost like feelers; and its nucleus of light. Surely this great and lovely creature must be alive, must have intelligent experience of itself and of things other than it.

Then comes one of those quick contradictions which endow Stapledon's narrative with its tensile strength:

> In the tide of these wild thoughts we checked our fancy, remembering that only on the rare grains called planets can life gain foothold, and that all this wealth of restless jewels was but a waste of fire.

Under the detached tone is an almost animist belief in life everywhere, sentience everywhere. One of Stapledon's last fantasies, *The Flames*, postulates a madman's vision of fire with intellect.

With such paradox, such bleakness and beauty, Fiedler is well-equipped to deal. 'Ecstasy' is one of Stapledon's favourite words, and the ecstasy is usually one of both pain and pleasure. For there is pleasure of a high order in making that desperate voyage to come face-to-face with the Star Maker, and pain in discovering that this universe is but one in a sequence of universes, each imperfect in its way. 'Cosmos after cosmos, each more rich and subtle than the last, leapt from his fervent imagination.' In the extraordinary Chapter XV, Stapledon describes a progression of these flawed cosmoses, each one in turn failing ultimately to satisfy its creator, who stores them away like so many old video games in a cupboard, as he turns to prepare a yet more complex strategy.

Our own cosmos is in turn about to be put away. In the succeeding cosmos, according to the thought of the Star Maker, the physical will be 'more patently phantasmal than in our own cosmos,' while the beings who inhabit it will be 'far less deceived by the opacity of their individual mental processes, and more sensitive to their underlying unity.'

What really sets this dramatic unfolding at odds with Christian doctrine is the Star Maker's ruthlessness. The point is made more than once. 'Here was no pity, no proffer of salvation, no kindly aid. Or here were all pity and all love, but mastered by a frosty ecstasy.' Later: 'All passions, it seemed, were comprised within the spirit's temper; but mastered, icily gripped within the cold, clear, crystal ecstasy of contemplation.' This is closer to Thomas Hardy than Thomas Aquinas.

As Fiedler emphasizes, it was this display of coldness, this sense – to quote Fiedler's chapter heading – that God is Not Love, which moved C. S. Lewis to characterise Stapledon as the possessed scientist, Weston, in *Out of the Silent Planet* and *Perelandra*. This pillorying, sadly enough, represents about the peak of Stapledon's fame. He did not respond to Lewis. He always maintained a low profile, probably preferring the ecstasies of contemplation and chrysanthemums. Or perhaps, from the distance of the Wirral, he imagined that C.S. Lewis was one of those Bloomsburyites.

* * *

There was an occasion when Stapledon failed to keep a low profile. He turned up at the Waldorf Astoria in New York in 1949, for a meeting of the Cultural and Scientific Conference for World Peace, organized by the Soviet Union. Stapledon was the only British delegate.

Fiedler makes a good deal of this event, probably because he can draw on an eye-witness, Mr. Sam Moskowitz, the well-known scholar of SF. Stapledon was then sixty-three and evidently feeling his age; he would die in the following year. Moskowitz represents him as being deeply troubled that his books were out of print. It is surely easy to extend sympathy to such a figure who – blind to appearing a gullible fellow-traveler – seized on this wretched opportunity to cut some kind of figure in a world whose attention he had failed to capture.

Moskowitz gives Fiedler a chance to play the former's old game of trying to assess a writer by his influence on other writers, as if this were a sole measure of fitness. Moskowitz lists Eric Frank Russell, Clifford Simak, Robert Heinlein, and others who, had they truly experienced Stapledon, would have written differently. Fiedler includes Philip K. Dick, Ursula Le Guin, and Stanislaw Lem, as well as an example from Poul Anderson which might more reasonably come under the heading of cribbing.

Stapledon is so inventive that many passages could be pointed to as notes which later, lesser, writers expanded into full-scale novels. One of such instances occurs in Chapter XIII of *Star Maker*: 'The huge dark worlds with their immense weight of atmosphere and their incredible breadths of ocean, where the waves even in their most furious storms were never more than ripples such as we know on quicksilver ...' Is not this the origin of Hal Clement's *Mission of Gravity*? The answer, almost certainly, is No.

What is certain is that Stapledon has had a real impact on British SF authors. Arthur Clarke has admitted his debt, and Fiedler has heard of Arthur Clarke. That prevalent 'pessimism,' as Americans like to label it, that preoccupation with the root causes of things, that suspicion of the Machine, that savouring of disaster, even that eye on what the Immanent Will may be up to next – all these are as English as apple pie, and flow strongly through Stapledon even if they do not ultimately derive from him. Possibly William Golding's name should also be considered here.

Only the American scene, of course, concerns Fiedler. As an intellectual and academic, his is a brave defence of science fiction; however, one cannot but notice that when he turns to address fans directly, as it were, his language becomes more lax, thus: '[Stapledon] seems to have remained finally unaware that by spinning yarns about the future in a narrative mode which eschewed the example of Henry James and James Joyce, co-founders – in the view of real highbrows – of the English art novel...' etc.

Following this passage, Fiedler goes on to quote another of Moskowitz's suggestions, that Stapledon was influenced by Edgar Rice Burroughs. To read Burroughs is one thing; but Stapledon is at the opposite pole to the author of *Tarzan*, that jolly old hack, and to refuse to recognize this is to do SF no service.

It is idle to imagine that, if Eric Frank Russell had been persuasive enough, Stapledon might have contributed to John W. Campbell's *Astounding*, and thereby have found fame. He never subscribed to the idea that one brave guy could lick the universe, given a big enough spaceship.

So in the end Stapledon, whose grand theme is communication, communication between woman and super-beast, between alien and human, between organic and inorganic, between soul and creator, largely failed to communicate. Not with his contemporary readership; hardly with his fellow-authors; rarely with the SF fans.

A failure? Far from it, unless success is to be measured only by the coinage. At least in his two great neurasthenic masterpieces, he soared to imaginative heights unrivalled in invention and *gravitas*. It would be only appropriate if Olaf Stapledon found his greatest readership in the future.

The Downward Journey: Orwell's 1984

'There is a word in Newspeak,' said Syme, 'I don't know whether you know it: *duckspeak*, to quack like a duck. It is one of those interesting words that have two contradictory meanings. Applied to an opponent, it is abuse; applied to someone you agree with, it is praise.'

Neologisms such as *duckspeak* and slogans like 'War is Peace' provide dramatic signposts in the landscape of George Orwell's *1984*, and direct our attention towards the oppositions and paradoxes of which it is constructed. The whole novel charts an example of enantiodromia, that is, the inevitable turning of one thing into its opposite; its strategy is to anatomise Winston Smith's progression from hatred to the time – dramatically achieved in that resounding last sentence of the text – when he comes to love Big Brother.

In this mirror effect, left has become right, right left. I shall deal here with some of the ways in which Orwell mirrors life.

One major mirror effect is proclaimed in the very title, for *Nineteen Eighty-Four* is itself a piece of wordplay, the year 1984 being a mirror image, at least as far as the last two digits are concerned, of the year in which Orwell was writing the novel, 1948.

The novel itself is full of similar oppositions. Winston Smith's barrack-like flat is contrasted with the love-nest over the antique shop. The elaboration and importance of his work at the Ministry is contrasted with its triviality. The astronomical number of boots manufactured on paper by the state is contrasted with the fact that half the population of Oceania goes barefoot. When O'Brien holds up four fingers, Smith sees five, in the final obscene triumph of doublethink.

There is another hierarchy of oppositions, the ones which most grasp our attention because they are mirror images of assumptions we make in the everyday world. We do not believe that IGNORANCE IS STRENGTH or that FREEDOM IS SLAVERY – although the novel shows clearly how these things can be. We believe that peace is the norm and war is the exception, unlike the rulers of Oceania. Nor do we readily accept that political confessions, extracted under duress, are true.

All these oppositions, which are word-oriented, are paraded in order to unsettle us. If the novel's title is 'merely' wordplay, then we are entitled to ask to what extent Orwell was actually trying to predict the future, or to what extent he was simply deploying 'the future' as a metaphor for his present; in other words, using the future for yet another mirror effect.

In many of its aspects, *1984* captures accurately daily existence in World War II for the civilian population. Here are the rundown conditions under which people in England, Germany, and elsewhere actually lived, here are the occasional bombs falling, the spirit of camaraderie, and the souped up hatred of a common enemy. The rationing, the propaganda, the life lived in shelters, the cigarettes which must be kept horizontal so that their tobacco does not spill out, the shortage of razor blades, the recourse to cheap gin: these are details of common-experience in the forties, gathered together for maximum artistic effect. At the same time, on a more personal level, Smith's work at the Ministry of Truth reflects Orwell's work at the BBC in Broadcasting House.

In such aspects, Orwell used a general present. It is this general present which provides the furniture of the novel.

More deeply part of the centrality of the book are some of Orwell's own obsessions. The familiar Orwellian squalor is in evidence throughout. The woman poking out a drain in *The Road to Wigan Pier* reappears as Mrs Parsons with her drain problem, and so on. Such matters are in evidence even in Orwell's first novel, *Keep the Aspidistra Flying*, and a preoccupation with illness and personal decay infect the novel – hardly surprisingly, in view of Orwell's deteriorating health. He died only a few months after *1984* was published and proclaimed. In the final scenes, when Smith and Julia meet for the last time, it is age as well as torture which has ruined them: 'her thickened, stiffened body was no longer recognisable from behind.'

But this is a novel operating beyond the compass of the ordinary realist novel. Being a political novel – that rare thing, an English political novel – it has more dimensions to it than the physical. Its principal preoccupation is with betrayal, betrayal through words. In this respect, it is a sibling of *Animal Farm*. ALL ANIMALS ARE EQUAL BUT SOME ANIMALS ARE MORE EQUAL THAN OTHERS is a step, or rather a long stride, towards *duckspeak*, and the betrayal of the deepest intentions of a revolution. Winston Smith, right from the start, is not only a secret enemy of the Party he serves. He also betrays himself by his enjoyment of the work he does for it. 'Smith's greatest pleasure in life was in his work' – and his work is bound up with words, distorting the truth by falsifying od records even when those records are themselves already fake.

Orwell's deployment of the philosophical entanglements inherent in words and phrases is masterly. He was early in life fascinated by G.K. Chesterton's unparalleled talent for paradox. *1984* may owe something to Chesterton's future-fantasy, *The Napoleon of Notting Hill*; it certainly extends its paradoxes. One example must suffice. When Smith asks O'Brien if Big Brother exists 'in the same way as I exist,' O'Brien answers immediately, 'You do not exist.' Here the paradox is that no paradox exists, for, in Newspeak terms, Smith has become an unperson and does not exist.

Nor is it too fanciful to imagine that Orwell believed that his novel would falsify the future. Certainly, that seems to have been one of its effects. Fear is a great hypnotiser, and some people are prepared to believe that we live in an actual Orwellian vision of the future, in that world whose image is a boot stamping on a human face forever. In a literal sense, of course, this is totally untrue. We still live in a world worth defending. War and peace are still distinguishable states of mind. (And in 1984 at least one atomic bomb has been dropped on Airstrip One; that has not happened in our real world – yet at any rate.)

The West may, like decadent Byzantium apeing the manners of its besiegers, ultimately betray itself from within to the enemy without. But we still live in a community where diverse opinion is tolerated, where individual salvation may be found, where TV sets have an Off button, and where we are not subject to that prevailing paradox which subjugates Orwell's proles: 'Until they become conscious they will never rebel, and until they have rebelled they cannot become conscious.'

To see 1984 as a nest of paradoxes is not to denigrate its power. Indeed, it may be in part to admit that to attempt to chronicle the future using the past tense is itself a paradox, one committed unwittingly every time a science fiction writer puts pen to paper. But 1984 is a more humorous novel than is generally acknowledged, though admittedly the humour is decidedly *noir*. In that respect, it bears a resemblance to Franz Kafka's work, about which learned commentators have rightly expended much serious thought. (Learned commentators are correct in regarding humour as subversive.) Yet when Kafka read extracts from *Der Prozess* to Max Brod and friends, they all laughed heartily, and Kafka often could not continue for tears of laughter. But Kafka and Orwell both acknowledged Dickens among their masters of grim humour.

When I first became interested in Orwell's play with paradox and mirror image, I conceived the idea that the plot of *1984* is much like that of an A.E. van Vogt science-fantasy novel, in which one man alone has a vision of the truth, sets out to overturn the world, and finally manages to do so ('Asylum' is one such example). Orwell took a great interest in trash literature. This interest manifests itself in *1984* in the passages where Smith, as part of his work, invents a story about a fictitious character called Comrade Ogilvy. 'At the age of three, Comrade Ogilvy had refused all toys except a drum, a sub-machine gun, and a model helicopter … At nineteen, he had designed a hand-grenade which … at its first trial, had killed thirty-one Eurasian prisoners in one burst…' This clearly is a kind of science fiction story at whose absurdity we are meant to laugh.

In pursuit of the Van Vogt connection, I once took the opportunity of asking Orwell's widow, Sonia, if Orwell had read much pulp science fiction (it existed at that period only in pulp magazine form). Had he ever read any A. E. van Vogt, with plots centering on world-wide conspiracy?

Her answers, like so many answers life gives us, were enigmatic. She thought he had read some science fiction. She did not know the name of Van Vogt.

About H. G. Wells Orwell was much better informed. He expressed his delight more than once in Wells's scientific romances, even going so far as to claim that 'thinking people who were born about the beginning of the century are in some sense Wells's own creation.' But he disagreed strongly with Wells as political soothsayer, and in particular with Wells's views concerning a world state, of which he said, 'Much of what Wells has argued and worked for is physically there in Nazi Germany.'

Shortly after World War I, Wells rebuked Winston Churchill for speaking of the Bolsheviks as if they were a different order of being. Orwell argued that Churchill was more realistic and that he was right and Wells wrong. With totalitarianism, a new order of men had come into the world, perverting science for their own ends. *1984* is the history of that new order. O'Brien and the Party members are Orwell's ghoulish mirror image of Wells's Samurai in *A Modern Utopia*, while at the same time representing the new totalitarianism rising to threaten the post-war world. The debt to Wells is unavoidable; he was the man who had created the future as a forum for debate on present ends and means at the turn of the century.

We can now see the answer to our question. Was Orwell trying to predict the future or was he using the notion of the future as a mirror for his present? Of course the answer is ambiguous. Most of the novel mirrors the past ('"The past is more important," agreed O'Brien gravely'), including the tradition of constructing utopias, but this is built about a core of futurism, that core in which Orwell conjures up the spectre of England under a totalitarian regime, a regime in which science is at the service of a new brutality, and in which the world is locked into a kind of dreadful unity through the war that is peace. The future and its polemics are given reality by the employment of the furniture of the past.

As with many novels, *1984* mirrors the author's own life and the books to which he is indebted. What is different about *1984* is that it utilises the most powerful lever available to science fiction; it places the events it depicts ahead of us, and so to be yet experienced, instead of behind us in the past, and so safely out of the way.

In Orwell's world, the very word 'freedom' has been banished. Whereas in our world, words like 'freedom' and 'democracy' are bandied about in everyday use on all sides. But has freedom in fact been banished for the fictitious inhabitants of Airstrip One? In order to maintain a boot stamping on the human face forever, the owner of the boot must suffer as well as the owner of the face. The price of loss of freedom is eternal vigilance.

There are few rewards for the Party faithful except power. Power is seen as an end in itself. The real, undeclared aim of the Party is, we are told, to remove all pleasure from the sexual act. This startling but negative aim, which Orwell does not consistently pursue, reflects the negativity of power; it is doubtful whether Big Brother actually exists, while higher up officials like O'Brien are merely inquisitors with some new, some ancient, tortures at their command. Orwell can imagine rats but not Stalin.

Power like money is useless in itself. There has to be something to spend it on. It is true that 'purges and vaporisations' are a part of the mechanism of the Party's regime of government, but this is scarcely enough to satisfy a Party member. Puritanism is all they get. Orwell himself was possibly dissatisfied with this arrangement. When Smith gets to O'Brien's flat, we see that it is not so austere as all that. There is wallpaper on the walls, the floors are carpeted, the telescreen can be switched off, the butler pours wine from a decanter, and there are good cigarettes in a silver box. Not sybaritic, exactly; more the sort of thing to which typical Old Etonians (Orwell was an untypical example) could be said to be accustomed.

Even in these elegant surroundings, O'Brien is discovered still working. The proles he helps to oppress enjoy greater freedom.

For the proles in their seedy bits of decaying London there are trashy newspapers, astrology, films 'oozing with sex,' pornography, rubbishy novels, booze, sport, and gambling. These are all in plentiful supply. Orwell shows his traditional mixture of despisal and envy of the working classes; Smith's attitude is very much that of Gordon Comstock in *Keep the Aspidistra Flying*, written thirteen years earlier. Gordon 'wanted to sink down, down into the muck where money does not rule.' The proles are free of worries, only the proles have double beds, and no one cares if there are bed bugs. Smith manages to reach that place mentioned longingly by Gordon: 'down, down, into some dreadful sub-world that as yet he could only imagine.' Orwell did finally imagine it, in his most extraordinary novel, and that repeated 'down, down' shows how far the journey was.

* * *

One can see how George Orwell enjoyed writing *1984* for its own sake. I believe the prophetic element to be only part of its attraction, and in any case the prophesy was apotropaic, intended to warn. Thus, the more it succeeded in conveying its warning, the less likely was its picture of the future to become reality. Its success is that it fails to paint a true portrait of the true 1984. However grim we may hold our 1984 to be, it is not Orwell's grimness. We perhaps owe Orwell some gratitude that his widely influential *1984* is not our 1984.

Some commentators have claimed as a weakness the fact that the dialectic of the novel is all with the Party, with O'Brien, with the Thought Police, and that nothing positive is offered by way of opposition. To my mind, such comments show a misreading of the book. In the long line of utopianists, Orwell has an honourable place.

H. G. Wells perceived that for a utopia to exist in a period of rapid communications it had to be world-wide; and for 1905, before the first World War, this was an acute perception. By the late nineteen-forties, after a second World War, Orwell saw that a countervailing paradox was required. His way to happiness on Earth lies in the subversive message which Julia slips Smith in the corridor, a note saying merely I LOVE YOU. And utopia, far from being worldwide, has shrunk to a shabby little room over a shop, with a willing girl, a double bed, and plenty of privacy.

Thus have our expectations diminished over the century.

Such a utopia needs no dialectic. Its strength is precisely that it does not require words. For the true enemy in *1984* is ultimately words themselves, those treacherous words which will serve any vile purpose to which they are put. Even Julia's message has a taint to it, since its three words hold the most important one in common with that other well-known three-worder, the much-feared Ministry of Love: indeed, in Smith's case, one leads almost directly to the other.

In place of words come objects, and the inarticulate life of proledom, personified in the old washerwoman singing under the lovers' window as she hangs out her washing. It is a distinctly nostalgic substitution. As Smith says, referring to a paperweight he has bought, a piece of coral embedded in glass, 'If the past survives anywhere, it's in a few solid objects with no words attached to them, like that lump of glass there.' Words are the allies of doublethink.

In a television broadcast made over the Christmas period, 1982, the novelist Anthony Burgess claimed to have read *1984* thirty times. He said of it that it was one of those rare books which tells us what we need to know, which informs us of what reality is.

Like all of Orwell's novels, with the brilliant exception of *Animal Farm*, *1984* is not a masterpiece judged purely as novel. Judged as a vehicle for putting over what Orwell wished to tell us, for conveying that pungent mixture of squalor, nostalgia, disillusion and analysis of betrayal, it is brilliant.

Although *1984* does not on the surface hold up a mirror to our 1984, I believe that Burgess was right on a more inward plane. In 1948, that drab year best never relived, the novel seemed indeed to be a prediction of the future, exact in each realistic detail. Read in the year of its title, it has turned disconcertingly into a secret history of all our lives. For we have lived in a parallel world of political bullying and hypocrisy, of wars and totalitarianism, of cultural revolutions and anti-cultural movements, of blind hedonism and wild-eyed shortage. Even if these things have not overcome us, they have marked us. Our shadows – to use the word in a Jungian sense – have conspired with the Thought Police and the Party. What has happened to us here is, in O'Brien's words, forever.

We see the novel's transformation through time: from prophecy of the future to a parable of our worldy existence, 1948–1984.

It will be interesting to see what becomes of Orwell's novel now the year 1984 is over and concentration on it has died away. It would be pleasant to believe that *Animal Farm* would then be more generally read and recognised, for it remains the book on revolution and revolution's betrayal, and one of the seminal fables of our century.

My personal feeling is that *1984* will continue to be read and loved by ordinary people; and this for a good reason. Though we prefer to overlook the fact, many aspects of *1984* closely correspond to the lives of those 'ordinary people.' For most, life is a battle against poverty, shortages, inadequate housing, ill health. They too experience betrayals which may prove fatal. They too come to experience in their own bodies – and without needing words – what Julia experienced, a thickened stiffened body, unrecognisable from behind. They too are manipulated by uncaring governments.

In one film version of *1984*, the ending showed Smith and Julia reunited, clinging happily to each other, unchanged by their ordeal. We have a contempt of that sort of thing. Not only is such nonsense untrue to Orwell's novel: it is unfortunately untrue to most people's experience.

What we value most about Orwell's work is not its prophecy or even its polemics, but rather the way it faithfully mirrors the experience of the majority of the people.

A Whole New Can of Worms

Philip Dick made me happy. I loved and still love his novels. Why be made happy over novels which show all too plainly how awful the state of the world is? Because they did just that, without flinching, without having soft centres and sloppy endings. And because of the way they were written – with a unique tang.

Cowardly critics have sometimes found my novels gloomy, but I never managed as much sheer silent disaster as Dick. He should have had a Nobel prize.

When Dick died, we held a memorial meeting for him in London. It was heat-wave time, with temperatures in the nineties. The dogs were crawling into dustbins to die. Nevertheless, the faithful turned up at the old City Lit rooms and crammed into the theatre. Even the molecules jostled each other.

I was one of the three speakers from the platform.

Here's what I said. And I hope you're still listening, Phil.

We're here tonight to rejoice. There is no reason to mourn – well, not too much. Bucket-kicking is endemic in the human race. Have you ever considered that it may be all of us who have gone, whisked into some terrible schizoid version of the present ruled over by Brezhnev, Mrs Thatcher, Pope John Paul, and the

Argentinian junta, while Phil Dick remains where he ever was, in Santa Ana, still jovially fighting entropy and kipple with a new, eighth, wife by his side?

We rejoice because Dick is one of the few writers to defy the First Law of SF Thermodynamics. This law states that exploitation in the SF field is so great that writers decay as they age instead of maturing, like bad wine, and that meaningfulness decreases in inverse proportion to number of words published.

Like all good SF writers, Dick was continually trying to figure out what made the universe tick. Even if there is a way to figure out the universe, it probably can't be done through SF, which forever throws in its own 'what ifs' to flavour the recipe. Figuring out the universe needs: long scientific training, the mind of a genius, and years of zen silence; three qualities antithetical to all SF buffs. Nevertheless such an attempt is worth making, and for the same reason that never quite reaching the peak of Mount Everest is better than never having climbed it at all. There really were times when it seemed as if Dick had the universe in a corner.

The more you try to figure out the universe, the more enigmatic it becomes. You know that ingenious U-bend in a toilet, which used to figure conspicuously in Harpic adverts; it keeps the stinks down the drain instead of in the room? Since the universe you are trying to figure out includes the mind doing the figuring, then – as Sir Karl Popper may have said in a back issue of *Planet Stories* – that mind acts as its own U-bend and refuses to let you get down to the real layers of fertiliser where growth and destruction begin.

All the same, Dick patented his own U-bend into ontology. Before our eyes, he kept opening up whole new cans of worms. Dick suffered from paralysing anxiety states which forays into the world of drugs did not alleviate; we see his mind constantly teasing out what is to be trusted, what let in, what discarded – and how far let in, how far discarded. The process applied alike to words, canopeners, wives, and worlds.

From this, anyone not knowing anything about Dick might

conclude that he was a gloomy and terrifying writer. Well, he was terrifying, certainly, but the gloom is shot through with hilarity. The worse things got, the funnier. His literary precursors are Kafka and Dickens. Actually, Kafka, Dickens and A. E. van Vogt: it's the secret schlock ingredient that makes Dick tick.

Let's just illustrate with a passage from A *Scanner Darkly*, one of Dick's best and most terrifying novels, where Charles Freck decides to commit suicide.

At the last moment (as end-time closed in on him) he changed his mind on a decisive issue and decided to drink the reds down with a conoisseur wine instead of Ripple or Thunderbird, so he set off on one last drive, over to Trader Joe's, which specialized in fine wines, and bought a bottle of 1971 Mondavi Cabernet Sauvignon, which set him back almost thirty dollars – all he had.

Back home again, he uncorked the wine, let it breathe, drank a few glasses of it, spent a few minutes contemplating his favorite page of *The Illustrated Picture Book of Sex*, which showed the girl on top, then placed the plastic bag of reds beside his bed, lay down with the Ayn Rand book and unfinished protest letter to Exxon, tried to think of something meaningful but could not, although he kept remembering the girl being on top, and then, with a glass of the Cabernet Sauvignon, gulped down all the reds at once. After that, the deed being done, he lay back, the Ayn Rand book and letter on his chest, and waited.

However, he had been burned. The capsules were not barbiturates, as represented. They were some kind of kinky psychedelics, of a type he had never dropped before, probably a mixture, and new on the market. Instead of quietly suffocating, Charles Freck began to hallucinate. Well, he thought philosophically, this is the story of my life. Always ripped off. He had to face the fact – considering how many of the capsules he had swallowed – that he was in for some trip.

The next thing he knew, a creature from between dimensions was standing beside his bed looking down at him disapprovingly.

72

The creature had many eyes, all over it, ultra-modern expensive-looking clothing, and rose up eight feet high. Also, it carried an enormous scroll.

'You're going to read me my sins,' Charles Freck said.

The creature nodded and unsealed the scroll.

Freck said, lying helpless on his bed, 'and it's going to take a hundred thousand hours.'

Fixing its many compound eyes on him, the creature from between dimensions said, 'We are no longer in the mundane universe. Lower-plane categories of material existence such as "space" and "time" no longer apply to you. You have been elevated to the transcendant realm. Your sins will be read to you ceaselessly, in shifts, throughout eternity. The list will never end.'

Know your dealer, Charles Freck thought, and wished he could take back the last half-hour of his life.

A thousand years later he was still lying there on his bed with the Ayn Rand book and the letter to Exxon on his chest, listening to them read his sins to him. They had gotten up to the first grade, when he was six years old.

Ten thousand years later they had reached the sixth grade.

The year he had discovered masturbation.

He shut his eyes, but he could still see the multi-eyed, eight-foot-high being with its endless scroll reading on and on.

'And next –' it was saying.

Charles Freck thought, At least I got a good wine.

This unusual ability to mix tragedy with farce is matched by a paranoid's ability to scramble – if not always unscramble – plots. The result is an *oeuvre* which presents a large scale portrait of the incursions of technological advance upon the psyche of the West, and its shattering under a series of hammer blows. Occasional protagonists may survive, but Dick never leaves us under any illusions about the magnitude of the incursion.

Thus his work represents an unrivalled unity in the SF field, a unity only reinforced by the way in which most of the texts of that *oeuvre* are staged – not far away in the galaxy, which might have afforded some relief – but in one of the epicentres of the disintegrating psyche, Southern California.

With the disintegrating psyche, as some might expect, the disintegrating family. The one portrait of a family in all of Dick's *oeuvre* is the four miserable junkies, spying on each other, dying or trying to die, together with their cat child-substitute, in *A Scanner Darkly*. With this absence of familial pattern goes a disconcerting absence of mother-figures, and indeed a certain lack of females all round. It's hard to imagine a Mrs Palmer Eldritch, and the policeman who wants his tears to flow has for wife merely a devilish sister.

For three decades, Dick unfolded this schizoid portrait of the coming age. Again, one must repeat, we can observe in his writing a steady deepening of his understanding and capacities, as we observe it in Dickens.

During the first decade, the fifties, we admire the surface glitter of his puzzles – *Time Out of Joint* – and all that. His prankish short stories become increasingly sophisticated. In the sixties, profound change continues: what was devised becomes felt; complexity of plot becomes matched to a complexity of thought. The Weltanschauung is not universally dark, though illusion is harder to disentangle. In this period stand three of Dick's surest memorials, *The Three Stigmata of Palmer Eldritch*, *The Man in the High Castle*, and *Martian Timeslip*. Slightly later, also in the sixties, is another group of three, though I think a lesser group, *Now Wait For Last Year*, *Do Androids Dream of Electric Sheep?*, and *Ubik*. Here, unrealities have multiplied to such an extent that the result is a confusion we are tempted merely to reject as abnormal; the threatened illusions of the earlier group strike much nearer home.

The seventies yield two remarkable novels in which the protagonists strive for reality, in one case finding and in one case failing to find it: *Flow My Tears, the Policeman Said*, and *A Scanner Darkly*. The 'explanation' of *Flow My Tears*, whereby a group of people move into transposed reality because of another person's, Jason Taverner's, failings, makes no scientific and even worse theological sense, though for all that it is a sombrely glittering novel, the real hero being a corrupt police chief who does not enter until half-way through the book. But *A Scanner Darkly* is all too terrifyingly plausible, on both scientific and theological grounds, with the terrible drug, Death, which splits the corpus callosum, rendering the victim dissociated from himself. This, it seems to me, is the grandest, darkest, of all Dick's hells.

My guess is that Dick at one time came to some kind of perilous treaty with psychedelic drugs, just as Anna Kavan did with heroin. Kavan never came off heroin; it was her doppelganger, her bright destroyer, killingly necessary to her. Dick's renunciation of drugs brought forth the eighties group of novels, again a trio, *Valis*, *The Divine Invasion*, and *The Transmigration of Timothy Archer*. It's too early to judge this group. The last novel is set in what for Dick is a curiously sunny Southern California, and opens on the day John Lennon is shot. It thrills with intimations of death – but when I said that to someone, he said, 'What Dick novel doesn't?'

I have to say, ungratefully, that I so vastly enjoyed Dick giving me bad news, opening up whole new cans of worms at every turn, that I become peevish when a can opens and angels come winging out. That the narrator of *Timothy Archer* is a lady called Angel hardly helps matters. Despite these reservations, it is a complex and interesting novel, fairly light and sunny in tone. It bears the hallmark of Dick, a hallmark discernable even in the minor novels, genuine grief that things are as bad as they are. That's a rare quality in SF.

So Dick began as a smart imitator of Van Vogt and ended up as a wizard. Most careers in the SF field flow the other way about. Maybe it's the Hobart effect.

Dick said that it was not the possibilities of SF that appealed to him but the wild possibilities. Not just, 'What would happen if...' but 'My God, what would happen if...'

This is partly why we like him. But ultimately the affection he inspires is beyond analysis. He had a way of dramatising his inner fears which made you laugh. His novels are full of gadgets, sentient hardware, and awesome entities, but nevertheless they are inward novels. He constantly invents new means of doom and destruction, but nevertheless a sense of gusto bounces up from the page. In some peculiar sense, he was a world-league novelist, yet he meekly burnt two mainstream novels when Don Wollheim told him they were no good. There's the paradox. If it wasn't for Don Wollheim at Ace, we'd possibly never have seen any Dick novels ever, and the universe would have been different. All our inner lives, ditto.

Dick's American readers appear only to have found Dick depressing. Was he too wild? Were there too many worms in his can? It was in Britain that he first found more realistic and welcoming appraisal. Accustomed by national temperament to sailing through seas of bad news without turning a vibrissa, we appreciated Dick's ingenuity, inventiveness, and metaphysical wit. We taught the Americans to see what a giant they had in their midst, just as they taught us to admire Tolkien. If we do admire Tolkien.

Now the tide has turned. Hollywood has made an over-heated, over-produced, and overtly immoral film from a lovely book, and called it by a crummy old Alan Nourse title, *Blade Runner*, an anagram of *Brunner Laid*. The rebarbative Stanislaw Lem said that Dick fought trash with trash. It looks like trash could win.

Meanwhile, the SF world rallies round, aware that some awful grey shagged-out thing on Mars has now got Dick by the short hairs. I've never liked the SF community more. A real spirit of affection is in evidence. Hence this meeting.

The SF newspaper, *Locus*, put out an excellent Dick memorial number just after he disappeared, with tributes and memories from many hands. Perhaps I may quote here a paragraph from what I said then, writing in New York:

Dick was never out of sight since his first appearances in those great glad early days of the fifties, when the cognoscenti among us scoured the magazines on the bookstalls for names that had suddenly acquired a talismanic quality: J.G. Ballard, William Tenn, Philip K. Dick. Now he's gone, the old bear, the old sage and jester, the old destroyer, the sole writer among us who, in Pushkin's mighty phrase, 'laid waste the hearts of men.'

Peep

When Jim Blish was yielding finally in the battle against cancer which he had fought for many years, my wife and I went to visit him in the ominously named Battle Hospital in Reading, England.

He lay in bed in a towelling robe, dark, bitter, lightweight – intense against the pallid room. As ever, he radiated great mental energy. Books were piled all over the place, by the bedside, on the bed. Oswald Spengler's *Decline of the West* lay open, face down, on the blankets.

Dear Blish! What tenacity of life and intellect! I thought of that incident in Battle Hospital when reading *The Quincunx of Time* once again. *Quincunx* is a rare thing, true SF with a scientific basis – the sort of story that readers have always been saying isn't written anymore. And it is something more than that. It is, in a way, gadget fiction; central to it is a marvellous gadget, the Dirac transmitter – but the Dirac leads to deep metaphysical water, into which Blish plunges with glee.

The science chiefly involved is mathematics, proverbially the queen of the sciences. New dimensions of time are opened in the novel; a more complex math has been achieved in the future, in which time is subsumed as an extra spacial dimension. Hence

Quincunx's world-lines. Hence, too, one of its most famous passages, when one of the characters who has been listening to the transmitter declares:

> 'I've heard the commander of a world-line cruiser, travelling from 8873 to 8704 along the world-line of the planet Hethshepa, which circles a star on the rim of NGC 4725, call for help across eleven million light years...'

The characters who overhear this extraordinary communication are perplexed, as well they might be. They work out the problem, the solution to which is neat and exciting. Their perplexity springs from the fact that they are looking into a future where different number-worlds from ours prevail. It's wonderful but also logical: *there is not, and there cannot be, numbers as such*. The line in italics is not mine but Spengler's. He put it in italics, too.

Spengler amplified his statement by saying, 'There are several number-worlds as there are several Cultures. We find an Indian, an Arabian, a Classical, a Western type of mathematical thought and, corresponding with each, a type of number – each type fundamentally peculiar and unique, an expression of a particular world-feeling ....'

Whether or not Blish derived some of his ideas direct from Spengler, we cannot now determine. In this case, it seems likely.

A different cultural base would naturally make the future difficult for us to comprehend, and vice versa. The future will no more understand our compulsion to stock-pile enough nuclear weapons to destroy the world several times over than we understand why the Egyptians built the pyramids.

'You'll know the future, but not what it means,' says one of the characters in *Quincunx*. 'The farther into the future you travel with the machine, the more incomprehensible the messages become ....'

One of the many original features of this novel is that it does actually concern the future. Most science fiction, if it is not fantasy, is about some extension of the present which only by agreement do we call 'the future.' It catches our attention because we see in it a mirror of the present day. Blish was after something different. *Quincunx* is like few other fictions, and does not resemble closely anything else Blish wrote.

Another strange feature is the fact that the story is about a galactic empire, although this does not appear to be the case at first. (I anthologised it under its original title, *Beep*, in my two-volume *Galactic Empires* (Avon Books, 1979)), Blish solves the vital question of how communications could be maintained over vast distances. The strange thing about Blish's galactic empire is that it is a utopia. This we have never heard before. Things always go wrong in galactic empires, as we know. In Blish's empire, things go obstinately right. Instant communication has brought perfect communion.

The long short story *Beep* has been only slightly expanded to make *Quincunx*. Most of the expansion is in the nature of philosophical exploration of the theme, and includes a portrait of Captain Weinbaum as seen through an extra dimension: 'a foot thick, two feet wide, five feet five inches in height, and five hundred and eighty-six trillion, five hundred and sixty-nine billion, six hundred million miles in duration.'

Blish in his introduction makes a typically prickly defence of his book, quoting a critic's comment that it is 'not redundant with physical action.' That may be so. But *Beep* achieved immediate popularity, and has proved unforgettable. There is no rule which says that science fiction has to be packed with action. Better a tale of real imagination and ingenuity – like this one.

One of the most ingenious features of the original story lay hidden in its title, *Beep*. *Beep* contains a wealth of meaning just like the beep in the story. Noise is information in disguise, Blish tells us. To ram the notion home, he has two people in disguise, plus a popular song also disguised. And free will disguised as rigid determinism.

We are not taken into the galactic empire. All we are allowed is a *peep*, because we are stuck here in the present, without benefit of Dirac transmitters. But that peep, like the beep, contains infinite worlds, once you consider it.

Quincunx is really a clever bag of tricks. No wonder readers loved it. Its story-line is shaped in an odd spiral, the world-line of which whirls you into a fiery heart of speculation, then out again.

I just wish Blish in his introduction had taken the opportunity to explain his new title, since that task now devolves on me.

The title refers to the five-dimensional framework within which the affairs of the story are conducted. A quincunx is an arrangement of five objects at four corners with one in the centre, in the figure of a lozenge or other rectangle. The structure of the story leads us to believe that Blish may have visualised his small cast of characters set out in some such quincuncial fashion:

This figure lines up the males on the left and the women on the right, with the indeterminate figure of J. Selby Stevens in the middle to represent the vanishing fifth dimension.

Blish seized upon the idea of a mystical all-pervasive quincunx from Sir Thomas Browne's curious work, *The Garden of Cyrus, or the Quincuncial Lozenge* (1658). Cyrus the Great, the founder of the Persian Empire, restored the Hanging Gardens of Babylon, planting out saplings in lozenge configurations. Our word 'Paradise' comes from the Persian word for garden, and *Quincunx* depicts a kind of paradise, where sins and crimes are easily forgiven and young lovers have guardian angels – in the shape of Event Police – watching over them.

Browne's tract is a discourse upon all the manifestations of quincunxes in nature, in mankind, on earth, and in the heavens. According to Browne, it is an all-pervasive sign, although little commented upon. This of course fits in with Blish's conception of world-lines and the math behind them. Despite all of which, I still think that *Beep* is a better title.

But Blish liked such archaic systems of knowledge as Browne's, and his books are choked with their fossils. We both had a passion for Browne's writings, though I lack Blish's ferocious appetite for archaic systems. Also by his bedside, that last time we saw him in Battle Hospital, lay a copy of Samuel Taylor Coleridge's *Biographia Literaria*. Coleridge described this book as 'sketches of my literary life,' but it consists mainly of discussions of Wordsworth's poetry and of the philosophy of Kant, Schelling, and the German philosophers. I had a vision of Blish about to enter the complex realm of Coleridge's thought. He seemed too frail to traverse those gusty corridors of metaphysics. Here was one more ramshackle structure of thought, tempting him in. But Time, with which he wrestled in *Quincunx* and other works, had run out.

When James Blish and his stalwart wife Judy received visitors in their Harpsden home during the last stages of Blish's illness, he would not be able to speak at first. In any case, he was not a man all found it easy to feel at home with, though his intimate friends had no problems on that score. When he had drunk a neat tumbler of whisky, he would liven up, and then would begin to talk. He spoke impersonally for the most part, eyes darkly gleaming in his skull; perhaps he would talk about opera, to which he listened on LPs. The operas of Richard Strauss especially appealed to him. He made dry jokes as he went along, creaking with mirth. He had great admirations, great hatreds.

At one time, when our mutual friend, Harry Harrison, was also present, Blish was going on at some length about Wagner's *Ring des Nibelungen*, *on* which he was an enthusiastic authority.

Harry grew impatient at last.

'Come on, Jim,' he said, 'it's only a bunch of krauts singing.'

At which Blish broke off into tremendous fits of laughter.

All Blish's novels repay reading and re-reading. He was never one of the most popular writers in our field, although his *Cities in Flight* series received great acclaim, and certainly *A Case of Conscience* – which won a Hugo Award – became popular even beyond the confines of SF. Perhaps it is because most of his books are 'not redundant with physical action' that he has otherwise not been so widely enjoyed. He is, however, one of the most original of writers, and *The Quincunx of Time* one of his most original books.

He would have been delighted to see this new edition.

A Transatlantic Harrison, Yippee!

Well, in case you don't catch the reference, you have probably read a forceful and amusing alternative world novel entitled *A Tunnel Under the Deeps*. That plonking title was wished on it by its American publisher; its real and more characteristic title – the one the author gave it – was *A Transatlantic Tunnel, Hurrah!* The author is that very transatlantic man, Harry Harrison. And the story's about an America which never parted company from Britain.

Harry is or was a New Yorker, but as soon as he made his first sale to John W. Campbell, with a little item called *The Stainless Steel Rat*, he bought an airline ticket and started off on a world tour with his wife Joan. They have now completed this tour several times over and are still going. Harry's a very energetic man.

He is also very popular, damn it, which means he keeps being made guest of honour at conventions all over the world. Or when that fails, Harry throws his own magnificent conventions in Dublin (at one of which World SF was born, but that's another story).

The consequence of which is that I have to keep writing intros to convention booklets, glossing over Harry's manifest vices (his rabid teetotalism for one item) and plugging his virtues (your guess is as good as mine). In fact, I was thinking of putting together a little book of *One Hundred Best Intros to Harry Harrison*. Instead,

I include just one Intro here. It appeared originally in the book for Rog Peyton's Novacon 12, in Birmingham, England. You can tell how desperate I was getting by then.

Harry and I are still the closest of friends after twenty-five years and I'm sure he didn't mind this tribute – much.

* * *

Funny you should ask me to introduce Harry to the multitude. This is where we came in. Harry and I are negotiating with Gollancz to do one last anthology together, consisting of my introductions to him and his introductions to me throughout the years. Gives us a chance to crack all our old jokes one more time.

Anyhow, folks, in case you need telling – in which case, what are you doing here? – our Guest of Honour at Novacon 12 is *Harry Harrison*, one of the most popular figures ever to heft a meat pie at a SF convention, as well as one of SF's most eminent, most readable authors. Prolific, too. Here I may be allowed to give away a small secret and say that Harry Harrison is a pen name only. The real name is Catherine Cookson, and only the SF is written under the name of Harrison.

He and I met when Rog Peyton was just a gleam in his father's eye; ever since then, I have followed Harrison's career with admiration and akvavit. Here are a few facts about this amazing man, some of which are known only to him.

In stature, he is exactly midway between Dave Langford and Harlan Ellison, which is quite some way.

He once lifted Bob Shaw shoulder high with his hand tied behind his back.

No Harrison novel contains the word 'diaphone,' though some of them come rather close (as for instance 'diagram' in *Beneath Us the Stars* and 'diaphragm' [twice] in *One Giant Step from Earth*).

He speaks seventeen languages, all of them for the first time.

He is a close personal friend of both Charlton Heston and Cliff Richard; the latter's famous song hit, 'Congratulations,' written in collaboration with Charlton Heston, was originally entitled 'Make Room! Make Room!'

Once to his eternal regret he referred to Christopher Priest – three times famed Aubrey winner – as 'Boy Science Fiction Writer.' This error has been perpetuated several times since.

He cleans his teeth with a patent puff adder poison while standing naked in a pool of stilboestrol.

He celebrated his golden wedding recently in the presence of masked men from the holy order of First Fandom.

There is a Mount Harrison on Mahé Island in the Indian Ocean, and another one, smaller admittedly but never yet climbed, in the secret basements of the Royal Angus Hotel.

Andrew Stephenson's parents planned originally to christen their child Harry Harrison Stephenson – until they saw the baby.

Harrison's workload means that he employs a computer to work his word-processor. To initiate a new trilogy programme, he simply types in key-words like 'DiGriz,' 'sensuality,' 'automation,' 'star-smashers,' 'progress,' and 'kicked the shit out of him' and the computer does the rest.

His shibboleth-breaking exposé faction-novel, *Loves of the Paraplegics*, was banned in sixty-nine countries.

He flies from his Dublin hideout round the world regularly once a month via Alaska. This is why many young eskimo boys and girls are called Harry Ootee and Harriet Kamoumee.

His wife Joan preserves the shrivelled remains of both John W. Campbell and E.J. Carnell in her deep-freeze. Her Campbell's soup is second to none. The chili concarnell is good, too.

His car – a Harrison Ford – does 20 light-years to a gallon; it's a special Campbell's souped-up version.

Both Harrison and his wife have clauses in their will leaving their kidneys to the main public urinal in Zagreb, Jugoslavia.

Twice last year Harrison was invited to become President of the Lebanon; he refused graciously through pressure of work.

All these amazing facts and more are explored in full Technicolor in our forthcoming publication, *A Transatlantic Harrison*, *Yippee*, on sale in the foyer, though it's not quite clear which foyer.

There is no doubt that Harry will derive enormous pleasure from this convention, and that we shall have an awful job keeping him in order. My suggestion is that all fans should cease their usual silly mindless self-indulgent drinking and rally round Harry with the pints while he keeps up the intellectual word-play (complete with sound effects, of course). That way we stand a chance of getting through the next three days with a minimum of chaos.

And just a word of warning here. Inwardly, Harry is a modest, quiet man, shrinking from human contact. This is the Harrison nobody has ever seen. Do not upset him by asking him for his signature on any of his books (supposing you should find a few kicking about in the book room or wherever). He regards this as an intrusion, a violation of personal privacy.

It is safer not to buy or to be seen carrying any Harrison titles. Better not upset the man. Remember, he is on holiday, relaxing on his way to a convention in Outer Mongolia, and among us merely to enjoy the Brum sunshine. He does not wish to be reminded of past masterpieces. *Play it safe.* Why not buy an Aldiss book instead? I'll sign it. I've no scruples. I'll even sign it with Harry's name. No extra charge.

This third section is about more general topics, where prose comes from, science fiction's relationship to science, and, more personally, the reasons why I wrote the three Helliconia novels.

The Atheist's Tragedy Revisited

Writers are still asked where they get their crazy ideas from. They are less often asked where they get their crazy prose from. In general, prose derives from all sorts of models long forgotten.

I would be unable to name all the writers – read when I was boy or adolescent – who helped shape my idea of what prose should be. The roll call would include poets as well as novelists and essayists.

Some of my novels were written with a consciousness of debt to one particular author. *Greybeard* owes a debt to Thomas Hardy, the English novelist I have enjoyed most, because of the sense he imparts of his characters being bound to nature. Even at the time, *Greybeard* seemed to me to have rather a lot of adjectives in it. I resolved to write a novel without adjectives, as far as possible.

By then, I had become heavily influenced by the French *nouveau roman*, as well as by that marvellous film on which Alain Robbe-Grillet and Resnais collaborated, *L'année dernière à Marienbad*. The result was *Report on Probability A*.

In other cases, I have had the work of Mary Shelley or Olaf Stapledon at the back of my mind.

Sometimes it is possible to insert a passage almost playfully which recalls, at least to the writer, a passage he read elsewhere and admired. Below – as an example – is a passage from my novel, *The Eighty-Minute Hour*, followed by the passage I had in mind, a wonderful piece of imagery from Cyril Tourneur's poetic drama, *The Atheist's Tragedy*, with its splendidly elaborate unfolding of clauses mimicking the flurry of waves up the shore.

There was a time when I had a passion for the dark plays of Webster and Tourneur, and saw most of them performed. This was how I doffed my hat to them, years later.

After England and all but the granite hip of Scotland sank beneath thermonuclear bombardment, thousands of tattered human bodies – sodden and hairless as handkerchiefs – were washed ashore by mighty tidal waves, year after year, all along the western coasts of Europe, from Narvik and the Lofoten Islands in the north, from Jutland and the Frisians, from the rocks of Brittany southward, where the Medoc grapes grow, driven by furious new currents through Biscay, to appear informally dressed as Mortality in the charades at Biarritz and San Sebastian, and along the rainy beaches of Asturas and Galicia, right down to Lisbon and beyond Cape St. Vincent, where one of the last time-nibbled deliveries of bodies was made as far afield as the estuary of the Guadalquivir, once the private hunting grounds of the Dukes of Medina Sidonia; there, herons, spoonbills, egrets, and birds fresh from nesting places in the permanent snowcaps of the Sierra Nevada gazed like museum-goers on the salt-pickled remains of the inhabitants of Southampton, Scunthorpe and South Ken, who were now part of some greater and more permanent snowcap. Even later than that, sometimes years later, arms still identifiable as arms, or children's hands resembling sleeping crabs, would be cast up in the Azores or on the black laval sands of the Cape Verde islands.

Walking the next day upon the fatal shore,
Among the slaughtered bodies of their men

Which the full-stomached sea had cast upon
The sands, it was my unhappy chance to light
Upon a face, whose favour when it lived,
My astonished mind informed me I had seen.
He lay in's armour, as if that had been
His coffin; and the weeping sea, like one
Whose milder temper doth lament the death
Of him whom in his rage he slew, runs up
The shore, embraces him, kisses his cheek,
Goes back again, and forces up the sands
To bury him, and every time it parts
Sheds tears upon him, till at last (as if
It could no longer endure to see the man
Whom it had slain, yet loth to leave him) with
A kind of unresolved unwilling pace,
Winding her waves one in another, like
A man that folds his arms or wrings his hands
For grief, ebbed from the body, and descends
As if it would sink down into the earth,
And hide itself for shame of such a deed.

The Pale Shadow of Science

A venerable Oxford story tells of the college which received a large private bequest. In the senior common room, the Fellows were discussing how the money should best be invested. The Bursar finally said, 'Well, let's invest in property. After all, property's served us well for the last thousand years.' And the old Senior Fellow in the corner chirped up and said, 'Yes, but you know the last thousand years have been exceptional.'

Well, we would probably all agree with the Senior Fellow. And we would probably agree that the years since the dropping of Little Boy on Hiroshima have been exceptional. We feel that civilisation is going somewhere fast; therefore we ought to know where it is going. There seems to be no pilot on our speeding craft. So we turn to prediction.

Like ESP, to which it bears some relationship, prophecy has never become legit. Despite the commendable efforts of Nigel Calder in this country, Herman Kahn in the States, and so on, prophecy and prediction remain a happy hunting ground for astrologers and science fiction writers.

There is a kind of prediction called extrapolation, a nice scientific-sounding word. How does it differ in fact from prediction? Well, you take all the known facts on a subject and simply double the number that you first thought of. At least, that is how it seemed when 'futurology' became one of the in-words of the sixties. Extrapolation always sounds disarmingly sensible – a cool look ahead. Nigel Calder's experts in his 1964 symposium were perfectly reasonable to extrapolate from that date that we would have a Moon base in operation by 1984. Had he got his experts together in 1944, none of them would have spoken about a Moon base. No Moon base exists. Should we therefore consider the hypothetical 1944 panel more correct than their successors, twenty years later? That would be silly. Extrapolation is really a way of thinking about the present, not the future; part of the world-picture in 1964, much more than of our present present, included a reasonable expectation of a Moon base within twenty years. The energy crisis and the recession had not then struck.

SF is another way of thinking about the future, and of the present masked as future. It is part of the function of some science fiction writers to keep on dreaming of Moon bases.

But not all science fiction writers. It is also the function of science fiction writers to be diverse.

When Neil Armstrong walked on the Moon in July 1969, Isaac Asimov went on record as saying, 'This justifies all the science fiction written in John Campbell's *Astounding/ Analog* since the nineteen-forties.' One sees what Asimov means, one understands why he was proud, one sympathises, and yet I believe that he was profoundly wrong. The only way that science fiction can be justified is if it is good science fiction, not if its predictions turn out correctly. It is on that point I wish to elaborate.

To begin with what science fiction writers and scientists have in common, I suppose we would all go even further than the Senior Oxford Fellow and say that we expect the *next* thousand years to be exceptional. The build-up of population, the build-up of technology, of communication, of information, and the creation of complex social infrastructures cannot but bring immense changes in life and thought, in diet and behaviour, in birth and death, in knowledge and intuition, in speech and silence, in our whole perception of existence.

We know that ... and yet the fine detail ... Who here will bet me a hundred pounds that there will be a Moon base in 20 years, in 2004? Who here will tell me which way the pendulum of sexual morality will have swung by the time the Moon base is built? Who can tell me where London's third airport will be in 2004?

The relationship between SF and science is complex. It became more complex when the space age began and SF writers were invited out of their obscurity to explain trajectories and escape velocity and docking procedures to laymen. They were experts all of a sudden: alchemists whose lead of fantasy had turned into the gold of knowledge. Ever since then, science fiction has had on the whole a better reception from scientists than from literary pundits. This is very gratifying, but to my mind the thing should be the other way round. I don't mean that scientists should not take SF seriously as a form of literature in which the current developments and obsessions of the age are given a dramatic airing, but rather that the *literati* should take it seriously for those same reasons – instead of ignoring it, as they do, because it doesn't conform to the conventions of the major nineteenth century novels they studied in the English schools of Oxbridge and Ivy League. Imagination is in short supply: a precious commodity that many fear.

A remarkable example of literary blindness could be observed in 1948, when Aldous Huxley published his prophetic novel, *Ape and Essence*, which deals with nuclear catastrophe, followed by the degeneration of humanity back to a stage where females undergo anoestrus. The novel also contains much about despoilation of natural resources, long before conservation became a popular slogan. In every respect, *Ape and Essence* is all that SF should be: it boldly elucidates a current dilemma in imaginative terms. Huxley's novel went to literary critics. None of them was capable of appreciating what Huxley was doing; they did not know how to read or process his book. Huxley got a bad, ill-informed press

– and that in spite of his stature as a futuristic novelist, author of *Brave New World*.

Such illiteracy by the literates has led to a situation where science fiction writers court the scientists; they turn towards that audience as flowers – all except the difficult daffodil – turn towards the sun. It also leads them occasionally to address bodies before whom they feel themselves scarcely qualified to speak ….

Frederik Pohl has been an assiduous speaker and lecturer between novels. At one time, he would accept invitations to address learned bodies on the population problem, which he regarded as the gravest issue of the sixties. In the sixties (if you remember) the nuclear issue had gone off the boil. Fred told me he gave up at the point when he realized that he was beginning to enjoy painting a picture of doom. He gave up the admired role of expert and returned to writing novels with a strong scientific content.

What is more dangerous is when writers start to regard their novels as if SF were in some way a branch of science. To do this, they may stress the predictive factor in their writing. For example, after the dropping of the atomic bombs on Japan, there were numerous stories written warning against the dangers of fallout in future wars. Many of them predicted that radioactivity would cause mutations in the human race. Henry Kuttner forecast a sub-race of mutants, hairless and with telepathic powers, against which the rest of humanity waged war. The idea sounds ridiculous now but, given the date of origin, like the Moon base prediction of 1964, it wore an air of alarming scientific plausibility.

But science fiction novels are not scientific experiments which move towards a desired end to clinch a hypothesis. A science fiction novel should contain within it what an eminent critic, Darko Suvin, calls a 'posited novum,' a new thing – whether object or concept – held up for our consideration. The novum may be, for example, an anti-gravity machine. The writer is under no obligation to tell us how it works. If he can tell us how it works, then he is wasting his time writing novels and his talent should be employed elsewhere.

What he should do, though, is to give us some form of description, some hint of theory, so that we can almost persuade ourselves that we comprehend how the anti-gravity machine works. Then he can show us what effect his machine has on the world.

Ursula Le Guin's ansible is an instantaneous communication device. It features in her novel *The Dispossessed*. We readily understand the need for such a device in a widespread galactic culture. Although we are not told how the ansible works, we know that it is one tangible result of Shevek's work on a unified field theory. Le Guin is not predicting the ansible; the important point about this posited novum is that it makes sense within Le Guin's own taoist thought, in a novel much concerned with utopian thinking and the difficulties of communication.

There can hardly be a less scientific concept, I imagine, than a time machine. H.G. Wells, who invented that blessed contraption, describes only its physical appearance, and that vaguely; the theory behind the machine's working is left even more vague. We know it works only because the prototype worked and disappeared into the future. Yet the novel, *The Time Machine*, is one of the most scientific of scientific romances, in that it dramatises for the ordinary reader two of the nineteenth century's most profound discoveries: the great age of the Earth, and the principles of evolution. The Eloi and the Morlocks are not there merely to titillate and shock; they are there as fascinating examples of what we as a race might become, given time.

And of course *The Time Machine* is a morality, based in part on Kelvin's reformulation of the second law of thermodynamics. Let me remind you of the end of all things on Earth:

The darkness grew apace; a cold wind began to grow in freshening gusts from the east, and the showering white flakes in the air increased in number. From the edge of the sea came a ripple and a whisper. Beyond these lifeless sounds the world was silent. Silent? It would be hard to convey the stillness of it. All the sounds of man, the bleating of sheep, the cries of birds, the hum of insects, the stir that makes the background of our lives – all that was over … At last, one by one, swiftly, one after the other, the white peaks of the distant hills vanished into blackness.

Here, imagination, scientific training, and a good prose style merge. The posited novum, the time machine, is a vital part of the story, but not the story itself. The story is not there to prove the machine exists. Literature and science work by opposite processes. The scientific method is to take particular instances and extract from then a general application which can then be demonstrated to apply to further instances. The method of literature, on the contrary, is to take a number of general applications, and embody them in a particular instance, which can then be felt to apply to other instances. Frederik Pohl and Cyril Kornbluth's *The Space Merchants* points to various ways in which advertising agencies lie to the public to fob off on them an indifferent product; the authors then show us the Fowler Schocken corporation selling the ghastly planet Venus to would-be colonists. We believe it. We know they'd sell real estate on Neptune as well, given the chance. But the literary method proves nothing, unlike a scientific experiment.

There is another way of looking at the two opposed modes of thinking represented by literature and science. Wells himself pointed to the distinction. He called the modes 'directed thought' and 'undirected thought.' We are all aware of the difference. In terms of human evolution we may suppose that undirected thought came first; undirected thought could be represented spatially as a ramble round and round a familiar object, perhaps seeing it anew. Whereas directed thought could be represented as walking towards a distant unfamiliar object for purposes of identification.

In *The Work, Wealth and Happiness of Mankind* (1913), Wells boldly entitles Chapter Two 'How Man Has Learnt to Think Systematically and Gain a Mastery over Force and Matter.' He speaks of undirected thought as imaginative play: close really to what we might now call a hypnoid state. He praises directed thought as leading to 'new and better Knowledge, planned and directed effort.' Directed thought, according to Wells, enters philosophy with Plato and defines the scientific aspect of modern civilisation.

It is doubtful if scientists today would endorse Wells's view of science as being purely the product of directed thought. His view too rigorously excludes what we may call the Eureka factor; it also excludes the character of the scientist. What is interesting about Wells's two different modes of thought is that he employs them both, serially, in his fiction. The early SF novels – *The Time Machine, The War of the Worlds, The Island of Dr. Moreau*, up to *The First Men in the Moon* (1901) – are by common consent regarded as among his best and most enduring fictions. Their power lies in Wells's wandering around familiar objects and seeing them anew; he is trying to prove nothing; he investigates ambiguities and contrasts in the universe which he need not resolve. It is necessary that young Selenites be adapted to society; that process causes pain to the individual. That's the way things are, and there is no remedy. In the words of Samuel Johnson:

> How small, of all that human hearts endure,
> That part which laws or kings can cause or cure.

In his later fictions, Wells attempts to produce cures. He switches to directed thought. The difference is marked. Gone are the ambiguities and balances we met on Moreau's island, the puzzle of the boundaries between human and non-human, between intelligence and reflex. In place of conundrums, instructions. We must submit to a world state for our own good. We must be governed by enlightened samurai. We must not have pets in our homes for health reasons. The mazes of human life are to be swept clean in exchange for a unitary answer. Mr. Polly, Mr. Kipps, Mr. Lewisham, give way to Mr. Britling, Mr. Blettsworthy, and William Clissold. In short, Wells forecasts. 'The great general of Dreamland,' as he once called himself, becomes a demagogue instead. As directed thought replaces undirected, we are addressed, but no longer enchanted. Demagogue is a pejorative word. Wells gave up literature in an heroic attempt to save the world from itself.

The Shape of Things to Come was published in 1933. It is hardly fiction; it forecasts. For instance, the Modern State emerges after the 1965 Conference called at Basra by – yes, you guessed it – the Transport Union.

The Shape of Things to Come has been much admired for forecasting World War II. Writing in 1933, Wells almost gets the year of the outbreak of war right: 1940 instead of 1939. But his is not the war that was fought. The real war was more savage than anything Wells describes; yet he has civilisation breaking down as a result of war, because that suits his didactic purpose. Only on the rubble of yesterday can the Modern State of tomorrow be built.

It is impossible today to read *The Shape of Things to Come* with any patience, whereas the earlier fictions remain fresh. We value Wells as both imaginative novelist and prophet, but never as both together, for what is imaginative is not truly prophetic, and what is prophetic not truly imaginative. Wells taught whole generations that things were going to be different. It is a lesson we have thoroughly learned – though the War Office appears not to have done – but it was originally Wells's lesson.

In short, Wells's great early novels are examples of undirected thinking; his later propagandistic novels are examples of directed thinking. To go into the prediction business is to give up the best way of making an imaginative novel. The imagination always haunts ambiguity. Science, child of imagination, is dedicated to abolishing ambiguity.

General Hackett's two recent books on World War III are already quaint period pieces, full of sunny optimism which takes no account either of the Kremlin and Pentagon planning of post-strike scenarios or the findings regarding the descent of nuclear winter following a strike.

Prophecies can, then, be ludicrously wrong. Of course they can also be ludicrously right. When an early telephone was installed in the office of a mayor of an American city, he was moved to prophecy. 'The day will dawn,' he said, 'when every city in the United States will have a telephone.'

That's a story Arthur Clarke tells. One of the best-known prophecies of recent times is Clarke's famous projection of communication satellites in geosynchronous orbits, made in 1945. If Clarke could have formulated a means of delivering the satellites into their orbits – a means non-existent in 1945 – he could have patented the idea. That would have made him, presumably, one of the richest men in the world. This stunning piece of forecasting appeared as an article in *Wireless World*. Wisely so. Had Clarke written the idea into a story, a fiction, and published it in a science fiction magazine, his prediction would have had less force.

After all, predictions are two-a-penny in SF magazines. We SF writers have predictions the way dogs have fleas. They are the furniture of our future. In one of my novels, *Barefoot in the Head*, written in the late sixties, I predicted Arab interference bringing European culture to a messy standstill – which was virtually what happened in reality in 1973. But it happened in ways I did not foresee – or wish to foresee within the particular context of that novel.

In any case, if you throw off a hundred predictions and two of them happen to be fulfilled, that does not make you a prophet, any more than a man shooting at a barn door a hundred times and hitting it twice can be called a marksman.

In sum, I think that a novel of science fiction must succeed on its own terms as a novel, and not on some extra-literary terms. We still read *The First Men in the Moon* with pleasure, not caring that the reality is otherwise. Prediction is a bad first priority for novelists.

If prediction is bad, can we turn the equation round and state that negative prediction is good? That holds true in at least one case – the case of Orwell's *1984*. Orwell was warning us; his forecast was apotropaic. Our real 1984 is probably less like the one Orwell imagined simply because he uttered his famous warning. But Orwell was a special case. We needed his warning because we believe the dangers of totalitarianism to be real; whereas we have not heeded John Wyndham's warning, and we remain totally unprepared for the triffid invasion. Prediction to be effective must deal with what is already in existence. Whereas most SF deals with something non-existent: from one of Italo Calvino's invisible cities the size of a pinhead to X's galactic empires, covering a hundred thousand planets.

And yet. Science fiction does have a relation to science, just as it does to literature. I only wish that the two cultures did not remain so far apart; then our bridges would be less difficult to built. Science fiction plays in that wonderful speculative world of possibilities which has been hard-won since the days of the renaissance – a world of speculation always under threat. To my mind, science fiction is of immense importance when it is being its imaginative self, when it offers us a metaphor for the varieties of experience life offers. It should be about the future. When it gets involved with telepathic dragons, I'm lost.

A contemporary SF writer like Gregory Benford, a scientist working in astrophysics and plasma physics, writes highly imaginative SF which attempts not to bend the rules of science while treating of the unknown. In such novels as *Against Infinity* and *Across the Sea of Suns*, Benford presents a holistic view of science which is fructifying. Both novels point beyond our present problems to the numberless possibilities of the future.

Philip K. Dick, another Californian writer, is far less optimistic than Benford. Yet his novels, too, in their dark inventive surrealism, light up our imaginations. I can't think of a single prediction in Dick's novels. Though he seems to operate under the general assumption that things in society get steadily worse unless a few modest little men keep patching things up as best they can. I am more sure about that than I am about a moon base in 2004.

A Monster for All Seasons

But first, a story. The scene is the main convention hall of a science fiction convention, Lunacon, held in the crumbling Commodore Hotel, New York, in 1975. Famous critic, fan, and collector, Sam Moskowitz, is holding forth from the platform. Fans are slouching around in the hall, sleeping, listening, or necking. I am sitting towards the back of the hall, conversing with a learned and attractive lady beside me, or else gazing ahead, watching interestedly the way Moskowitz's lips move. In short, the usual hectic convention scene.

Fans who happen to be aware of my presence turn round occasionally to stare at me. I interpret these glances as the inescapable tributes of fame, and take care to look natural, though not undistinguished, and thoroughly absorbed in the speech.

Later, someone comes up to me and says, admiringly, 'Gee, you were real cool while Moskowitz was attacking you.'

That is how I gained my reputation for English *sang froid* (or *snag froid*, as my typewriter puts it). The acoustics in the hall were so appalling that I could not hear a word Moskowitz was saying against me. To them goes my gratitude, for my inadvertent coolness in the face of danger may well have saved me from a ravening lynch mob.

Few reviewers stood up in support of my arguments in *Billion Year Spree*. Mark Adlard in *Foundation* was one of them.[1] Yet it appears that some of my mildly ventured propositions have since been accepted.

Sam Moskowitz, of course, was pillorying me on account of heretical opinions in *BYS*. I did not gather that he said anything about my major capacity as a creative writer. One unfortunate effect of the success of *BYS*, from my point of view, is that my judgements are often quoted but my fiction rarely so, as though I had somehow, by discussing the literary mode in which I work, passed from mission to museum with no intermediate steps.

Such is the penalty one pays for modesty. I mentioned no single story or novel of mine in my text; it would have been bad form to do so. Lester del Rey, nothing if not derivative, repays the compliment by mentioning no single story or novel of mine in his text,[2] though to be sure disproportionate space is devoted to del Rey's own activities.

This particular instance can perhaps be ascribed to jealousy. To scholarly responses we will attend later.

First to rehearse and repolish some arguments advanced in *Billion Year Spree*, in particular the arguments about the origin of SF. On this important question hinge other matters, notably a question of function: what exactly SF does, and how it gains its best effects.

BYS was published in England and the U.S. in 1973, the English edition appearing first, from Weidenfeld & Nicolson. It is a good edition, illustrated. The Doubleday is less good. Owing to negligence on Doubleday's part, the corrected proofs I returned to them were not sent on by them to the printer. So a number of needless errors are embalmed in that edition (which the Schocken paperback edition then perpetuated by hurrying into print without

---

1   Mark Adlard, 'A Labour of Love,' *Foundation* 6.
2   Lester Del Rey, *The World of Science Fiction* (1980).

consulting me). I apologise to American readers for many fatuities of which I was well aware – as well as for many that have been pointed out to me since.

The book took three years to write. I had no financial support, and was assisted by no seat of learning. I favoured no clique. I used my own library. I consulted no one. Really, it was a bit of a gamble, since I have a wife and children to support by my writing. But there were two bestsellers to fund the venture (*The Hand-Reared Boy* and *A Soldier Erect*), which were – and still are – going strong. I looked both inward to the SF field itself and outward to the general reader, Samuel Johnson's and Virginia Woolf's common reader; I wished to argue against certain misconceptions which vexed me, and I hoped to demonstrate what those who did not read SF were missing.

There was no history of science fiction in existence. I wrote the sort of book which it would amuse and profit me to read.

Of the two initial problems facing me, I overcame the second to my satisfaction: how do you define SF, and what are its origins? Obviously, the questions are related. My ponderous definition of SF has often been quoted, and for that I'm grateful, although I prefer my shorter snappier version, 'SF is about hubris clobbered by nemesis,' which has found its way into *The Penguin Dictionary of Modern Quotations*. The definition in *BYS* runs as follows:

Science fiction is the search for a definition of man and his status in the universe which will stand in our advanced but confused state of knowledge (science), and is characteristically cast in the Gothic or post-Gothic mould.

Not entirely satisfactory, like most definitions. It has the merit of including a consideration of form as well as content. On the whole, criticisms of this definition have been more effective than those directed at my proposals for the origins of the genre.[3]

---

3 An instance is 'The SF Story,' a typically scatty review of *BYS* in Robert Conquest's *The Abomination of Moab* (1979).

It needs no great critical faculty to observe that most SF is not about 'a search for the definition of man'; it is about telling a story to please the reader – and in that it is no different from any other literature. Only when SF texts are piled together do we see a common restlessness about where mankind is heading through its own blind efforts. More questionable is that phrase about the Gothic mould.

I am not one hundred percent sure about the phrase myself, but this much is clear: I got it from Leslie Fiedler. Leslie Fiedler writes the kind of criticism one can read with enjoyment, unlike most of the criticism which originates within the orbit of SF academia. Fiedler has this to say of the Gothic mode, following on a discussion of Monk Lewis's *The Monk* of 1796:

> The major symbols of the gothic have been established, and the major meanings of the form made clear. In general, those symbols and meanings depend on an awareness of the spiritual isolation of the individual in a society where all communal systems of value have collapsed or have been turned into meaningless cliches. There is a basic ambivalence to the attitude of the gothic writers to the alienation which they perceive. On the one hand, their fiction projects a fear of the solitude which is the price of freedom; and on the other hand, an almost hysterical attack on all institutions which might inhibit that freedom or mitigate the solitude it breeds … The primary meaning of the gothic romance, then, lies in its substitution of terror for love as a central theme of fiction … *Épater la bourgeoisie*: this is the secret slogan of the tale of terror.[4]

Spiritual isolation, alienation – these lie also at the heart of SF, like serpents in a basket.

Passages like the above defined the sort of fiction that most of my admired contemporaries were writing. I saw in them, too,

---

4 Leslie Fiedler, *Love and Death in the American Novel* (1960).

a reflection of my own responses to society which prompted me towards science fiction. The love of art and science I developed as a child was a rebellion against the smug bourgeois society in which I found myself. Art and Science were what *They* hated most. In this way, I reinforced the solitude I felt. This also: I merely wished to *épater* society, not overthrow it; the satirist needs his target.

This stinging function of SF was always apparent, from the days of Mary Shelley (*Frankenstein*, like its progenitor, *Caleb Williams*, contains more punitive litigators than punitive monsters within its pages), through H.G. Wells, and Campbell's *Astounding*, until the time when I sat down to write in *BYS* in 1970. During the 70s and 80s, SF has become widely popular, widely disseminated. Its sting has been removed. The awful victories of *The Lord of the Rings*, *Star Trek*, and *Star Wars* have brought – well, not actually respectability, but Instant Whip formulas to SF. The product is blander. It has to be immediately acceptable to many palates, most of them prepubertal. Even the sentimentality of such as Spider and Jeanne Robinson's 'Stardance' is not considered too sickly sweet for consumption. As Kurt Vonnegut ripened on the tree and fell with a thud to earth, so too did the nutritive content of SF.

The nutritive content has been fixed to suit mass taste. Now the world, or the solar system, or the universe, or the Lord Almighty, has to be saved by a group of four or five people which includes a Peter Pan figure, a girl of noble birth, and a moron of some kind. The prescription thus incorporates an effigy for everyone to identify with. In the old days, we used to destroy the world, and it only took one mad scientist. SF was an act of defiance, a literature of subversion, not whimsy.

Notice Fiedler's comment on the basic ambivalence which gothic writers feel towards their alienation. Leaving aside Instant Whip SF, one can perceive an ambivalence in science fiction which goes deep – perhaps one should say an ambivalence which is the subject. The emphasis of this ambivalence has changed over the years. Gernsback's *Amazing* was decidedly technocratic in bias, and purported to demonstrate how the world's ills could be solved by increased applications of technology – a reasonable proposition, if a century late – yet large proportions of the fiction concerned experiments etc which went terribly wrong. Hubris was continually clobbered by nemesis.

Another fundamental ambivalence is less towards technology than towards science itself. Even technology-oriented authors like Arthur C. Clarke show science superseded by or transcended by mysticism and religion; such surely is the meaning of his most famous short story, The Nine Billion Names of God.' It is not science but the fulfillment of religion which brings about the termination of the universe. The world ends not with a bang but a vesper.

Another ambivalence is the attitude of writers and fans to SF itself. They declare it publicly to be far superior to any possible 'mimetic' fiction; yet privately they laugh about it, revel in the worst examples of the art, and boast of how little SF they read.

SF is a function of the Gothic or post-Gothic. So, for that matter, are the novels of Peter Straub, and they also – in such examples as the tantalisingly named *Ghost Story* – bestraddle customary definitions of ghost stories and mainstream literature.

What I wish I had altered was the final word of my definition, to have said not 'mould' but 'mode.'

One of the difficulties of defining SF springs from the fact that it is not a genre as such, just as the absurd category 'Non-fiction' is not a genre. Taking my cue from Rosemary Jackson,[5] I suggest that our problems in the area of definition will be lightened if we think of SF as a mode. Jackson says, It is perhaps more helpful to define the fantastic as a literary *mode* rather than a genre, and to place it between the opposite modes of the marvellous and the mimetic.'

This may not help with the question of to what extent SF is a department of fantasy; 'fantasy' as a literary term, like 'classical' and 'romantic,' has come through usage to be defaced; but it helps

---

5   Rosemary Jackson, *Fantasy: The Literature of Subversion* (1981).

us to appreciate SF as the obverse of the realistic mode, and to see that SF can itself assume various generic forms. There is, for instance, a fairly well-defined category of 'disaster' SF and this in itself can be sub-divided into cautionary disasters (like *1984*) and into what I have termed 'cosy catastrophes' (such as *The Day of the Triffids*), in which the hero ends with the power and the girl, and is personally better off than he was at the beginning. No form which includes more than one genre can itself be a genre.

The relevant dictionary definition of 'mode' is, 'A way or manner in which something takes place; a method of procedure,' and 'A manner or state of being of a thing.'

While my critics argued, as well they might, with the *BYS* definition of SF, they rarely advanced a more convincing alternative. The same must be said for the response to my proposal for a great SF progenitor.

My search for ancestors went back no further in time than Mary Shelley, with *Frankenstein* (1818) as the first model of the SF mode. The wide acceptance of this proposal by academics may have been prompted by relief – a sensible relief occasioned by their not therefore having to teach *Gilgamesh*, Dante, and Otis Adelbert Kline to their classes.

One sees that this argument of origins can never be definitively settled, for conflicting genres have contributed to the modern mode. But it is an argument worth pursuing, just as paleontologists pick over the so far insoluble question of the early origins of mankind.

When first claiming for *Frankenstein* such a pre-eminent role in SF, I intended to put forward an argument, not an avowed truth. In particular, I wished to present a counter-argument to those two entrenched views which claimed either that SF was as ancient as literature itself or that 'it all began with Gernsback.' Some commentators managed to hold both assumptions at the same time.

If we claim as SF anything which includes a departure from the natural order, or which exhibits Darko Suvin's cognitive estrangement, we gather to ourselves a great body of disparate material, so disparate that it renders the term 'SF' meaningless and the material impossible to study in any effective way.

Beyond this argument of necessity is a philosophical objection to lumping together, say, Plato, Lucian, Paltock, Swift, and Poul Anderson. Although sophisticated analysis may reveal what these writers have in common, the sensible reader will be alienated; he will remain aware that the cultural differences are greater than any unifying thread of wonder, speculation, or whatever.

As Darko Suvin puts it, if such books as Hardy's *Two on a Tower* and Wilkie Collins's *The Moonstone* are SF just like Wells's *The Invisible Man*, then in fact there is no such thing as SF[6].

That there is a kind of tradition of the fantastic is undeniable, but it does not admit to easy study, possibly because many of the popular texts are missing, as we might imagine that popular SF of our age (the magazines of the forties, for example) would be missing, were it not for a few devoted individuals (Moskowitz is an honoured example) who defied a general contemporary neglect. Equally, the writers in this tradition had a nose for their predecessors, and generally reveal themselves as familiar with their writings – though to be familiar with was not always the same as to understand. Writers are impatient creatures and take only what they need; thus, H.G. Wells can say that Frankenstein 'used some jiggery-pokery magic to animate his artificial monster,' whereas this is precisely what Frankenstein does *not* do.

The argument that SF began with Gernsback hardly needs refuting anymore, and I will detain no one with the obvious counter-arguments. Yet when I wrote *BYS*, the refutation was necessary, and I had some fun with that old phrase about Gernsback being 'the father of SF.' Edgar Allan Poe has received

---

6   Darko Suvin, *Metamorphoses of Science Fiction* (1979).

the same accolade. This quest for father-figures reached what we hope will be its nadir when, in the same year *BYS* was published, Isaac Asimov wrote one of his Introductions, entitled 'The Father of Science Fiction,' and nominated John W. Campbell for that role.[7] It was a relief to be able to appoint a mother-figure instead.

The seminal point about *Frankenstein* is that its central character makes a deliberate decision. He succeeds in creating life only when he throws away dusty old authorities and turns to modern experiments in the laboratory. One of Victor Frankenstein's two professors scoffs at his reading such ancients as Paracelsus, Agrippa, and Albertus Magnus – 'These fancies, which you have imbibed, are a thousand years old!' – while the other professor is even more scathing: the ancients 'promised impossibilities and performed nothing.'

Frankenstein rejects alchemy and magic and turns to scientific research. Only then does he get results. Wells was absolutely mistaken in his remarks about 'jiggery-pokery magic'; it is jiggery-pokery magic which Frankenstein rejects.

This is qualitatively different from being carried to the moon accidentally by migratory geese, or being shipwrecked on Lilliput, or summoning up the devil, or creating life out of spit and mud. Victor Frankenstein makes a rational decision: he operates on the world, rather than vice versa; and the reader is taken by plausible steps from the normal world we know to an unfamiliar one where monsters roam and the retributions of hubris are played out on a terrifying scale.

I say that the reader is taken by plausible steps. In fact, the interwoven processes of the *Frankenstein* narrative are better described by Suvin – 'the ever-narrowing imaginative vortex ...' etc. (*ibid.*)

To bring about the desired initial suspension of belief, Mary Shelley employs a writerly subterfuge which has since become the

---

7 In *Astounding: John W. Campbell Memorial Anthology*, ed. Harry Harrison (1973).

stock-in-trade of many SF writers. Wells imitated her method some decades later, to good effect. She appeals to scientific evidence for the veracity of her tale.

It is no accident that Mary Shelley's introduction to the anonymous 1818 edition of the novel begins with a reference to one of the most respected scientific minds of her day, Dr Erasmus Darwin. Darwin, grandfather of Charles Darwin, and an early propagandist of evolutionary theory, was referred to by S.T. Coleridge as 'the most original-minded man in Europe.' The opening words of the Introduction are, 'The event on which this fiction is founded has been supposed, by Dr Darwin, and some of the psychological writers of Germany, as not of impossible occurence.' Thus Mary Shelley makes it clear that the first aspect of her novel which she wishes to stress is the scientific-speculative one.

This is the most revolutionary departure of *Frankenstein*. This is the one which separates it most markedly from the Gothic (another factor being the absence of simpering heroines). We must not ignore another novelty. The monster in his isolation operates as a criticism of society, as later does Wells's Invisible Man and the central figure in Algis Budrys's *Who*? When the monster cries, 'I am malicious because I am miserable,' he is dramatically reversing received Christian thinking of the time. This atheistic note echoes the central blasphemy of Frankenstein's diseased creation. SF was to become a refuge for anti-Christian and anti-establishment thinking, and some criticism of society is present in most successive SF, save in the trivial examples of Instant Whip.

In his edition of *Frankenstein*[8], Leonard Wolf argues that the novel should not be considered as SF, but rather as 'psychological allegory.' This is like arguing that *The Space Merchants* is not SF because it is 'political allegory.' There is no reason why both books should not support both functions. The strength of SF is that it is not a pure stream.

---

8   Leonard Wolf, ed. *The Annotated Frankenstein* (1977).

David Ketterer, who has written perceptively about Mary Shelley's novel,[9] agrees with Wolf, while saying that the concerns of *Frankenstein* might more broadly be described as 'philosophical, alchemical, and transcendental, and psychological or scientific.' Ketterer is also keen to deny that *Frankenstein* can be described as SF.[10]

The novel is alchemical in so far as it is firmly anti-alchemy. The science is not very clear – impossible, if you like – but we can recognise it as science rather than alchemy, although Mary was writing some years before the word 'scientist' was coined. As for the philosophical and transcendental qualities, they arise from the central science-fictional posit, just as they do in Arthur Clarke's *Childhood's End*, and rule the novel out of the SF stakes no more than does Wolf's psychological element.

Arguments against *Frankenstein* being SF at all rest on very uncertain ground. Not only is there Mary Shelley's own intention, as expressed in her Introduction, but her sub-title points to where she believes its centre to lie; she is bringing up-to-date the myth of Prometheus. Her fire comes down from heaven. It was an inspiration – and one that Universal Studios would later make much of – to utilise the newly captive electricity as that promethean fire. Later generations of writers, with neither more nor less regard for scientific accuracy, would use 'the power of the atom' with which to energise their perceptions of change. Nowadays, telepathic super-powers get by under the name of SF.

The argument against *Frankenstein*'s being the first novel of SF could be more convincingly launched on other grounds, historiological ones. The more a subject is studied, the further back its roots are seen to go. This is true, for instance, of the Renaissance, or of the Romantic movement. So perhaps the quest for the First

9   David Ketterer, '*Frankenstein's Creation: The Book, The Monster, and Human Reality* (1979).

10 David Ketterer, '*Frankenstein* in Wolf's Clothing,' in *Science Ficition Studies* #18, July 1979.

SF Novel, like the first flower of spring, is chimerical. But the period where we should expect to look for such a blossoming is during the Industrial Revolution, and perhaps just after the Napoleonic Wars, when changes accelerated by industry and war have begun to bite, with the resultant sense of isolation of the individual from and in society. This sense of isolation is a hallmark of Romanticism, displayed in the opening paragraph of that milestone of Romanticism, Jean-Jacques Rousseau's *Confessions*: 'I feel my heart and I know men. I am not like others whom I have seen; I dare believe that I am not made like anyone else alive.'

This is the region of *Frankenstein*. Mary Shelley found an objective correlative for the cold intellectual currents of her day. It has maintained, and even implemented, its power to our day.

We need to resist a temptation to classify rigidly, thinking to achieve intellectual clarity by so doing. There is no contradiction involved in regarding this remarkable transitional novel as a Gothic story, as one of the great horror stories of the English language, *and* as the progenitor of modern SF.

Nobody seeks to argue that *Frankenstein* is not a horror story. The influence of the movies has greatly persuaded us to concentrate on the horror aspect. Yet the movies have always cheapened Mary Shelley's theme. The creature is turned into a dotty bogeyman, allowed only to grunt, grunt and destroy. It is presented as alien to humanity, not an extension of it.

Mary Shelley depicts the creature as alienated from society. Just when we have learned to fear the creature and loathe its appearance, she shows us the reality of the case. This is no monster. It is a lost soul. Above all things, it wishes to reverence its absent creator.

Every good Frankenstein-watcher has his own opinions about the monster. It is the French Revolution, says Suvin. It is Percy Bysshe Shelley, says Christopher Small.[11] I have come to believe that the stricken creature is Mary herself, that she found in the

11 Christopher Small, *Ariel Like a Harpy: Shelley, Mary, and* Frankenstein (1972).

monster a striking objective correlative for her childbirth. Later in her career, in her other SF novel, she projects herself as Verney, the Last Man in a world of death, wandering alone without a soulmate.

The monstrous Things populating traditional horror stories are presented as inimical to mankind; they are externalised. Frankenstein's monster represents a departure in this respect, from horror towards SF. Again, Wells picks up the hint, in *The Island of Dr. Moreau* and also in *The War of the Worlds*. In the former, we have a clutch of manmade monsters who also go in fear of their creator. In the latter, the Martians – following the first powerful description of them as disgusting and frightening – are shown to be as humans might become at a later possible stage of evolution.

If I were re-writing *BYS* now, I should qualify *Frankenstein*'s preeminence by allowing more discussion of the utopianists of eighteenth century France, and of such works of the Enlightenment as Sebastien Mercier's *The Year 2440* (1770).[12] The hero of this work wakes up seven centuries in the future, to a world of scientific and moral advance. But between such examples and later ones come the guillotines of the French Revolution, to deliver a blow to pure utopianism from which it has not recovered. The prevailing tone was to be set, at least in the Anglo-American camp, by the glooms of Gothic-Romanticism.

I began by saying that the question of function was wrapped up with the question of origin. To regard SF as co-existent with literature since Homer is to bestow on it no function not also operative in literature; which contradicts the experience of most of us who study and enjoy both literature and SF.

To regard SF as 'all starting with Gernsback' is to impoverish it to an unfair degree. SF then becomes a kind of gadget fiction, where every story more than ten years old is hailed as a 'Classic,'

---

12 Discussed in 'Since the Enlightenment,' in Brian Aldiss, *This World and Nearer Ones* (1979).

and reputations can be made by rewriting one's previous story ad infinitum. SF may be a microcosm, but it is larger than a back yard.

To speak practically, one has to consider how best to introduce historical SF to new readers or students. Should one confront them with Homer's *Odyssey*, Mercier's *Year 2440*, Mary Shelley's *Frankenstein*, or the wretched crust of Gernsback's *Ralph 124C41 +*? I trust that the answer is obvious.

It was a passage in *BYS* concerning Hugo Gernsback which most offended readers. This, it appears, was what Sam Moskowitz was attacking me for at the Lunacon. Later, the enthusiast David Kyle took me to task[13] for saying that Hugo Gernsback was arguably one of the worst disasters ever to hit the SF field. Well, admittedly I stated the case strongly in order to be heard above the sound of choristers praising Old Uncle Hugo, but there was truth in what I said. Ten years later, I would qualify the remark: worse disasters have struck since, notably commercial exploitation.

Kyle's history scores slightly better than Lester del Rey's. It actually manages to mention the title of one of my novels, *Barefoot in the Head* ('extravagant if not incomprehensible'). The gain is offset by a veiled threat. The last time anyone said such rough things about Gernsback, we are told, 'was at the 1952 Chicago con; a fan named Chester A. Polk was sent to hospital and Claude Degler, head of the Cosmic Circle, drove Don Rogers out of fandom for good.'

Alexei Panshin, reviewing *BYS* in *F&SF*, also threatened to have me drummed out of the regiment.

Despite which, I have much sympathy for the Kyle–Moskowitz position. Fans like Kyle have had to watch SF taken out of their hands, when once they must have thought it was in their pockets. Well, chums, it belongs to Big Business now, so we're all losers. The media have taken over – and First Fandom was preferable to the Fourth Estate.

---

13 David Kyle, *A Pictorial History of Science Fiction* (1976). I call Kyle an enthusiast because he disdains the name of critic.

More ambivalent is the attitude of general critics of the field. There's a feel of punches being pulled. Tom Clareson, in 'Towards a History of Science Fiction,'[14] evades the issue entirely, with a bland paragraph on *Frankenstein* which follows on a reference to Asimov's *The Gods Themselves*. In James Gunn's history of SF,[15] he gives *BYS* a more than friendly nod, but cannot resist delivering the familiar litany of defunct magazines, backed by displays of gaudy covers. Like del Rey, Gunn names none of my fiction; like del Rey he lumps me in with the New Wave, though obviously without malice. In his later four-volume critical anthology,[16] Gunn becomes more Venturesome; he is a 'safe' scholar moving slowly to a more individual, creative, position.

Clareson and Gunn, like Kyle and Moskowitz, may be regarded honourably as old-timers in the field. Robert Scholes and Eric S. Rabkin, one gathers, are relative newcomers – as their 'thinking person's guide to the genre'[17] demonstrates. This means they cannot reel off litanies of dead stories in dead magazines. It also means they adopt *Frankenstein* as the progenitor of the species. Hooray! No matter if they don't acknowledge where exactly they derived the idea from. They are genial about *BYS*, and mention in passing that I have written fiction, though only *Barefoot in the Head* is named. Perhaps someone somewhere taught it once. Charles Platt, are you blushing?

All the critical books I have mentioned are quirky, including my own. I am less conscious of quirks in two recent encyclopaedic works, Neil Barron's *Anatomy of Wonder: Science Fiction* (1976) and Peter Nicholls' *Encyclopedia of SF* (1979), both of which seek to be dispassionate in judgment. Both take cognisance of the range of my work over the last twenty-five years, short stories as well as novels.

---

14 In Marshall Tymn, ed., *The Science Fiction Reference Book* (1981).

15 James Gunn, *Alternate Worlds* (1975).

16 James Gunn, *The Road to Science Fiction*, 4 volumes (1977–81).

17 Robert Scholes and Eric S. Rabkin, *Science Fiction: History. Science. Vision* (1977).

Both these reference books pride themselves on being as up-to-date as possible (the Barron title is currently available in a second edition). In *BYS*, I decided that there were insufficient perspectives from which to judge anything later than 1960 (a decade before I began writing the book), and so followed the example set by most histories of literature in tempering commercial considerations with discretion.

On the whole, my book was treated kindly. I have gained fewer black marks for it than for my defence of the New Wave writers in England during the sixties, when I fought for their right to express themselves in their own way rather than in someone else's. Despite the attempts of persons like del Rey to lump me in with the New Wave, I flourished before it arrived, and continue still to do so. That experience taught me how conservative readers of SF are, for all their talk about The Literature of Change. But perhaps the study of SF, virtually non-existent when I began *BYS*, has brought in a more liberal race of academics; one hopes it is so.

This must also be said. I know, am friendly with, or at least have met, all the living writers and critics mentioned in this article. Such is part of the social life of a science fiction writer, nor would one have it otherwise. David Kyle I have known since the fifties – a charming man who would not set the head of the Cosmic Circle on to me unless I really deserved it. This gregariousness, reinforced by such SF institutions as conventions and fanzines, with their informal critical attitudes, forms a kind of concealed context within which – or against which – most SF writers still exist, long after the collapse of Gernsback's SF League.

Samuel Delany has pointed to this concealed context,[18] urging

---

18 Samuel R. Delany, 'Reflections on Historical Models of Modern English Language Science Fiction.' *Science Fiction Studies*, Vol. 7 Pt. 2, July 1980, reprinted in *Starboard Wine* (1984)

formal critics to take note of it. Certainly, I was aware of it when writing *BYS*, even if I missed it at Lunacon, when it became flesh in the form of Sam Moskowitz.

My brief here has been to talk of adverse responses to *BYS*. So I have not talked about the praise it has received in many quarters, outside and inside the SF field. I intended the book to be enjoyed, and rejoiced when it gave enjoyment. It brought me a Special BSFA Award, and the much-prized Pilgrim Award from the SFRA. On the congenial social occasion when I received the Pilgrim, Scholes, Rabkin, Suvin, Clareson, and many other distinguished names were present. Truly, friends are better than critics.

BYS concluded by forecasting a great increase in academic involvement in science fiction. The involvement has developed rapidly, as all can testify. Watching from the sidelines, I see some of the difficulties from which academics suffer.

Humanities departments are under threat in times of recession, in a way that science departments – though themselves not without difficulties – are not. In self-defence, academics in humanities posts write their papers in a form of language which imitates the jargon of their colleagues in the harder sciences. The result is frequently an inviolable form of gobbledegook. An example of what I mean is taken almost randomly from a respected critical journal:

> The most serious difficulty with the genre concept comes from the fact that the existence of a particular genre structure (variant) in a given epoch is usually accompanied by literary consciousness of writers, critics, and readers who recognise this structure as different from the synchronic structures of other genres. This intersubjective recognition, depending as it does on the general level of education and culture, on the familiarity of the reading public with traditional and modern literatures, and on the state of criticism in the epoch, is, of course, often arbitrary.

While not entirely resisting attempts at divination, these two sentences seem to say little, and say it in an ugly way remote from the graces of our language as she is spoke. A defence mechanism is in operation. To speak plainly is to risk being taken for a fool. Difficulty must be seen to operate in the texts, or else there may be difficulty with grants in the future. SF criticism, being new, is particularly vulnerable to the administrative chopper.

Beneath the tortured language, what is said rarely carries malice. At least not openly. Our boat is still new and not properly tested; it must not be rocked. Thus criticism and its object have come full circle since the eighteenth century. Then, judgments were expressed with clarity and style, and were often designed to wound:

> Cibber, write all your verses upon glasses;
> So that we may not use them for our —.

Helliconia: How and Why

For many years I had contemplated writing a story about a world where seasons were so long that all one's life might pass in spring, say, or in the winter. The idea had a powerful emotional appeal. Some while ago, I walked into a Northern town and discussed this idea with another writer, Bob Shaw, who was also powerfully attracted to it.

The creative part of the brain works at its own pace, and in its own way. In the summer of 1977, I wrote a letter to a friend setting forth in outline how I imagined conditions would be for a human-like race inhabiting a planet resembling Earth with a year which endured for several thousands of ordinary years. 'Let's say this planet is called Helliconia,' I wrote, on the inspiration. The word was out, the name named. The process of conjuration had begun. From then on, I had to proceed consciously.

I worked with great concentration and dedication. The novel was to be in three volumes, with each volume completed in little more than eighteen months, averaging approximately 150,000 words per volume. The whole story was finished by the end of June 1984.

It was clear from the start that I would need advice for all the disciplines needed to fortify the narrative: history, biology, philology, and so forth. At the basis of everything, the astronomical and geophysical aspects – the details of the Helliconian binary system – had to be as correct and current as could be. Today's theories were wanted, not yesterday's.

So I consulted the various authorities whose names are acknowledged in the novels. Most of them entered into the game of Helliconia readily, and had fruitful suggestions to make. Most specifically, it was Iain Nicholson's description of the binary system and how it came about which opened up what I regard as one of the most profound themes of the novel, the process of enantiodromia, by which things constantly turn into their opposites; knowledge becomes by turns a blessing and a curse, as does religion; captivity and freedom interchange roles; phagors become by turns conquerors and slaves. As a means of making concrete this amorphous but deeply felt theme, the binary model was ideal. (Only later did I turn back to one of my short stories, 'Creatures of Apogee,' to perceive that I had already deployed the process on a miniature scale.)

Ambition grew in me to construct a great story, a new kind of scientific romance which would look substantial even when set beside the epics of the science fiction writer I most admire, Olaf Stapledon.

A number of factors fostered this determination. I will mention only a general and a personal one.

The general first. All was not well with the science fiction field in which I had worked so long. I had been proud to be considered a rule-breaker, a renegade, a man who followed his own star regardlessly. My strong opinions – in particular those concerning the impossibility of exceeding the speed of light in a heavier-than-light vessel and the improbability of finding intelligent life elsewhere in our galaxy – had made me enemies. Nevertheless I saw myself as part of a field which had its own dynamism, and within which some sort of rational debate went forward.

Now the *massif central* of science fiction was crumbling. SF which adhered to rational posits was becoming rarer. Younger writers, particularly in my own country, were hedging their bets by writing a form of science fiction which might, with luck, pass for ordinary fiction, or by creating texts which lodged themselves comfortably in a nostalgic past rather than the future. Everywhere, everyone was writing fantasy; novels abounded in which the hero – or the hero with his miscellaneous gang – is impossibly heroic, where what prevails is an air of general implausibility or, to give implausibility its euphemistic name, magic. In short, it seemed as if the rational was out of favour, along with the ancient art of story-telling.

This crisis may be attributed to several causes, some working within the medium, some outside. The older type of science fiction, looking ahead to an expanding future, is difficult to write in the depressed decade of the eighties, when the world is undergoing recession. The insistent threat of nuclear warfare, too, makes us appear trivial or falsely optimistic if we write about a prosperous future. With the Third World on our conscience, dreams of technological glory ahead are apt to ring hollow. Too many schemes which once seemed excitingly utopian have ended in disaster and disarray, like the scheme to 'develop' (a word regarded with scepticism nowadays) the Amazon basin.

Science fiction writers are demoralised by the megabuck-earning SF films of recent years, and often try to imitate their follies. While the writers of rubbish can always eke out a living, middle-echelon writers are being squeezed hard by changes in the market and marketing philosophy. The opportunity extended to famous writers of an older generation, such as Asimov, Clarke, and Heinlein, to turn out poor imitations of earlier work and be overpaid for it is also demoralising.

To the personal factor. Even my earliest novels, such as *Non-Stop*, *Hothouse*, and the chronicle-novel (as its first publishers called it) *Galaxies Like Grains of Sand*, have reflected my concern for the paradox that mankind, a part of nature, has seen itself apart from nature, opposed to nature. It is a faulty perception which will lead to disaster, and has led to disaster. When I defined SF as 'Hubris clobbered by Nemesis,' I was thinking of this divorced element in the human psyche, which I have in the past defined in Toynbeean terms as the division between the head and heart.

This fatal divorce is something we suffer from as individuals, and not merely as a species. In the present day we seem to have, in general, lost an awareness of our closeness to the earth. Our perspectives have narrowed. Our reason has not helped us to see that we are sustained by a number of non-rational sources such as our instincts, our sense of empathy with others, and all those pleasant promptings about life, birth, death, and the mythological level of life (in short, those numinous qualities which were once labelled 'God,' or something similar, in times when the heart had dominance over the head). The cities have spread the poison. We are flimsier creatures than we should be. We can't see the stars for street lamps. We live in a world of fences. We build the fences, to hide our incompleteness.

Such intimations came to me more clearly when I found that my existence had passed through a disturbing phase into one more richly productive, which Carl Jung refers to as 'individuation.' I felt that what was perceived more clearly might be expressed more clearly, and that this time I might add a diagnosis. Whether I was right or not, I was certainly confident.

So there was the will to make a general romance about Helliconia of, let's say, a semi-scientific nature. And there was the will to go beyond that and construct a drama which could accommodate my diagnosis of the world's ills. But more importantly, there was the will of the novelist to seize upon the large stage of Helliconia to tell that drama in the most effective way.

At first I had some hope of cramming everything into one book. This soon proved to be impossible. To give any adequate idea of the scale of Helliconian life, then at least three points – sample points – in the mighty arc of the Great Year had to be taken and displayed with all the vigour at my disposal. That meant telling stories about characters to which an ordinary reader might lend sympathy: people not given over to heroics, though sometimes to heroism; not faultless people, set apart by virtue; but people, men and women, caught in the toils of life, often unclear about where they were going, and involved in their feelings for one another; in short, courageous people without a great deal of insight. And these people would be shown in contrast to the gigantic background of their planet at periods when both the climate and history were undergoing change.

From the start, it was apparent that my characters were going to suffer vicissitudes even greater than those in my previous novels. Readers know what critics often forget, that it is oddly comforting to read of fictional suffering. Nevertheless, I wanted to reward my readers with what optimism was inherent in the system: the possibility that human life might be happy, and the way there. Since I had reached a period of stability and happiness myself, that way could be found, and finding it shaped the pattern the overall story took.

It all sounded straightforward, once I had familiarised myself with my own intentions. But before I began to write, I decided to make the game a little more complex by staging the drama on more than one plane. There should be five layers to this cake.

We should explore life on Helliconia. Fine. But this was without relevance unless we also learnt something about life on Earth. And, as an intermediary between the two planets, we must have the Earth Observation Station, orbiting Helliconia, in which human beings are suspended like souls in limbo. But to venture further, to the fourth layer, let's see what happens to the Helliconians when they die, let us pursue them into the afterlife.

And, since in large measure this is a drama of evolution, let's see what kind of post-Christian gods control Helliconia and Earth. So we come to the highest level, the level of the tutelary deities, who emerge fully in the third volume.

Once I began writing, all else was forgotten but the interest in the story, the saga of Yuli wandering from the snowy wilderness into the dark citadel of Pannoval: then to be followed by the growth of Embruddock, and the people who live there, the dedicated Shay Tal, the intransigent Aoz Roon, diffident Laintal Ay, and all the others, whose lives are lived out as Spring unfurls and veldt emerges from the snow-plains.

In the second volume, as Helliconia and its sun Batalix draw nearer to Freyr at the time of perihelion, the drama is a more subtle and complex one, concerning the holding of territories and kingdoms, the triumph and eclipse of religions, and the difficulties of a headstrong king divorcing his beautiful queen, the Queen of Queens, in order to make a dynastic marriage with a child. This particular story, by the way – or the germ of it – was borrowed from the history of the early Serbian state and the reign of the doomed Nemanijas. King Milutin took as his fourth wife the child Simonida, daughter of the Byzantine Emperor Andronicus. In Thessaloniki he was married to his six-year-old bride. You can still see Simonida staring out at you, tense and doll-like, from frescoes in Jugoslavia, most notably in the lovely monastery of Gracanica. But child marriages were common in the Middle Ages.

The second volume has the richest prose. Among other things, I read and attended performances of Shakespeare's *A Midsummer Night's Dream* to prepare myself for its writing.

The final volume relates what happens in the northern hemisphere of Helliconia, Sibornal, after a campaign, when the army returns home with the plague in its ranks. The central character is Luterin, a young man who does not understand the truth about his parentage – an echo of the situation regarding humanity itself. He is infatuated in turn by two ladies, his intended bride, Insil Esikananzi, and a slave woman whose husband he has killed, Toress Lahl. The novel has its strong romantic elements, although the ending is anti-romantic; this is the case with the first two volumes also.

Helliconia is presented as a strange and wonderful planet. So it is. But so is Earth, and there is little that happens on Helliconia which has not happened in one form or another on Earth. The one major difference is the existence on Helliconia of other intelligent or semi-intelligent species: most notably the phagors, that ancipital race perpetually warring with humanity for possession of the globe.

Although deadly enemies, phagors and humans exist in a commensal relationship with each other. Much of the story is taken up with this painful relationship, which must be broken and yet would be fatal to break. On Earth we have no phagors, only the animal sides of our natures, with which we are similarly at war, and with which we must come to some kind of agreement. This problem, exciting as any encounter with a mounted phagor, finds explicit place in the final volume.

For me, one of the happiest moments in the whole story is when a terrestrial human being, one of our descendants, points to the whereabouts of Helliconia in the tropical night sky, in the constellation of Ophiucus. This is one way of indicating that the book is not a fantasy. Helliconia has, in Shakespeare's phrase, 'a local habitation and a name.' It is a world where you can be flung into prison for debt. For these reasons, and because of the strong sub-theme of evolutionary progression, I have used H.G. Wells's term and called the book 'a scientific romance.'

But sufficient room has been left between the lines for every reader to make what he will of it. Half the attraction of having such a broad canvas is that it can be filled with terrors and adventures and excitements.

Readers ask if everything in all three volumes was planned before I began to write. The answer must be no. I knew what I wanted to happen and where I had to go. And I had the guidelines suggested by my experts. But most of it was my own devising, and I allowed myself to surprise myself day by day.

Eventually I got, with some astonishment, to where I intended. But during my seven years of work, the world itself had moved on. There were two areas of scientific discovery in particular which brought interesting news.

Our sun is believed[1] to have a companion, dubbed Nemesis, which at its nearest comes within half a light year of Earth. Its passing disturbs the Oort comet cloud, so that Earth is bombarded by cometary material, the result of which is a kind of short and natural 'nuclear winter,' with a cooling of Earth's surface sufficient to bring about the extinction of various phyla. These conclusions are supported by findings in the fossil record, with mass extinctions occurring every 26 million years (the dinosaurs being victims of the most famous extinction), and by patterns of impact craters on the Earth's surface.

Other research, into the likely effect of detonation of nuclear weapons in our atmosphere, has led to the coining of the unpleasant if picturesque phrase used in the preceding paragraph, nuclear winter. The impact of even a 'modest' nuclear war, say something in the region of ten thousand megatons, would be such that the filth released into the upper layers of the atmosphere would precipitate changes in the climate of the northern hemisphere. Photosynthesis could not take place. Not only human beings but trees and many other phyla would die. Europe might come to resemble Greenland or, at best, a chilly steppe. Nor would these effects necessarily remain contained within the atmospheric circulation of the northern hemisphere.

For neither of these two interesting advances in knowledge had I, sitting in my study in Oxford, originally planned. Yet it could not be said that I was unprepared; my narrative and its concerns were such that both sets of findings settled readily into the script! Indeed, the nuclear winter scenario went to reinforce the metaphor of Helliconia's harsh seasons.

---

1 This hypothesis has already been challenged by later ones.

Encouraged by this act of serendipity, I determined to go further than intended, and develop the hypotheses of James Lovelock to some degree; thus my novel would fulfill all the obligations of true science fiction by encompassing, not only scientific knowledge still under debate, but speculation based on that knowledge. Time will test the accuracy of my guess. At least the guess is an optimistic one. And it would be a pity to end this three-volume parade of gallantry and folly on anything but an optimistic note.

... AND THE LURID GLARE
OF THE COMET

Introductory Note

The idea of this book is to preserve some of the articles I have written over recent years which may be of more than ephemeral interest. It follows on from my earlier Serconia Press book, *The Pale Shadow of Science*, and is the mixture as before. Except.

Except that here I include a brief autobiography, presenting it to my readers with some trepidation. Gale Research Books in Detroit have begun a rather astonishing series of volumes, entitled *Contemporary Authors – Autobiography Series*. Gale sent me a copy of Volume I, asking me if I would write for Volume 2. Writers are allowed to have photographs of their choice to accompany the text. It all looks amateur and artless, but from it a reader can learn a great deal about that ever-mysterious subject, other people's lives. I decided to have a go at Volume 2.

It is difficult, perhaps impossible, to be truthful about oneself. I did my best. The exercise opened up a new area of writing. Gale limits its writers to a certain number of words. In the greatly revised sketch, here presented as 'The Glass Forest,' the thing has grown almost half as long again. My trepidation is, in consequence, almost half as great again.

Incidentally, it is worth anyone's while looking up the Gale books in their library. The first volume contains autobiographical sketches by Marge Piercy, Richard Condon, Stanislaw Lem, and Frederik Pohl, among other familiar names, the second Poul Anderson, James Gunn, and Alan Sillitoe.

'The Glass Forest' is the *pièce de resistance* on this menu; but I hope that the other courses will also please. As before, science fiction and writing rub shoulders with travel, history, and other arts.

My thanks go as ever to the stalwarts of Serconia Press and to Marshall B. Tymn, President of the International Association for the Fantastic in the Arts, in connection with that august event, the Seventh Conference of the IAFA in Houston, Texas on 12-16 March 1986, which I was privileged to attend as Guest of Honour.

B.W.A.

Bold Towers, Shadowed Streets ...

As I was finishing the compilation of this book, it happened that I received a letter from a reader in Churubusco, Indiana, Mr Gary J. Anderson. Not only was this the first time I had ever heard from any of the citizens of Churubusco, but Mr Anderson had encouraging things to say to me.

He and his friends had much enjoyed my Helliconia novels. My opinion of Churubusco went up in leaps and bounds. And in one sentence, Mr Anderson said what an author would most like to hear. He said, 'Your books have made a profound change in the way I observe things in this world.'

Your books have made a profound change in the way I observe things in this world. It's a fine sentence. I started thinking of all the books which have changed the way I observed things. When I wrote back to Mr Anderson – as I did immediately, even dropping the darling new novel on which I had just begun work – I mentioned one such book to him, *Civilisation*, by Clive Bell.

Civilisation profoundly changed the way I observed things. Let me see if I can explain the small miracle.

After over three years in the Far East, I had returned to England. 'So, you're back to civilisation at last,' said old friends. I believed the Far East to be a civilised and decent place, but I understood what

133

they meant. Also, my role had supposedly been that of defender of civilisation. That was what you were told when you were sent to fight the Japanese, and the savage behaviour of the Japanese lent credence to the claim. And I believed the claim in the way you believe things as an adolescent, neither believing nor disbelieving, indeed hardly listening. Another thing was that at the end of the war a lot of people talked about restoring civilised values.

So I went into this used bookshop and found a book called *Civilisation* and bought it. It presented a whole new concept for consideration. Such a matter had never entered my head before. Nor had I realised what a barbarian was. Clive Bell was one of the Bloomsbury set. He married Vanessa Stephen, Virginia Woolf's sister. He was one of the elite. He would not have had a good word to say about me. I was one of his barbarians.

All the same, I liked his book greatly. Books – yes, even novels – should tell us all the things we need to know which our parents, in their ghastly struggle for a living and a false image, fail to tell us. I recognised that what Bell was saying was true (in other words, more accurately, I was swayed by his argument). For Bell, civilisation was a fragile and rather artificial structure, the chief characteristics of which were a love of music, humour, broadminded tolerance, and reason. In order to say what a revelation this was to me, I have to make the admission that until then – child of war shortages that I was – I had believed that civilisation could be defined mainly by plentiful consumer goods. In a flash, I saw how despicable was this materialist assumption. Civilisation was not a Mercedes but an attitude of mind.

This may make me sound very silly. In youth we are very silly, and things are often no better in age. The point was, I suppose, that no one had bothered to inform me of these things before, just as possibly no one had told Mr Gary Anderson that all life on Earth forms a unity.

There is another point, come to think of it. Only on certain people can such gobbets of information or revelation have effect. Stony ground abounds. I was ready for the words of Clive Bell because I had, since early childhood, been secretly aghast at the materialism of my own family. And my sojourn in the East had persuaded me that there was more than one sort of civilised behaviour.

While we are about it, I have another confession to make. Clive Bell was a great admirer of the eighteenth century. At that time, I knew rather less about the eighteenth century than I did about the moon. (About the moon I reckoned to know most of what was going, and had every faith in its being visited by mankind within the next thousand years ...)

So I started reading about the eighteenth century, devouring some of the writings of those who lived then, studying its artists. Samuel Johnson presented himself to me, and he too changed the way I thought, rather in the way that bulls change china shops.

But I must not go on this way or I shall lose credibility. Let's stop there. Let's not make too much of *Civilisation*. It has come to seem slightly precious, *presque* Bloomsbury. But supposing Bell, who died in 1962, returned to Earth and picked up my novel, *Dark Light Years*. Would he be able to see in it some of his own teaching? I hope so.

Avid for more writings which would provide an overview of our culture, I lighted on Lewis Mumford, author of *Technics and Civilisation*. He also wrote *The Condition of Man* and *The Culture of Cities*. These I read with avidity. Like Bell, Mumford had wit, which requires a fine eye for detail.

I turn to my bookshelves to find one or other of my two copies of *Civilisation*. I have Kenneth Clarke's volume of that name, but not Clive Bell's. Somehow, they had gone, borrowed or lost in one of the Aldisses' many moves. Somehow, I had managed to live several years without wanting to look inside those covers again. Maybe the umbilical cord had been severed.

My idea had been to quote something apposite, to give a flavour of the man. Perhaps it is as well I have no copy; even good wines lose their flavour with time. Some Mumford will serve instead.

My copy of *The Culture of Cities* belonged to Arnold Toynbee, and has his signature. The book was published in 1938. Mumford is a kind of socialist-liberal or liberal-socialist much like H. G. Wells. His style, I see now, is more bombastic than my present taste enjoys. But here's what he says about metropolises, taken pretty much at random.

> This metropolitan world ... is a world where the great masses of people, unable to have direct contact with more satisfying means of living, take life vicariously, as readers, spectators, passive observers: a world where people watch shadow-heroes and heroines in order to forget their own clumsiness or coldness in love, where they behold brutal men crushing out life in a strike riot, a wrestling ring or a military assault, while they lack the nerve even to resist the petty tyranny of their immediate boss: where they hysterically cheer the flag of their political state, and in their neighbourhood, their trades union, their church, fail to perform the most elementary duties of citizenship.
>
> Living thus, year in, year out, at second hand, remote from the nature that is outside them, and no less remote from the nature within, handicapped as lovers and as parents by the routine of the metropolis and by the constant spectre of insecurity and death that hovers over its bold towers and shadowed streets – living thus the mass of inhabitants remain in a state bordering on the pathological.

And so on. To be honest, I am less carried away by such arguments than I was when I went into my Mumford phase at the end of World War II. I found myself trapped in an English city – admittedly the pleasantest of cities, Oxford – and this American voice was a comforter, not a rabble-rouser. For my time in the East had been spent mainly outdoors. The Army is not a domestic institution. The sun, the wind, the rain, were immoderate elements. None of your English compromises, when it is hard to tell whether or not the sun is up. Protestantism would never have taken root in India. There, they must have gods with fifty arms, to match the manic dexterity of nature.

Somehow, I had to fit myself into the hole of urban living, and it went hard. Mumford gave voice, with a Shakespearean command of detail, to my discontents. The city as civilisation's lens and destroyer! This was what Shelley was talking about when he wrote to his friend Maria Gisborne

> You are now
> In London, that great sea, whose ebb and flow
> At once is deaf and loud, and on the shore
> Vomits its wrecks, and still howls for more.

Success is a city much like London. It too can welcome us in, only to destroy us. But is it better to fail in the countryside?

The answer to that question seems to be that those who amass fortunes, and who are therefore most able to choose, prefer, on the whole, the vivid physical life of the hunt, whether the quarry be fish, fox, or fallow deer, at a good distance from the nearest metropolis.

In those bold towers and shadowed streets of which Mumford speaks, decisions are being taken which will influence all of us. We cannot expect with any confidence that those decisions will have our good at heart. We are surrounded with plenty, with a hailstorm of technological marvels, with a variety of foods and drinks such as the ancient pharaohs never knew, with immense personal freedoms (freedom from slavery, for instance a rare thing in the history of civilisation), with access to lakes and oceans of knowledge, with ceaseless imagery, and with the abounding creativity of our century. And yet ... and yet the shadow of physical and spiritual famine stalks us. The lurid glare of the comet reveals the poverty of our 'dark, compressed lives,' to borrow Wells's phrase.

This is the great dilemma. Somehow, we have to control ourselves. Clive Bell, a member of the elite, believed in rule by elite. So did Plato in his *Republic*, and More after him, in *Utopia*, and most of the utopianists since. In my novel, *The Malacia Tapestry*, I tried to draw a city state utopia ruled by an elite. Malacia is a sunny, not unhappy place, but eventually the sheer human injustice of it becomes intolerable, even to those – like my hero, de Chirolo – who don't wish to think about such matters.

We have to believe in the equality of mankind, even though our daily experience tells us that equality does not exist. At least equality can exist in the mind.

Equality implies self-discipline. If my neighbour is my equal, I shall not mug him. If I am the equal of my neighbour, again, I shall not mug him. If those shadowy decision-makers in the bold towers think we are all equal, they will not metaphysically mug us.

Well, I can see that these are topics I ought to confine within the perimeters and ill-defined shores of my new and yet unwritten novel. As a popular writer, I believe in the success of the popular arts, and in the duty of those arts to demonstrate that there is more to life than a succession of Rambos and Conans. No one can be equal in the lands of Rambo and Conan. There is a better world, where complex issues are decided by other than blows and bullets.

May it long continue so, in Oxford and Churubusco!

... *And the Lurid Glare of the Comet*

'Others abide our question – thou art free,' said Matthew Arnold
in his sonnet on Shakespeare. Among past science fiction writers,
many, I fear, abide our question and are gone. Wells, on the other
hand, seems in many respects to increase in stature. He is our
Shakespeare.

We know little of William Shakespeare outside his writings. Of
H. G. Wells, we are well informed. His is a tightly documented
life. Not only are his fictions grounded in his own life, however
finely above ground they fly; he took care to leave various records
of what he was up to. He lived at a brisk pace and did not easily
separate life from literature. This trait it was that lured him into
much of the hasty journalism with which he became involved,
and which has obscured his real achievements.

Bernard Bergonzi's seminal work, *The Early H. G. Wells*, has
established a kind of orthodoxy: that the early science fiction is
the best of Wells, and that little he wrote after *The First Men in the
Moon* in 1901 is of much consequence. This is not entirely true,
or is at best a simplification. There is the almost unconsidered *In
the Days of the Comet*, for instance.

Of recent years, we have had to adjust our views of Herbert George

139

Wells. It was becoming easy for a general reader simply to dismiss him as a failed prophet, or to classify him with such writers of a fading epoch as Arnold Bennett, Gissing, or Hilaire Belloc. But Wells is amazing; Wells had a time-bomb waiting. In 1984 was published – thirty-eight years after his death – his secret story of his love-lives, under the title *H. G. Wells in Love*.

Wells wanted to be happy, that most immodest of ambitions. He took great pains to be happy, and devoted much of his remarkable energy to that end; what was rare in his strivings was that he tried to make the women with whom he so regularly got himself involved happy too. He set them up in houses, paid their hotel bills, and for many years put up with the most difficult of them (there the palm goes to Odette Keun) in a vague placatory way which must have aggravated as much as it mollified. The most famous of these involvements, apart from that with his breathtakingly tolerant second wife, Jane, was with Rebecca West.

There was, of course, Rebecca West's side of the question; but our later age can see sympathetically that many of the vexing contrivances these lovers were put to, as for instance the occasional pretence that Wells was merely his son Anthony's uncle, were forced upon them by the social conventions of the time.

This great amorous warfare of flesh and spirit comes fresh to mind as one reads *In the Days of the Comet*. The book was first published in 1906, at a time Wells labelled 'the promiscuous phase of my life'; not that he was able exactly to stay chaste until well into his seventies. By 1906 Wells was extremely famous in a way that writers these days are not, who sink instead into obscurity, produce plays, or become 'media personalities.' Wells went travelling about the world, enjoying intercourse of one kind or another with presidents and prostitutes, reporting and being reported on. He was confident that a new world was emerging, uncertain how it would emerge, eternally lively and curious. A natural advocate of free love.

Once his book of essays, *Anticipations*, had been published in 1901, Wells was listened to increasingly as a prophetic voice, competent to speak about the real world, rather than to indulge merely in his ingenious fantasies. *In the Days of the Comet* is a balance between the dissatisfactions and hope of the real world and constructive fantasy. It's a visionary novel. Visionary novels are always disappointing in some way, since words never correspond exactly to either facts or wishes; but this is a prize exhibit of the species.

Wells's first readers were most struck by his vision of the new world emerging, a world of free love and social equality. We in our generation are more likely to be impressed by his portrait of things as they were – and by their resemblance to today. The comet has yet to come.

A profile of the novel appears disarmingly simple, a case of 'Look here upon this picture, and on this.' We are shown the old world; the comet passes; we are shown the new world. There is a Biblical directness in the parable: 'We shall all be changed, in a moment, in the twinkling of an eye.' The comet is the mechanism, the lurid visitant, which carries us from the one picture to the other, and Wells is properly offhand in his pseudo-scientific talk of the nitrogen in the comet's tail having its benevolent effects upon mankind.

This sensible method of argument by contrast is one that others have followed, before and since. We hope for a better world, we see it clear. But how to get there? Wells in 1906 could see no bridge to utopia; he forged a miracle instead, with legitimate didactic intent.

This forging is performed with great literary skill, something with which Wells is too little credited (though Nabokov and Eliot have acknowledged Wells's powers). The strengths of the book have also been widely underestimated, even by those writers and readers who traffic in comets and similar wonders.

The story is told in Wells's easy manner. After a crisis, we get the throwaway remark, 'Then, you know, I suppose I folded up this newspaper and put it in my pocket,' which catches without pretension the absent-minded listlessness following a lover's quarrel. The prose grows more spirited when Wells's traditional dislikes are paraded. Despite many attempts at it since, no one has bettered Wells's description of places where commerce has invaded nature – perhaps because he finds a kind of desolate beauty there. When Leadford, the central character, arrives at a seaside town, we come on the following passage:

> The individualistic enterprise of that time had led to the plotting out of nearly all the country round the seaside towns into roads and building plots – all but a small portion of the south and east coast was in this condition, and had the promises of those schemes been realised the entire population of the island might have been accommodated upon the sea frontiers. Nothing of the sort happened, of course; the whole of this uglification of the coastline was done to stimulate a little foolish gambling in plots, and one saw everywhere agents' boards in every state of freshness and decay, ill-made exploitation roads overgrown with grass, and here and there at a corner, a label, 'Trafalgar Avenue' or 'Sea View Road.' Here and there, too, some small investor, some shopman with 'savings' had delivered his soul to the local builders and built himself a house; and there it stood, ill-designed, mean-looking, isolated, ill-placed on a cheaply fenced plot, athwart which his domestic washing fluttered in the breeze amidst a bleak desolation of enterprise.

Of course we recognize it. What was happening in Shapham-bury in 1906 is happening in Florida today.

The tale of Leadford's thwarted affair with Nellie, of his love which turns to hatred, and of the business with the gun, is occasionally melodramatic; a similar theme is more subtly handled in the 1924 novel, *The Dream*. But the narrative proves enough to allow Wells to string out before us a series of ghastly cameos, the finest of which is probably the picture of the industrial Midlands, when twilight settled over a tawdry scene of sheds, factories, terrace houses, and blast furnaces.

> Each upstart furnace, when its monarch sun had gone, crowned itself with flames, the dark cinder heaps began to glow with quivering fires, and each pot-bank squatted rebellious in a volcanic coronet of light. The empire of the day broke into a thousand feudal baronies of burning coal.

Such passages brim with imaginative energy. In his book, *Language of Fiction*, David Lodge makes an eloquent defence of *Tono-Bungay*, which Wells was to publish only three years after *In the Days of the Comet*. Lodge points out that there is a way of reading Wells, just as there is of reading Henry James, and speaks of *Tono-Bungay* as a 'Condition of England' novel: a novel neglected because its style, its whole thrust, does not accord with preconceived ideas of the English novel as formulated by Henry James and F. R. Leavis. To a large extent, the same principle applies to *In the Days of the Comet*.

All its vivid imagery of physical chaos serves a purpose directly geared to the meaning of the novel. It links the tangible world with the chaos of mankind's thinking, and in particular with Leadford's lost and murderous state of mind. As we are told,

> The world of thought in those days was in the strangest condition, it was choked with obsolete inadequate formulae, it was tortuous to a maze-like degree with secondary contrivances and adaptations, suppressions, conventions, and subterfuges. Base immediacies fouled the truth on every man's lips.

Clarity was blocked as thoroughly as the way to the sea.

In fact, Wells offers his readers a red herring in the extract quoted above. The 'world of thought' may indeed have been choked by 'contrivances, adaptations, suppressions, conventions, and subterfuges'; but this emotive description applies even more closely to Wells's private 'world of emotions,' to what he termed 'the promiscuous phase of his life.' The utopia of the novel is no extensive plan of rational living, as were previous utopias such as Bellamy's, whose rationale Wells had borrowed for *When the Sleeper Wakes*, or even as were Wells's earlier approaches towards utopia. Rather, it is a sphere where love requires no 'contrivances,' etc.

Linking *In the Days of the Comet* with *The Dream*, Patrick Parrinder, in an article on Wells's utopias, says that the novel stresses 'not the perfection of social organisation in a utopia but the contrast between the individual contentment it would offer and the emotional storm and stress of twentieth century life.'[1]

For ten years, Wells had poured out his mythopoeic stories and novels in extravagant, generous, and startling fashion. Really, a decade of such prodigality is all we should expect from any writer: burning out is also part of the giving process of creativity. There is textual reason to believe that Wells, that intuitive creature, was aware of the passing of his gift. In the same year that *In the Days of the Comet* appeared, one of Wells's best short stories was published in a daily newspaper; its theme runs parallel to the theme of the novel.

In 'The Door in the Wall,' Lionel Wallace, the central figure, grows up to be a successful public figure. At the age of five, he is wandering the city streets near home when he discovers the door in the wall. He enters, to find himself in a garden of delight, the original primal garden, where panthers are harmless and gentle mother figures attend him. There are other children in the garden. They greet Lionel with friendly cries. He plays with them. The garden is a personal utopia for one.

Once he has left the garden, Lionel can never find it again. He grows up. He becomes a member of parliament, a Cabinet

---

1   Patrick Paninder, 'Utopia and Meta-Utopia in H. G. Wells'; *SF Studies* 36, July 1985.

Minister. Occasionally, after long intervals, he sees the door again, but can never spare time to enter it. Always some worldly business prevents him: he is hurrying to see a woman or he is late getting to the House of Commons. His sense of lost vision grows as he grows older.

> This loss is destroying me. For two months, for ten weeks nearly now, I have done no work at all, except the most necessary and urgent duties. My soul is full of unappeasable regrets ...

Wells celebrated his fortieth birthday in 1906. 'The Door in the Wall,' like *In the Days of the Comet*, shows a weariness with the humdrum world, a longing for illumination, a hatred for the smallness of everyday life. Yet Wells was fated to enter that life, to become a businessman of ideas, now that his creative fire was dying. Bergonzi puts it differently: 'His imagination became increasingly coerced by his intellectual convictions.'

It may be so. What is less arguable is Bergonzi's perception that the door in the wall, which remained forever closed and eventually resulted in the death of Lionel, stands as a symbol of the highly original talent which Wells sensed he was losing.

The experienced writer has his strategies. Most of Wells's writing life still lay before him. He found a way to eke out the imaginative with various intellectual speculations which were interesting in themselves. And he found subjects nearer home than Mars and the Moon. In particular, he found England and the twentieth century.

Consider two brief passages from *In the Days of the Comet*, in which we are asked respectively to perceive the inner and outer lives of men of the twentieth century, and of the central character in particular.

> We young people had practically no preparation at all for the stir and emotions of adolescence. Toward the young the world

maintained a conspiracy of stimulating silences. There came no initiation. There were books, stories of a curiously conventional kind that insisted on certain qualities in every love-affair and greatly intensified one's natural desire for them, perfect trust, perfect loyalty, lifelong devotion. Much of the complex essentials of love were altogether hidden … We were like misguided travellers who had camped in the dry bed of a tropical river. Presently we were knee deep and neck deep in the flood.

And

To the left spread a darkling marsh of homes, an infinitude of little smoking hovels, meagre churches, public houses, Board schools, and other buildings out of which the prevailing chimneys of Swathinglea rose detachedly. To the right, very clear and relatively high, the Bantock Burden pit-mouth was marked by a gaunt lattice bearing a great black wheel, sharp and distinct in the twilight, and beyond, in an irregular perspective, were others following the lie of the seams. The general effect, as one came down the hill, was of a dark compressed life beneath a very high and wide and luminous evening sky, against which those pit-wheels rose. And ruling the calm spaciousness of that heaven was the great comet, now green-white, and wonderful for all who had eyes to see.

Over the chaos shines the comet, growing larger night by night. It forms a contrast to the 'dark, compressed life' on which it shines. Wells wrote with the predicted 1910 appearance of Halley's comet in mind. Equally topical for us is the miner's strike, with its pickets and attacks on cars. Wells's power as a fantasist derives from his firm grip of the world-as-it-is.

Since *In the Days of the Comet* was not well received when it appeared, as frequently happens when visionary books are set before a largely unprepared public, it seems appropriate to offer a new reading of the novel to a new set of readers.

This is not a 'Condition of England' novel, though in some respects it may be seen as a precursor of *Tono-Bungay*. Rather, it is a skilfully conducted 'Condition of Mind' novel. The Change effected by the comet is a change of mind. Striking descriptions of physical states are always linked to mental states – as when the hideous towns are designated 'cities men weep to enter.' The sick state of the people before the Change is dramatised cunningly in a variety of ways as Europe drifts towards war, the ultimate waste, the ultimate confusion. 'Humanity choked amidst its products.'

This sickness of mind is nowhere better embodied than in the character of its central figure, Willie Leadford, who tells the story. On the first page of his narrative, Leadford speaks of his 'crude, unhappy youth.' Throughout the story until the Change, he reveals himself as brutal, troubled, murderous, and ineffective. This is precisely the state of the world in which he lives. Despite the tide of bottled emotions, everything is reduced to pettiness. 'It seems to me even now,' says Leadford after the Change, 'that the little dark creature who had stormed across England in pursuit of Nettie and her lover must have been about an inch high ....'

Leadford is deliberately not elaborately characterised. The same applies to the few other actors – a point to which we return later. But on the details encumbering Leadford's physical existence Wells is sharply precise. We particularly understand the nature of this 'dark and sullen lout,' as he calls himself, by his treatment of his mother, the woman who endured much to ensure her son's comfort, minimal though that comfort is.

The portrait of Mrs Leadford is undoubtedly based on Wells's memory of his mother at Atlas House in Bromley, Kent, where he was born. The exasperated love he felt for her is always present, nowhere more so than in the description of the old woman's dreadful kitchen. Even George Orwell never bettered that kitchen of Mrs Leadford's, where the business of deforming the human soul is carried on quite as efficiently as in any factory. Mrs Leadford is growing old in her foul kitchen. Her hands are distorted by ill-use. She coughs. She shuffles about in badly fitting boots. Even her son wants nothing to do with her.

Wells turns to the historic present for the climax of these scenes of domestic misery. Leadford, betrayer and betrayed, says, 'And while she washes up I go out, to sell my overcoat and watch in order that I may desert her.'

In the Days of the Comet is full of such compelling moments, which crystallise the whole point of the book while being sufficiently powerful in themselves as moments of tragi-comedy in Wells's best manner.

So the entire first part of the novel represents an acute and brilliantly drawn picture of the mind of England and the industrialised countries at the turn of the century. Leadford, taken up with his wretched emotional relationships and his socialism, pays little attention to the comet drawing nearer to Earth. His counterweight, Parload, is the astronomer; it is through Parload that we see the contrast between earthly squalor and heavenly beauty, while Leadford is still having trouble with his boots.

The comet arrives and brings the Change. Wells now draws the utopia that could be. He was always a master of symbols, in his swift, careless-seeming way. Among the first objects the changed Leadford sees are a discarded box of pills and a wrecked battleship, a 'torn and battered mass of machinery' now lying amid ploughed-up mountains of chalk ooze. From now on, it will be possible to make love, not war.

Despite all these excellent preparations, the utopian world of might-be is a shadowy place when we come to it. Wells has to resort ultimately to traditional stereotype, of a place with trees of golden fruit and crystal fountains, tenanted by people who look exalted. He confronts a difficulty that Dante and Milton faced before him; the *Inferno* and *Paradise Lost* have more readers than a thousand *Paradisos* and *Paradise Regaineds*. Not only is a better world hard to realize, even on paper; but Wells had addressed himself particularly to that subject in the previous year, with the publication of *A Modern Utopia*, and his real interest lay elsewhere.

A Modern Utopia is a full-fleshed blueprint for a better, healthier, and happier world, in which a regulated capitalist economy is presided over by an elite (the 'samurai'). Since it appeared in 1905, *A Modern Utopia* has been much sneered at. Many of the book's ideas are sensible and rational – in a word, Wellsian; but an irrational streak in us prevents our putting our knowledge into practice on any effective scale. Wells was essentially rather a simple person (an adjective he applies affectionately to Kipps), and it was this simplicity which gave him the confidence to put forward his less-than-simple plans for mankind, generally in the expectation that they would be immediately taken up.

The rather shadowy utopia to which we are introduced at the end of the present book contains two well-dramatised elements not markedly present in *A Modern Utopia*, the death of warfare and an outspoken argument for free love. The argument for free love is carried on into the 'frame' of the story for extra emphasis.

Critics have accused Wells of wanting war. Certainly he was obsessed with war, almost as greatly as we are in our time. Certainly in 1914 he applauded the call to arms, as many people did – and wrote a rather silly book whose title coined a cliché, *The War that will End War*. But nobody reading *In the Days of the Comet* would call him a war-monger. I am thinking particularly of the lovely moment after the Change when the common soldiery on its way to war – as it might be, in Flanders – returns to consciousness by the roadside.

The men do not fall into ranks. They discuss the causes of war with incredulity. 'The Emperor!' they exclaim. 'Oh, nonsense! We're civilised men … Where's the coffee?'

It did not work out that way in 1914. Hailey's comet passed without effect.

But the new thing in Leadford's utopia which caught the attention in 1906 was emotional freedom. Love, not war, to suit that 'promiscuous phase' of his life.

Wells advocates free love: cleverly, he has a woman put forward the argument. Nellie is changed from a rural faceless creature to a 'young woman of advanced appearance' (to borrow a description jokingly applied to Christina Alberta in Wells's later novel *Christina Alberta's Father*). She puts forward the argument tentatively at first, but in the end conclusively: marriage is not what she wants; she wants to love where she chooses; she wants both Leadford and his rival. 'Am I not a mind that you must think of me as nothing but a woman?'

What infuriated the righteous, and Wells's enemies in the Fabian Society, was that Wells not only advocated free love, but had the cheek to practise it. He defied the conventions of the time. There is an amusing example of this in *H. G. Wells in Love*. Before the First World War, Wells was enjoying an affair with the Gräfin von Arnim, the Irish lady whose book, *Elizabeth and her German Garden*, was beloved in stately and less stately homes up and down the land.

One day Wells and von Arnim found something in the correspondence columns of *The Times* which amused them. It was, says Wells,

> a letter from Mrs Humphrey Ward denouncing the moral tone of the younger generation, apropos of a rising young writer, Rebecca West, and, having read it aloud, we decided we had to do something about it. So we stripped ourselves under the trees as though there was no one in the world but ourselves and made love all over Mrs Humphrey Ward. And when we had dressed again we lit a match and burnt her.

A word should be said finally about the form of *In the Days of the Comet*. Although it has been referred to here as elsewhere as a novel, it is in fact a separate if allied form, a novella. A novella, as properly understood, restricts itself to a single situation or event. It has few characters, and they mainly function in a symbolic role: the protagonist, the woman as love object, the rival, the mother, the statesman, and so on. Goethe's *Elective Affinities* is a good example of a novella. And *In the Days of the Comet* is a rare English language example of the mode – a much more perfect example than has hitherto been recognized.

In it, H. G. Wells shows his characteristic dissatisfaction with the existing order, his spirited haterd of the mess we have got ourselves into, his striving for better things. No doubt if he were alive today he would still find ample reason for dissatisfaction, hatred, striving, and contrivances.

When the Future Had to Stop

Some science fiction novels stay in the repertory too long. Others, for no good reason, never establish themselves. Or they may fail to establish themselves for a bad reason, because the author does not produce enough to keep his name perennially before the audience.

The name of Kingsley Amis is well enough known as a novelist. It is also fragrant to the SF audience as that of the author of the first general survey of SF – and an acute one at that – *New Maps of Hell*. There is also a short story or two, one an amusing parody of Ernest Hemingway, and the alternative world novel, *The Alteration*. But *Russian Hide-and-Seek* (1980) has failed to find an established place in the hearts of readers.

Perhaps it is because *Russian Hide-and-Seek* is both a rather forbidding novel and a rather complex one. This is a plea for better attention to it.

In a sense, the central topic of the novel is straightforward, even time-honoured. Britain, owing to its lack of vigilance, has been taken over by the Russians, and is now a satellite of the Soviet Union. This seems to place the book in the dire warning category of *The Battle of Dorking* and *When the Kissing Had to Stop*.

But matters are less simple than that. It is part of Amis's cunning that he does not show us the invasion of the island.

Like an Ibsen play, a lot of history has flowed under the bridge before the curtain goes up. We are confronted with a Britain fifty years after the coup.

The opening is magisterial. A grand English country house is surrounded by pasturage. The son, Alexander, an ensign in the Guards, is vexing his family, and indeed everyone else. The mother worries about flowers and dinner arrangements. We might be embarking on a leisurely nineteenth century novel. The one blemish to the rural picture seems to be the hundreds of tree stumps which disfigure the grounds of the mansion. That, and the family name, Petrovsky.

What we at first may assume to be threatened is in fact absolutely overwhelmed. There is no way to undo fifty years of history. This is an England no longer England. It is now the EDR, Soviet-occupied.

There is nothing futuristic about the EDR. It has been reduced to an imitation of pre-revolutionary Russia. This is a world of stately country homes with a vengeance, with the English as servants. Parties are thrown, dances are held, and dashing young fellers ride about on horseback. This reversion follows the somewhat similar patterns the victorious Nazis impose on Europe in Sarban's *The Sound of His Horn*, which once appeared in an edition with an admiring introduction by Kingsley Amis.

The novel is one of fine surfaces and corrupt interiors. Here is another large house. White-coated servants move about, supplying drink and food. Tennis is in progress on two courts. A small orchestra is playing old-fashioned waltzes. Everything is supposedly done in high style.

But: 'No one thought, no one saw that the clothes of the guests were badly cut from poor materials ... that the women's coiffures were messy and the men's fingernails dirty, that the surfaces of the courts were uneven and inadequately raked, that the servants' white coats were not very white, that the glasses and plates they carried had not been properly washed, or that the pavement where the couples danced needed sweeping … No one thought any of that because no one had ever known any different.'

Ignoring the fact that this is rather obtrusive authorial comment, we see embodied here the fine surface / corrupt interior principle on which the novel hinges. To every thing there is another aspect.

Alexander Petrovsky starts like a hero out of Fielding, young and spirited. He makes a fine initial impression on readers – and on Commissioner Mets, the power in the land. He impresses Mets by addressing him in good English, the language of the conquered. Alexander has gone to some pains to learn a few useful phrases and to pronounce them properly. 'But his vocabulary had remained small and his ability to carry on a conversation smaller still.'

Alexander bullies his subordinates. His sexual appetites are gross, and scarcely satisfied when he encounters Mrs Korotchenko, who likes being trampled on before the sexual act, and introduces her twelve year old daughter Dasha to join in her lusty variety of fun. They perform in a kind of sexual gymnasium.

If the occupying force is shown as corrupt under its polished veneer, the English are no better. The good ones were killed off in the invasion and the Pacification. Those left are mainly a pack of docile tipplers, devoid of morale and culture, living in a kind of rustic sub-world. It is a dystopia quite as convincing and discomfiting as Orwell's urban warrens.

To parallel this total loss of English qualities, the occupying force have lost all belief in their motivating creed, Marxism, which died out about 2020.

Among the younger Russian set, men and women, English phrases are fashionable. '*Fucking hell,*' says Elizabeth. The younger set imagines it is fond of England. Certain of them, including Theodore, the fiancé of Alexander's sister, are plotting to take advantage of a Moscow-generated New Cultural Policy. 'Group 31,' to which Theodore belongs, plans to restore England to the English.

'Group 31' wish to get Alexander involved. He is willing enough. To be a revolutionary is a great romantic pose which panders to his narcissism. He is callously prepared to assassinate his liberal father, if need be. And of course he will get a vital list off Mrs Korotchenko, who is the wife of the Deputy Director of Security, under Director Vanag.

Unexpected deaths follow, yet the underground theme proves less exciting than it should. What is more interesting, perhaps because more unusual, is the attempt, prompted by Moscow, to launch a performance of a once banned Shakespeare play, *Romeo and Juliet*. The play is to be the climax of a festival in which English culture is handed back to the English.

The Russians do not and cannot care for the past they have obliterated. Nor do the English care – except for a few over-fifties, who scarcely count. It is true that they refer to their conquerors as *the Shits*, but this is a fossil appellation, almost without malice. By such small authentic notes, the originality of the novel declares itself.

An audience is somehow raked up to attend the great event. The music recital is moderately successful. It includes works by 'Dowland, Purcell, Sullivan, Elgar, the composer of "Ta-ra-raboom-de-ay," Noel Coward, Duke Ellington (taken to have been an English nobleman of some sort), Britten and John Lennon.' But with *Romeo and Juliet*, it is different.

Alexander has a drink at the Marshal Stalin in St. John's Street before attending the theatre. The play about the death of innocence – although it has been cut to an hour in order not to tax people's patience too greatly – is a disaster. There is a near riot, the theatre is set on fire, Alexander decides not to rescue the girl playing Juliet.

In scenes of ghastly comedy, Shakespeare's island race rejects its old culture and religion when they are offered. It prefers to queue quietly for food – a typical meal being cabbage soup, belly of pork with boiled beets (since there's now a third fresh-meat day in a week), and stewed windfalls. Or it will booze at the Marshal Grechko (to become The Jolly Englishman under the New Cultural Policy).

Once a culture ceases to be common coinage, it has gone forever. It is a grim warning, one which elevates the novel far above the jingoistic military warning, Be Prepared! Sadness rather than jingoism is the imprint of these pages.

'Group 31' itself turns out to be a veneer over something nastier. And the insatiable Mrs Korotchenko betrays Alexander. Nor is this the only betrayal. One of the most chilling moments comes at the end, when Director Vanag is interrogating Theodore, after the latter's coup has failed. Vanag relates something of the history of the so-called Pacification, fifty years earlier. 'It was our country's chance to take what she had always wanted most, more than Germany, far more than the Balkans, more even than America. And she took it, after serious difficulty at first, after being on the point of having to withdraw entirely in order to regroup.'

Theodore asks, 'What did the Americans do?'

Vanag begins to laugh. He never bothers to answer the question.

Fittingly, the usual Amis humour is, in *Russian Hide-and-Seek*, suffused into a permeating irony. Detail is piled on disconcerting detail – each unexpected but just – like the young English woman girlishly longing to get to Moscow (an echo of Chekhov here), until the whole disastrous tapestry of a lost England hangs before us.

All that we value has been swept away. Culture is irrelevant. Nihilism prevails.

I have to declare an interest of a special nature in *Russian Hide-and-Seek*. The novel is dedicated to my wife Margaret and me. It's a fine novel, and I'm grateful.

What Happens Next?

This piece was composed for special circumstances, which I had better explain.

My last school, referred to elsewhere in this volume, was West Buckland, in North Devon. Although I was glad to leave, one of the masters there kept in touch with me, my old housemaster, Harold Boyer. We corresponded sporadically, even when I was in the Far East.

While I was meeting with a measure of literary success, Harold became a government Inspector of Schools, and, later, a Governor of West Buckland. The school by this time had acquired a forward-looking headmaster, Michael Downward.

I always sent copies of my books to the school library, hoping they might enliven the hours of some of those incarcerated there, as the writings of Aldous Huxley, Evelyn Waugh, and H.G. Wells had enlivened my period at school. There was also a certain ironic pleasure to be had in knowing that science fiction was cordially enshrined in the establishment where, in my time, it had been forbidden. Had not our Maths master, 'Chicken' Coupland (a wartime conscientious objector) torn up a valued issue of *Astounding Science Fiction* before the eyes of the whole form, at a time when I was in the middle of reading Theodore Sturgeon's 'Biddiver'?

As if to mark how greatly things had changed, one room in the school library was now officially designated 'The Aldiss Room.' I was invited to open it.

Driving down to Devon, I took with me a carton of presentation copies and the best reproductions I could find of two paintings to hang in the room which might have some appeal to the boys there. Both paintings held an exciting essence for me, and had helped towards a cohesive imagery in my writing. The hope was that someone else would glance at them occasionally and find imaginative escape from the routines of school.

This is the talk I gave about those paintings at the opening of the Aldiss room.

The grave, marvellous beauty of Pieter Breugel's *Hunters in the Snow* speaks for itself. If you find a prevailing sadness in it, that is in part because all the characters in the painting – and there are over fifty of them – are turned away from us, otherwise engaged. They have no concern with the external viewer, being entirely involved with their own world, their own pursuits. They remain inaccessible to us.

Hunters in the Snow is one of a series of canvasses Bruegel executed on the great secular topic of the months or seasons. Some of the series still exist after four centuries, some of them are lost. The original measures 114cm by 158cm – that is about 44 inches by 61 – and hangs in the Kunsthistorisches Museum in Vienna. Its power combines with apparent simplicity like a moral force.

We know little about Bruegel, but we do know that he painted this picture in 1565. Shakespeare had been born the year before. Those luminaries of the Renaissance, Veronese and Tintoretto, Bruegel's contemporaries, were working in the grand style in Italy; Palladio was building the church of St. Giorgio Maggiore in Venice. As you see, Bruegel did not paint at all like the Italians. His preoccupations were different and, for my taste, more profound.

This was the period when the Spanish were making a great noise round the world. It was the age of Sir Francis Drake, when Protestants and Catholics were engaged in bitter combat, when Mary Queen of Scots married Lord Darnley, and the Duke of Alva with 10,000 troops was all set to tyrannise the Low Countries. The plague raged. And plague, war, tyranny, the beastliness of man, all find forceful expression in Bruegel's paintings.

Not in this one. This painting reminds us of the other side of that cruel period. It reminds us that renaissance means re-birth, that the world was opening out, and that, as one critic put it, a sort of 'reclassification of the universe' was taking place. It is easier to see in Bruegel than in his Italian contemporaries the birth of our own age, with his concern not for princes or religion but with common people and common pursuits.

The very shape, the stances, of his people, make them our kin. Veronese's people are classical, patrician, Bruegel's are peasants. Veronese may show us languid men, never tired ones. He has a message to proclaim; Bruegel has a new awareness.

If you visited Mao's China, you saw art bent to the common end of glorifying the state, just as one sees the art of the Italian Renaissance directed to glorifying the worldly shows of religion. Bruegel had nothing to do with all that. His paintings show him to be a sceptical man, for whom 'glory' was a relative affair.

One's response to art operates on several levels. There's the academic level – and to derive full appreciation from a work of art requires training – and the personal level. For me, the point at which Bruegel and I meet is where he demonstrates exuberantly that an organic relationship exists between humanity and nature, that mankind has his due place in the affairs of the biosphere, and that whatever he does he is wedded to the seasons and the sweep of the sun –

Rolled round in earth's diurnal course,
With rocks, and stones, and trees.

Against the might of the universe, man's shows count for little (it is there that Bruegel parts company with the grand Italians). In his paintings, he expresses such commonplace but profound matters in many ways. In two of his more religious paintings, *The Conversion of St. Paul* and *The Procession to Calvary*, the events described in the titles – St. Paul's conversion and Christ's procession with the Cross – take place. Both St. Paul and Christ are placed in the traditional centre of their respective canvasses; but the crowds swarming about them, the landscapes and mountains which rise on every side, eclipse the main event. Most of the people depicted are scarcely concerned with St. Paul and Christ – they have their own lives to live. This profound and novel psychological observation, this populist view of history, must have shocked the first viewers of those canvasses to an extent that we, in a less religious age, can hardly appreciate. Perhaps the humanist in Bruegel found men more interesting than gods.

There's a similar effect in one of Bruegel's most famous paintings, *The Fall of Icarus*. The mythical flier plunges down into the water. All we see of him are legs, framed in spray. The legs are a mere detail lost in the large canvas. All about lies a golden imperishable landscape, constructed in the manner of *Hunters in the Snow*, with sea in the distance and ships upon it; close at hand, on the left, a peasant follows the plough, oblivious to Icarus's tragic drama of ambition. Sailors, fishermen, a shepherd, also carry on work as usual, ignorant or innocent of the mythological event which flashes in their midst.

W. H. Auden is thinking of such a synthesis when he claims that the old masters were never wrong about suffering. Dreadful dramas were enacted on the canvas. Meanwhile,

> the dogs go on with their doggy life and the torturer's horse
> Scratches its innocent behind on a tree.

The ploughman must be important, for he is in the foreground. Like so many of Bruegel's figures, he is generalised, not particularised. He stands for all ploughmen. But Icarus, the visionary, also has his place: it is for him the canvas is titled, just as the other canvasses are titled for St. Paul and Christ. The earth's work may rest on the shoulders of the peasants but they are rarely individual, being sunk in the subculture of labour. We also need the individual, the artist, the sufferer, the thinker, who flashes across the scene, who is – unlike the peasant – remembered when gone.

Studying *Hunters in the Snow* more closely, we can observe some of the emblems which were never far from Bruegel's thinking, The first men on our planet were hunters, and these Flemish hunters are scarcely better equipped for the hunt than were Neolithic men. They're passing a primitive inn, its sign awry, where the occupants are evidently concerned only in a very basic existence, the life of food and drink. They're roasting a pig.

The hunters are in transition. They're descending into the valley, where life is more civilised. It's a medieval world down there, still dominated by the mill which for centuries represented the latest technology and permitted an increase in the population. On the frozen stream and fields, children play, skating or sliding, permitting a glimpse of that ceaseless activity of the poor which so interested Bruegel. You may be reminded of the modern painter, L.S. Lowry, but Lowry's urban crowds are always isolated and hold no communion with each other. The hurlyburly of Bruegel's crowds is different, jollier, far more earthy.

Life looks quite tolerable. But the slow plod of the hunters, their poor catch, their lean curs walking dispiritedly behind them, as well as the fact that the mill is frozen up and looks like remaining that way for some time – all these serve to remind us that life's a serious affair. Over everything lies the spellbound silence of a severe Flemish winter's day.

Nothing of Titian's voluptuous countrysides here. This is Northern winter – perhaps its most striking depiction in all art

– before which everything must bow. Except perhaps the human spirit. Each of the little towns in the valley has a church, its spire pointing upwards in hope. It is towards these spires that the hunters move. The cold has separated them one from another; they're not talking, but they are heading towards home.

The painting appears to have more in common with Japanese art than with the Italian masters. The strong verticals, supplied by the receding trees which take us into the landscape, the subdued palette – browns, russets, greens, greys – are all tokens of a severe self-discipline controlling the prodigality of vision.

Here is what we most seek in an artist: a universal awareness, to which is coupled an empathy with the human detail.

The comparison between Bruegel and his southern contemporaries is instructive; to appreciate the originality of Bruegel, however, we should note the contrasts between his intentions and those of painters who preceded him.

It happens that about one hundred and fifty years earlier, other artists also left a record of the seasons. *Les Tres Riches Heures du Duc de Berry*, often referred to as *The Book of Hours*, was illustrated and illuminated by more than one artist, working under the direction of the Duc de Berry. It was completed some time after 1416. The most famous section of the book depicts the months of the year. In the twelve months, we observe that people have shadows, and that there are reflections in the water. As far as we know, such representations of natural phenomena had never appeared before.

The bright, clear miniatures of *The Book of Hours* give us a view of medieval life in more than its physical dimension. The peasants toil beneath the castle walls, whatever the season. They are stiff sturdy figures, mere emblems of God's purpose. When nobles appear, gorgeously clad, they are willowy, their hands small, their gestures decorous. The gulf between the two groups is unbridgeable.

Serf or duke, above them looms the castle. Great chateaux dominate the fields and vineyards – and Heaven stands above the chateaux, and there is not a darn thing anyone can do about it. Duke regally welcoming guests to his feast in January, peasants warming their genitals by a fire in February – all are God's creatures, all confined within narrow margins. Hierarchy, and the unthinking obedience hierarchy instils, dominated the Christian mind.

A century and a half later, the varied and lively world of Pieter Bruegel tells another story. We understand what the Renaissance means in terms of the freeing of the spirit of mankind. In the middle of the sixteenth century, when Bruegel was painting, a marked change in climate occurred. From then on, for another century and a half, all parts of the world endured probably the coldest conditions since the end of the last major ice age. *Hunters in the Snow* in fact depicts the onset of the Little Ice Age. Still a more enquiring spirit prevailed. Bruegel celebrates the fact that, although Icarus may have plunged into the sea, he at least aspired and flew.

So we turn from a painting for which one feels profound respect, even awe, to a painting of which I'm fond but cannot help thinking is really rather awful as a painting. It's the sort of picture that demanded the expression 'as pretty as a picture' be coined. We don't think today, as some of our Victorian predecessors did, that pictures and stories need be pretty or improving – mainly, I suppose, because the the comforting idea of moral progress has gone down the drain after two world wars.

The Hireling Shepherd, by William Holman Hunt, portrays a rustic scene. There are two human figures in it, a young man and a young woman, and a lot of sheep. The month could be August.

If we know as little about Bruegel as we do about Shakespeare, we know almost too much about William Holman Hunt. He was one of the Pre-Raphaelite Brotherhood; he was born in 1827 and died in 1910, to be buried in Westminster Abbey with due honour. His most famous canvas is *The Light of the World*. *The Hireling Shepherd* was painted in 1851, the year of the Great Exhibition.

Hunt was an unhappy man; his Christian principles seem to have been at war with his creative impulse. Fame and success brought him little joy.

The Hireling Shepherd is a well-constructed picture, the shepherd and his wench forming a solid triangle, with the girl's head pretty well in the centre of the picture. Parts of the background are attractive and have an airy sense that looks forward to the Impressionists; yet somehow they remain not properly integrated, as if we were looking at spring on the left and high summer on the right. The two country copulatives appear specially dressed for the occasion, like characters in a BBC TV Victorian drama.

The sense of artificiality reinforces the main impression of the painting: that Hunt is not depicting an episode in the everyday life of country-folk, but telling us an improving tale, while standing rather too close to our elbow. The moral appears to be 'When the cat's away, the mice will play.' Only we have sheep instead of mice and while the shepherd is making overtures to the wench, the riotous-looking sheep are getting out of hand, and will soon be despoiling a field of wheat. The lamb on the wench's lap will soon make itself sick on green apples.

Holman Hunt never entirely trusted his paintings to speak for themselves. They did not quite escape from the literary, and a moral had to be added. In this case, our red-faced yokel represents, in Hunt's words, 'The type of muddle-headed pastors, who, instead of performing their services to the flock – which is in constant peril – discuss vain questions of no value to any human soul ...' Very few today would be reminded of a clergyman by looking at our robust bucolic.

These days, we are less keen to deduce morals, and will probably content ourseves with speculating on what the lad and lass plan to do next on their inviting bank. One curious touch is the death's head moth which the shepherd is trying to show the girl – whether with or without success is for every viewer to decide for himself.

I chose this picture because it is the one I used as a pivotal point in my novel, *Report on Probability A*. The novel – though perfectly easy to read – is often regarded as difficult, because it deals with a situation frozen in time. No unfreezing takes place. Most novels present the reader with a problem to be overcome. The ramifications are carefully built up, we are confronted with a crisis or climax, and then comes resolution. Art copying orgasm. In *Probability A* we have a crisis of a kind, but we never know exactly what kind, since its ramifications are withheld; nor is the situation resolved. This leaves many readers dissatisfied; but a few – those who remain to the end – often receive a heightened sense of time and human drama.

To reinforce the imagery of my suspended situation, a typical nineteenth century painting was needed. My choice was *The Hireling Shepherd*, which I knew well, because it seems to represent in itself the concept of frozen time. In many Victorian pictures, the main interest lies not so much in the composition or the execution or the colour harmony, or in the statement, or even in a way in the actual subject, but in the question we as viewers are forced to ask: *What happens next?* Most Victorian painters were scarcely aware of the existential dilemma, but, living at a time of hectic and unprecedented progress with its concomitant uncertainty, they developed a mode of circumstantial art which managed to make a kind of materialist sense until the question was asked of the canvas, *What happens next?* Why this moment, why not next moment? (Some painters like Augustus Egg, following Hogarth, chose multiple moments and sequential canvasses.)

Although *What happens next?* is a question which expresses uncertainty – mingled anxiety and hope, perhaps – it appeased the anxieties of the Victorians, and does the same for us in our formidable age. The question is not posed, I think, before the nineteenth century, even in the so-called genre pictures of the Dutch school.

The great seventeenth century artist Vermeer painted interiors with ladies reading letters; we take his paintings at their face value, as paintings. To use an old-fashioned word, it would be vulgar to ask of Vermeer, Why this moment, why not next? But a nineteenth century English painting called 'The Letter' is sure to dramatise a situation; there will be clues as to whether someone has died, or a heart has been broken, or a soldier is coming home from the wars, or the mortgage is demanded. The interest is external to the composition. The future is part of the palette. We and the painter ask, *What happens next?* Between Vermeer and Holman Hunt and the two centuries dividing them has come a great change: Change itself. Tomorrow is no longer going to be like the present or the dear dead past. The sheep will be at the corn.

We call the division that brought such change the Industrial Revolution. The first generation to feel that great divide, which separates our modern world from the old lumbering world of mail coaches and infinite leisure, with the squire and parson lording it over the quiet villages – or whatever simplistic images you have of the past – the first generation to feel the pinch of change felt it severely. They were such men as Tennyson, Edgar Allan Poe, Thackeray, Charles Darwin, and Charles Dickens, all born between 1809 and 1812. For them, the railways and railway timetables arrived. In the works of each of them we can gauge the quickened pulse of change (though we catch that pulse already in Shelley's poems, and in that wonderful novel his second wife wrote).

Thackeray puts it like this:

We who have lived before railways were made, belong to another world .... It was only yesterday, but what a gulf between now and then! *Then* was the old world, stage-coaches, more or less swift, riding-horses, pack-horses, highwaymen, knights in armour, Norman invaders, Roman legends, Druids, Ancient Britons painted blue, and so forth – all these belong to the old period .... But your railroad starts the new era, and we of a certain age belong to the new time and the old one .... Towards what new continent are we wending? to what new laws, new manners, new politics, vast new expanses of liberties unknown as yet, or only surmised? ...

We who lived before railways, and survive out of the ancient world, are like Father Noah and his family out of the Ark ....

Ever since Thackeray, each generation has experienced similar dislocation. My father suffered in the trenches of World War I. I well recall the dropping of the two atomic bombs on Japan. My children remember the test flights of Concorde, men walking on the Moon. What happens next? All these dislocations are severe, but less severe than the first, because dislocation has become a part of change and change a way of life. All are the result of scientific and technical developments.

Science fiction is a kind of literature springing from the world of change in which we live. It also asks the question, *What happens next?* That was why I used the Holman Hunt picture as a kind of touchstone in *Report on Probability A*. You might find the novel a bit of a riddle, but then the question itself is a bit of a riddle. In many situations, to ask, *What happens next?* is tantamount to asking a more searching question, *What's going on now?*

There are my two pictures. I selected one that is unquestionably great, one that I think rather chocolate-boxy; but I considered both were interesting enough to catch the imagination.

When I was at WBS, a long while ago, I paid great attention to the pictures which then hung in the dining hall. I was astonished to come back, over thirty years later, and find them still hanging there, looking a great deal the worse for wear. There was Hobbema's *Avenue*, a rather ordinary picture which caught my fancy, and several others I recalled. They are moved now, since the hall has been redecorated, but art is important, not least because it can tell you things you don't realise you know until a lot later. It enriches your life by improving your appreciation of the world. The vistas that Bruegel spreads before us represent a terrific imaginative leap, a way of reclassifying the universe. After four centuries the freshness of its vision still has power.

Perhaps you will come back to the school when you are men and find, with some surprise, that you remember the Bruegel and the Holman Hunt from your days as a boy here – and you may then, with the benefit of another few years, understand them in a different way from my generation.

Perhaps you'll then be able to answer the riddle, *What happens next?*

Grounded in Stellar Art

How do you put a novel together?

So many intuitions and incidents from everyday life go into a novel that they could hardly be listed. Once the writer is launched on a theme with which he is happy, the stray pieces fall into place almost without thought.

Several times, I have attempted a complex novel which was designed to trawl much of what happened to be passing through my mind at the time. Such novels are *The Malacia Tapestry*, *Life in the West*, and the three volumes of *Helliconia*. And, of course, *Barefoot in the Head*.

Two notorious characters, Ouspensky and Gurdjieff, are talking to each other.

Ouspensky says to the Master, 'Tell me what you think of recurrence. Do we live only this once and then disappear, or does everything repeat and repeat itself, perhaps an endless number of times, only we do not know and do not remember it?'

And Gurdjieff replies, 'The idea of repetition is not the full and absolute truth, but it is the nearest possible approximation of the truth. In this case, truth can never be expressed in words.' Hedging his bets, as usual.

They're shabby sooth-sayers, O. and G., tippling wine, playing tricks, dossing in old Armenian houses, ending up whipping Katherine Mansfield in Fontainebleau. O. and G. are the first hippie philosophers, and as such ideal models for the psychoblasted Europe portrayed in *Barefoot*. They took over a bit as I wrote. Their confident expectation of the miraculous, their quest for it, their finding of it in everyday life, on railway platforms, in steamy cafés, in the suburbs of our pleasure, is very attractive. Maybe it's more fun to go in search of the miraculous than the truth. As Charteris does.

That having been said, the idea of the eternal return is a horrifying one. It fuels the most alarming episode in *Barefoot*, 'The Serpent of Kundalini.'

A novel is like a dream in that it is not a linear event, although the events within it may be described later by critics in a linear way. When we stand back and hold a novel up to the light of day, it reveals many dimensions. *Barefoot in the Head* was built to display many dimensions, that being one of its themes.

Here's a dimension the critics might not think of. When the novel was launched in England, its dust jacket bore two prices, one in old currency, one in new. Thus: 30s. / £1.50. The times trembled like reeds in rippled water. What critics make of the novel is inevitably less than the novel. Each critic angles his or her interest, brings up different coloured fish. James Joyce scholars find that Ouspensky meets Joyce.

Scholars weaned on music and drugs will find, I ween, music and drugs. European critics fish out the connection between Jugoslavia and the rest of Europe.

The beginnings of the book were indeed Joycean. Driving through the night in that confused region of Europe where France, Belgium and Holland comprise one large *laager*, where the Meuse becomes the Maars, I saw a broken neon sign flaring purple in the dark. STELLA ART it said. In fact, the name of the lager is Stella Artois, but I drank to Stellar Art. I forgot the first half of a French bird. In the mood of the sixties, with all possibilities possible, the sign started amazing wings of thought in my crane. The Meuse and the Maars, the same river under different names, symbolised the changing stream of Europe's many pat.

A united Europe, united in the chaos of LSD, the drug then conquering the world. An automatic culture of the automobile. Under the influence of mescalin, which has a structural biochemical relationship with LSD, Aldous Huxley saw a car. 'A large pale blue automobile was standing at the kerb. At the sight of it, I was suddenly overcome by enormous merriment. What complacency, what an absurd self-satisfaction beamed from those bulging surfaces of glossiest enamel! Man had created the thing in his own image ... I laughed till the tears ran down my cheeks.'

A touch of caricature was all I needed. For the future had alighted in the mid-sixties, and everything was an exaggerated version of its old self. That was true for me too. At a time of greatest happiness, I had vision. The great public world was my secret, and I travelled it openly.

Was Western culture, the 'Westciv' of the book, going down the great water-closet of history, and I alone privy to it?

This business of language. A novelist's problems are not a critic's. I wanted to talk about my acid heads, and I could see no other way to get close to them than to copy their thought and speech patterns. But what I was doing was boning up on Europe, not on James Joyce. I wrote from life, not books – give a man enough Europe and he will hack himself. I wanted to diagnose out the actual situation developing. People came to me and said, 'You're not writing about what the future will be like, Brian, you're writing about what it's like around Europe now.' I jotted down notes for the novel in Belgium and the Netherlands and France and Germany and Italy and up in the Scandinavian countries. And in Loughborough. I stayed in the hotel in Metz which features in the 'Just Passing Through' episode.

The confusion of language parallels the confusion of landscape as well as the confusion in the minds of Charteris & Co.

I'm a bit sceptical about having this Joyce thing hung on me. James Blish, a confirmed Joycean, started it. He carried on at great length about the language of the novel; I said, 'Yes, Jim, but the language is about something.'

Of course there are some good puns. Vaginisthmus of Panamama. Dungeoness. Agenbite of Auschwitz. Etc. The groundlings must be amused. But such matters, and such sportiveness with language, are not unique to this book. For instance, a discerning critic picked out the one sentence in *Barefoot* which appears also in *Report on Probability A*.

All authors who write half-way literate English owe much to few writers, to Shakespeare, Johnson, and – if you are going to remint the coinage – James Joyce. But we have such a flexible tongue. The game's infinite and easy as walking, that learned instinct. I think therefore I amble.

There are parallels between Joyce's 'Old mutther-goosip' and *Barefoot*'s 'Old Mumma Goosetale'; but there are so many associations to words. Goose: a silly girl, a tailor's iron; geese saved the Capitol, you go to goose fairs, goose month was the lying-in month for women; the Nazis did the goose step; there are geese you can't say Boo to, and others that lay golden eggs; there is also the royal game of goose, which I assume you play with women. But more important to the story and to the instance of 'Old Mumma Goosetale' is the fact that the goose is Angeline's pet bird – it comforted her when she was sad as a child. The language is not there for its own sweet sake, but for the effects it generates.

Page 92. 'He gave a sort of half-laugh by a wall, his beard growing in its own silence.' Perfect English, perfect sentence. One of the best I ever wrote. When I'd got that sentence down, I knocked off for the rest of the day.

I tried to convey confusion as clearly as I could.

You would possibly get more mileage by comparing this novel with my other novels than with *Finnegans Wake*. As the Irishman said, 'Sure, I couldn't rade it in a wake of Sondays.' One device I used was not contracted or even expanded from Joyce, the insertion of holophrastic words – using a single extant word to express a complex of ideas. An example is on page 137: 'The Serb had ceased to think what he was saying. It was the migratory converse.' Here, 'converse' can mean either 'conversation' or the converse of conversation. Which is a way of expressing the war within Charteris's mind; he is not thinking with his conscious brain but with his cerebellum, from the Latin 'cera,' wax, and 'bellum,' war – a war waxing and John Wayning in the skull.

I intended this confusion of language to be more a fusion than a con.

I took more from Ouspensky than from Joyce, more from Baedeker than from *Ulysses*. One critic, hooked on Joyce, came up with a car called 'Leopold II' as a tribute to Bloom. The reference is to page 176; that's where this phantom vehicle appears: 'Tumultaneously, the broad Leopold II sloughed its pavements for grey sand and cliffs cascated up where buildings were.' It shows what a clever commentator can read into a book. But in Brussels there's a broad highway called Leopold II; it is named to honour not literature but the King of the Belgians.

Through this monster plan of mindpattern comes the serpent, the serpent of Kundalini, an ancient conservative Hindu force rising from the older tributories of the brain into the neocortex. This primitivism has to fuse with the new world of speed and motorways. It is an energy Gurdjieff believed in, which he tried to flog into Katherine Mansfield, Aldous Huxley, and the other fashionables who visited his clinic at Fontainebleu. The energy is in Charteris, but we may believe he masks it by changing his name from the Serbian 'Dushan' to Charteris, the writer of the Saint stories. He comprehends the multiplicity of I's, of which Gurdjieff speaks.

Ancient wisdom has to be transmitted to man's higher centres. *Barefoot* embraces the eternal return. The first Charteris dies on reaching England, in Brontosaurus Broadway, detained by philosophy and love and a dose of Glenn Miller. He asks a final question, 'Cannot one act *and* dream?' (page 49). And that is what the next Charteris does, acts and dreams, mainly in England, the land of his dreams. We can never be sure whether the 'real' Charteris did not remain in Serbia. Is this literally 'his imagined England'? (page 28). We may be dealing only with a multiplicity of cast-off I's, rather like the multiplicity of universes in *Report on Probability A*.

But, as Charteris says, '*Here* is the permanent position' (page 260), provided 'you hold fast to dreamament.' My own feelings enter the novel at this point, focussed on the notion of eternal return. Much of life is dreamament. It is enough to *be*. Christian ethics form no part of Charteris's thinking; fortified by the psycho-chemicals, he sees only 'the infinite points of intersection' (page 246). Because of this – almost too late – he refuses the cross, which he perhaps regards as a Crucifiction.

But demented Europe still clings to the Judeo-Christian ethos; it's 'the old worn Westciv groove.' Saviours are part of a big cliché in the sky. If Charteris is to be a real saviour, Cass is ready as Judas, and Charteris is in line for the Cross. That is further down the line than he is prepared to go.

He becomes more of a saint by ceasing to play the Saint, and opts for a quieter way of life, in conformity with Gurdjieff's dictum, "As long as a man takes himself as one person he will never move from where he is.'

A raddled pastoral follows. 'All the known noon world loses its staples and everything drops apart.' At least one of Charteris's alternative I's can alter native thought and live peacefully to be ninety, revered by all but Angeline. Eternal recurrence ends the book, with forests dwindling again and new travellers blowing in from the north. The laws of energy see to that.

Although self-improvement is a crooked trail, Charteris gets somewhere. He learns to notice neglected Angeline, whom he has sometimes in the past carelessly called Angelina, as if even her name was a matter of indifference. Angeline is an important figure. She remains constant and stays with Charteris, although he has killed her husband. Then 'she broke with elmed summer into twain' and bore him a child; this marks a new independence for her.

The last Charteris we see achieves love instead of his previous self-centredness, and some perception of the woman. She is 'no longer the greylagging little girl' she used to be. Angeline complains a lot in old age. As he goes out, near death, to speak to the disciples, he recalls how he loved her, 'loved her in my way loved her being in many women,' and attempts in awkward fashion to tell her as much. Bent double, muddled, gnarled, confused, he can only say when she wakes, 'I had a little speech for you.' Angeline, cross and ancient, ticks him off. 'Heard too many of your speeches in my time.' She would have no time for Molly Bloom's monologue.

With the self-improvement comes more self-knowledge. As the disciples wait under the final tree, Charteris plays a last crafty Gurdjieffian trick. 'He would give them holy law okay but spiced with heresy.' And he pronounces the sentence which every reader must riddle for himself, 'All possibilities and alternatives exist but ultimately – ultimately you want it both ways.'

Perhaps what is represented is a human inability to verbalise the deepest things – the very barrier *Barefoot* tries so hard to transcend through its prose and its integral poems.

As for memory, it is an enemy to new lives. (The spirit of the sixties itself failed, and we were doomed to live through the stonier seventies and eighties, replaying the old records.) The old life does not digest. Charteris is always conscious of his father, the good old Serbian Communist, his death and his funeral. These images come back from another time, another land. 'My capital crime nostalgia.' So similarly Angeline dreams of her lost garden, befriended by geese.

From such seminal memories there is no waking, just as the psychochemicals do not provide the forward evolutionary thrust for which some hope but rather reproduce a Neanderthal vagueness of thought. The physiology brings fuzzy ologies.

It seems as if nothing of the old Westciv way of life survives – except the Head, from whence come all capital offences. There's a golden glow over the decay, laced with the irony of the final paradox, which would surely appeal to Gurdjieff: 'Keep violence in the mind where it belongs.'

There is an aspiration to higher consciousness. But ultimately this must rest with the reader.

It Takes Two to Tango

The absurdities of history are well illustrated in the case of the western attitude to China. A deadly enemy at one time, China changed overnight to everyone's favourite Communist country – 'the glory, jest, and riddle of the world.'

The story of how President Richard Nixon made contact with Chairman Mao, at least as that story is told in the memoirs of Henry Kissinger, is a remarkable piece of modern day fantasy in itself. Kissinger's mission to Peking was so secret that he flew to Pakistan, feigned a cold, and retired to the President of Pakistan's mountain retreat. There a Chinese plane was awaiting him. His escort pulled their guns on Kissinger; their orders were that he should travel in no kind of vehicle not made in the USA and not driven or piloted by a military man with full security clearance. Kissinger out-talked his guard and they all climbed into the cramped plane. That night in Peking, when Kissinger was in his pavilion in the Forbidden City, there came a knock at his door. Enter one of the most remarkable men of our century: Chou En Lai. And the talking began.

Within a few months, Richard Nixon was walking the Great Wall of China, and everyone was falling over themselves a) to say nice things about the hitherto hated Chinese, and b) to get to China, preferably at someone else's expense.

I found a) easy, since I had always admired the Chinese. By a bit of luck, b) fell into my lap also. So, at an interesting moment, when China was once more avid for breezes from outside, I became part of a special historical process. A plane carried me over the Himalayas from Islamabad on roughly the same course that Kissinger had followed, and, in October 1979, I found myself on Chinese soil in a state of wild excitement. After all those years, it had proved possible to visit another planet.

Kunming is a pleasant city to the south of China, with a climate of perpetual spring. There are good buildings and a sense of leisure. Only two hundred miles away is the Burmese frontier. It was evening, after sunset, and I strolled into Kunming Park.

A line of twenty-five watt bulbs burned above one of the walks. Beneath the dim lights, a crowd of young people was gathering. Some were dancing to the music of a wind-up gramophone. Old ten-inch records were being played. Couples were tangoing.

So the repercussions of the Cultural Revolution became manifest. It was not simply Beethoven who had been banned. Guy Lombardo and Edmundo Ros had also gone to the wall.

Yet here was Guy, here was Edmundo again, giving out under the mild night sky, as if the Twenties had never passed away. The old records had not been smashed, or the old rhythms forgotten, despite a million Little Red Books. No South American ever did a smoother tango than those Chinese. Six of them would share the local equivalent of a 7-Up while others danced in the limited space. They did not need alcohol; they had happiness. The dull visibility did not dim their beautiful spirits. They were young and free and all things were possible.

I'll never forget that tango. China was full of items I had never thought of before. Every day a fresh surprise. Courtesy. Mountains. Beautiful spiders on a flower-bed full of giant French marigolds and cactus. Close-up view of a hysterectomy undergone with acupuncture anaesthesia. The Ming tombs. Calligraphy.

Standing beneath the gate from which the silk caravans once left for Trebizond and Bokhara. The taste of persimmons. The impossible questions we asked the Chinese. The impossible questions they asked us: 'What precisely is the difference between American and English literatures?'

Travel is a perverse passion. Why do we leave home, with its comforts and routines, and subject ourselves to the indignities of airlines? Why, to enjoy discomfort and broken routine elsewhere. In many ways, I am an easy customer to satisfy when abroad; I just want something to go wrong.

Nothing went wrong in China – the reverse, in fact – but the prospect remained. At Xian airport, a storm grounded planes for a while. When I told a chap in the bar (well, it wasn't a bar actually, but that's another story) that I was flying to Kunming he pulled a face and said, 'That'll mean an Ilyushin 18. Lousy old planes. They're always crashing nose first. The Chinese keep the first six rows of seats empty to lower the casualty rate.'

I thought of these words as we crossed the tarmac to board our delayed flight. There, in CAAC insignia, stood an aged turboprop. It was an Ilyushin 18. These machines had been acquired from the Soviets in the nineteen-fifties, before the USSR and China fell out with each other. Aboard, a hostess brings you sweets and fizzy mineral water, and all the passengers wear green. The seats are canvas.

Once we were airborne, I evaded the hostess's detaining arm, went forward and peered round the curtain to where the first class seating should have been. There stood six rows of empty seats, shrouded in white, the Chinese colour for death.

So it was true. After thirty years of arduous service, the turboprop was due for a crash at any time.

The Chinese admit they are short of various sorts of transport. They also appear to be short of roads. Shortages of roads and vehicles in all provinces form a severe obstacle to increasing tourism and exports. The China any visitor sees is limited by this factor as much as by political calculation.

So you may find yourself faced with the prospect of a forty-eight hour train journey. Seize it. You will never have a rarer experience. By rail, one gains a faint notion of the scale of Chinese distances, the scenery is good to amazing, and the dining car stays open all day. The car attendant doubles as barefoot doctor.

The train stops occasionally at very long deserted stations. Everyone gets out. Hard class has a wash in long stone troughs provided on the platforms. Old ladies sell cakes, fruit, and bread. One stares through locked station gates at a peaceful village in the middle of nowhere which one will never see again. A mother plays ball with her child; one cannot wait long enough to see how the little game ends. An English lady asks a peasant through an interpreter, 'But are you really happy in China, *really* happy?'

Once we stopped at Chang-Sha, and were taken to visit a museum which featured a long dead Bronze Age princess, naturally mummified. We looked down on her; she was withered but tranquil, and her reproductive organs were separately displayed. Nearby was a perfect crossbow made in 1860 BC.

Oh, there were plenty of marvels, large and small. Large: the Great Wall, greater than can be imagined; the so-called Buried Army, where six thousand terracotta soldiers of the first Emperor of China march out of the soil to a daylight they have not visited for two thousand years. Small: a bed where Chou En Lai slept before the Revolution; schoolgirls we met in a Peking park, when asked what they wanted for their birthdays – no, no make-up sets, no CB radios – longingly, they said 'Pens and paper.'

But the most marvellous thing, if you discount the light itself and the wondrous politico-geographical fact of yourself actually standing on Chinese soil, is the Chinese people. Particularly in country districts men and women look at you and smile with genuine friendship – don't they? They give you something. They are multitudinous humanity. They are confident, yet no more aggressive than deer. In such a peaceful country, the terrors of the past are hard to believe.

And they speak of those terrors without malice. An artist was beaten up by Red Guards. He lay wounded in a gutter. No one dared go to his aid. But a dog ran over to him and licked his face. Seeing this, a Red Guard dashed up and killed the dog with one blow. Since then, the artist, now recovered, paints only animals. Animals don't suffer from ideology, a more deadly malady than rabies.

The people are long-suffering. 'Eat bitterness,' small children are taught. Suffer and endure. Most lives are lived on very little, captains of industry earn £15 per week. Villages at night are dark, almost unlit. During an interview with Vice-Premier Deng Xiao Ping, I watched him smile slyly as he pointed out the spittoon by his chair. 'I'm the last head of state to use one of those,' he said. 'I'm just a countryman … You probably earn four times as much as I do.'

This poverty has a transcendent quality, different from, for instance, the Stone Age poverty prevailing in parts of India. Despite periodic madnesses, China is a well-run country, and run for the poor, since there are only poor. Many of the production brigades, with their shared incentives, were admirable, though they are now being absorbed into larger units. It would be wonderful to think that China might solve problems which still confront the rest of the world. Better that than that China should follow some half-cocked Western model, as Mao followed Marxism. The future lies as thick – and as enigmatic – as does the past over Deng's domain.

All one can say is – go and see for yourself: China is different. People's expectations are different. In three weeks, you can feel that difference in your bones. You may not be able to express it, but you will never forget it. And it may make a difference in you.

Robert Sheckley's World: Australia

Travel does not merely broaden the mind. some-times it lengthens it.

That is certainly the case if you fly from England to Australia. By one of those primitive old Boeing 747s, it takes about twenty hours instead of the ninety minutes any reasonably minded SF reader would expect. Time passes with preternatural sloth, marked only by one plastic tray full of food following another like the flapping of a great bat's wing. One tries to read. Here at last is the heaven-sent chance to digest *Moby Dick*.... But concentration and the stratosphere are enemies. One tries to recite silently one's favourite poems, or at least the poems one remembers, which rarely happen to be one's favourites.

At Flores in the Azores Sir Richard Grenville lay ...

But the words twist and distort themselves, turning into hitherto unknown nonsense versions of nursery rhymes.

Pease pudding hot, pease pudding cold,
I'm in the parlour clock, half-past mould.

What does it mean? One arrives at destination in a surrealist frame of mind. Which is just as well if the destination is Australia.

Australia was something of an eye-opener. From Singapore, the plane flew straight till it was over Darwin. It then turned right a bit and spent several hours suspended over utter desolation. Have you noticed that about desolation? It is always either utter or unutterable?

Very little had ever happened down there and very little ever could. The very processes of creation had been skimped. Passengers looked down in horror, bar sales rocketed. Jerry-built people in a jerry-built world.

My mind, like a caged bird seized by a terror or a touch of the trots, darted back a million years, then forward a million years. As it banged its little feathered breast against the cage of centuries, all it could visualise was flash floods followed by droughts, flash floods followed by droughts, flash floods followed by droughts, and so on, punctuated only by inundations and dry spells. Bar sales rocketed again, reaching a new highball.

It made you ashamed to be an Earthman. What would aliens think of this cutprice planet?

After some hours of this mind-mincing nothingness, the plane achieved a point over Alice Springs. There the legendary city was, two miles below us: numerous tiny roofs and a bar or two, with outer defences of broken-down car bodies. Singapore Airlines took a half-left turn for the worse. Before you could say 'Emergency Oxygen Equipment,' we were dawdling over the Simpson Desert, several hundred million years back in the past, before life was patented.

Topography reached its nadir. What was that stuff down there? No general geographical term applied; it wasn't a desert or plain or savannah or steppe. No, a new term had to be invented for it, an essentially Australian term. The Outback. Up went the bar sales again.

By the time we landed in Sydney, to confront the new terrors of blue gums and toy koalas made from genuine kangaroo fur, I had twigged. The truth dawned. This was SFland. I had been transferred to a planet designed by Robert Sheckley. Who else could have invented the Australian continent with all its implausibilities? The author of *Dimension of Miracles* had been at work here.

I suppose it was this sense of the extraordinary which made my trip so memorable. Frankly, I was surprised to find ordinary congenial human beings living in the place. Well, I say ordinary... I did notice a tendency on the part of the population of Sydney to grab any passing Pommie, drag him to the Heads of that celebrated harbour, and point eastwards across the ocean, asking, 'Do you know what the nearest city is?' Pause, two, three – then their answer to their own rhetorical question: 'Valpar-bloody-aiso, seven thousand, two hundred and sixteen miles away.'

Once, I took the liberty of pointing in the opposite direction and enquiring the name of the nearest city to the west. Here the ordinary citizens were less sure of their facts. One said 'Canberra,' and fell to the ground weeping, where he was quickly eaten by a passing platypus. (Ah, we travellers could tell some tales ...)

Once I was with two ordinary citizens, and, in crazed response to my question, they fell to quarrelling.

'Perth,' one said.

'Dar-es-Salaam,' said the other, 'you stupid git!'

'No Perth's much nearer.'

'No Dar-es-Salaam is nearer – about five thousand miles nearer.' The argument came to blows. Which was embarrassing, since they had been engaged for a week only. In the end, the girl won on a technical knockout.

Wherever I went, I found the same obsession with distance. I can say without contradiction that, in the minds of its inhabitants, Australia is the biggest country in this or any other Sheckley-inspired nightmare. No matter where you go, it's always nearer to Dar-es-Salaam. Chris Priest, when staying in Melbourne, was invited to give a talk at a small school in Noojee or Nagambie or Bininyong, or one of those places about a hundred miles outside Melbourne with names that make us roar with laughter in Ashby-de-la-Zouche, Budleigh Salterton or Maidenhead. The teacher lady introducing Chris to the class said, 'And our guest has come a really long, long way to be here with us this morning. We're very grateful to him, since we've never had the privilege of a visit from someone from that part of the world before. So let's give a warm welcome to Mr Priest, who has made it all the way from Melbourne to be with us.'

I bypassed Noojee and Nagambie to take in the science fiction convention in Melbourne. It was all I had been led to expect, except for the general shortage of drink and the amazing number of teetotallers attending. Also attending was a party from Perth. Because of religious and political objections, they had decided not to fly. So they spend five days on the train and six on camels, polishing off the last hundred miles by yak and wallaby.

They were splendid people. I said to one, 'Perth's a bit far from anywhere, I gather.'

'Too bloody near Dar-es-Salaam for my liking,' he said.

As the contours of our bodies are shaped by the skeletons trapped inside, so, it seems, is the Australian psyche shaped by the alien geology of the country. A bizarre quality prevails over the most innocent landscape, reminding the visitor that he treads ancient Gondwanaland, and that time must still be – somewhere, secretly – early Paleozoic. This sense of a brutal landscape untrodden by the classical gods is well conveyed in Patrick White's marvellous novel *A Fringe of Leaves*, in which Mrs Roxborough, an English lady visiting Australia at the beginning of last century, is shipwrecked on the Queensland coast and captured by aborigines. It is a novel choked with the harsh Australian version of nature.

Of course the Australian psyche is also haunted by a sense of transplantation to alien soil. The effect can be felt in North

America, but never so strongly as in Australia. It is not simply that Australia was once used as a dumping ground for British criminals; the Indians of North America were practically wiped out by the colonists, whereas in Australia one is constantly aware of the aborigines, displaced, dispossessed, despairing. A sense of ancient past cheek-by-jowl with raw newness does not easily fade.

To visit Australia is to understand in a small way the difficulties which would attend the establishment of a colony on an alien planet.

This prevailing wind from the past is soon forgotten when one is sitting talking to the SF fraternity Down Under. Their preoccupations are the same as elsewhere. The old teasing relationship with England pops up only occasionally.

Lee Harding is one of the most interesting SF writers Down Under. In his fiction, he frequently tries to come to terms with the particular burden of the past which is Australia's. An excellent example is his novel *Waiting for the End of the World* (1983), in which the main character, who lives in the Australia of next century, is haunted by visitors from a remote past. Lee and his wife, Irene, took me out to their place in the Dandenong Ranges to the north of Melbourne, a beautiful spot filled with all the varieties of gum tree you could or could not name.

One day, we were walking through the forest which encroaches on Lee's back door. We followed a winding track among the trees. As we got to a wooden bridge over a dried gully, I looked down into the gully and said, casually, 'Oh, look, Lee, there's a lyre bird. And there's another one over there.'

Lee and Irene almost fell over. He had walked in this forest for twenty years and had never seen a lyre bird. To me, they were part of the stock repertory of odd Australian fauna, like wallabies and koala bears. Lee knew, as I did not, how scarce the birds were.

Deeper in the forest, we were surrounded by ferns and cycads. The very sounds in the air seemed different, the intensity of the light was different. Again came the feeling of being overtaken by something ancient. I said something of the sort to Lee. My exact words came up at me from the printed page when – several years later – I read a copy of *Waiting for the End of the World* and got to page 9, where those words are printed in italics. That was the way Lee played a time-trick on me, and built me into his book. Not for the first time, I felt like a plaything in *Dimension of Miracles*.

The Sheckley Effect was still working.

In Nicolas Roeg's marvellous Australian movie *Walkabout* a lost girl and her little brother consort with aborigines and in particular with an aborigine boy. The sister, played by Jenny Agutter, comes to realise when returned to civilisation that the richest part of her life had been when she was lost in the wilderness with the aborigine who died for love of her. Nevertheless, she must live out the rest of her days in cities. That is her destiny.

Mrs Roxborough, in Patrick White's novel, comes to the same perception but, as it were, from the opposite viewpoint. She is lying in filth in a low hut, the slave of an aborigine, naked but for the fringe of leaves. She thinks of her previous existence in England.

> She realised that most of her life at Cheltenham had been a bore and that she might only have experienced happiness while scraping carrots, scouring pails, or lifting the clout to see whether the loaves were proved.

Since so much of Australia is almost uncreated, almost uninhabitable, it provokes such thoughts. Those thoughts never lie comfortable, as Mrs Roxborough lay comfortable beside the dead fire in the hut. They remind us that we are prisoners inside whatever freedoms we enjoy. They remind us that humanity did a deal long ago, when, with spear and bow-and-arrow and the first flickerings of technology, men decided to separate themselves from the encompassing natural world. This was what Christians would term The Fall. They remind us that we have lost something; however fast 747s fly, they do not let us escape our domesticated selves.

They remind us that Australia is not just a place you fly to via Singapore Airlines. It is also a state of mind. However far we travel, we are stuck with it. Brains have taproots into the soil.

If God had intended us to think, surely he would have provided us with cut-off switches?

Sheckley, you've got a lot to answer for.

Sturgeon: Mercury Plus X

Sturgeon? The name was magnetic. There it was, perpetually crop-
ping up attached to the stories I most admired. Sturgeon: quite
an ordinary Anglo-American word among exotics like A.E. Van
Vogt, Isaac Asimov, Heinlein, Simak, and Kuttner. Yet – spiky,
finny, odd. And it was not his original name. Theodore Hamilton
Sturgeon was born Edward Hamilton Waldo. To the usual boring,
undeserving parents. That was on Staten Island, the year the First
World War ended.

So there were two of him, as there are of many a good writer. A
bright side, a dark side – much like our old SF image of Mercury,
remember, so much more interesting than banal reality. He had a
mercurial temperament.

The bright side was the side everybody loved. There was something so damned nice, charming, open, empathic, and elusive about
Ted that women flocked to him. Men too. Maybe he was at the
mercy of his own fey sexuality. If so, he was quizzical about it, as
about everything. One of his more cutesy titles put it admirably:
'If All Men Were Brothers, Would You Let One Marry Your Sister?'
Not if it was Sturgeon, said a too-witty friend.

He played his guitar. He sang. He shone. He spoke of his
philosophy of love.

Ted honestly brought people happiness. If he was funny, it was a genuine humour which sprang from seeing the world aslant. A true SF talent. Everyone recognised his strange quality – 'faunlike,' some nut dubbed it; faunlike he certainly looked. Inexplicable, really.

Unsympathetic stepfather, unsatisfactory adolescence. Funny jobs, and 'Ether Breather' out in *Astounding* in 1939. So to an even funnier job, science fiction writer. It's flirting with disaster.

I could not believe those early stories: curious subject matter, bizarre resolutions, glowing style. And about sexuality. You could hardly believe your luck when one of Ted's stories went singing through your head.

'It,' with Cartier illustrations, in *Unknown*. Terrifying. 'Derm Fool.' Madness. The magnificent 'Microcosmic God,' read and re-read. 'Killdozer,' appearing after a long silence. There were to be other silences. 'Baby is Three': again in the sense of utter incredibility with complete conviction, zinging across a reader's synapses. By a miracle, the blown-up version, *More Than Human*, was no disappointment either. This was Sturgeon's caviar dish. Better even than *Venus Plus X* with its outré sexuality in a hermaphrodite utopia.

As for those silences. Something sank Sturgeon. His amazing early success, his popularity with fans and stardom at conventions – they told against the writer. Success is a vampire. In the midst of life we are in definite trouble. They say Sturgeon was the first author in the field ever to sign a six-book contract. A six-book contract was a rare mark of distinction, like being crucified. A mark of extinction. Ted was no stakhanovite and the deal did for him; he was reduced to writing a novelisation of a schlock TV series, *Voyage to the Bottom of the Sea*, to fulfil his norms.

At one time, he was reduced further to writing TV pilot scripts for Hollywood. He lived in motels or trailers, between marriages, between lives. Those who read *The Dreaming Jewels* or *Venus Plus X* or the story collections forget that writing is secretly a heavy load, an endless battle against the disappointments which come from within as well as without – and reputation a heavier load. Ted was fighting his way back to the light when night came on.

About Ted's dark side.

Well, he wrote that memorable novel, *Some of Your Blood*, about this crazy psychotic who goes for drinking menstrual discharge. Actually, it does not taste as bad as Ted made out. That was his bid to escape the inescapable adulation.

One small human thing he did. He and I, with James Gunn, were conducting the writer's workshop at the Conference of the Fantastic at Boca Raton, Florida. This was perhaps three years ago.

Our would-be writers circulated their effusions around the table for everyone's comment. One would-be was a plump, pallid, unhappy lady. Her story was a fantasy about a guy who tried three times to commit suicide, only to be blocked each time by a green monster from Hell who wanted him to keep on suffering. Sounds promising, but the treatment was hopeless.

Dumb comments around the table. I grew impatient with their unreality. When the story reached me, I asked the lady right out, 'Have you ever tried to commit suicide?'

Unexpected response. She stared at me in shock. Then she burst into a hailstorm of tears, collapsing onto the table. 'Three times,' she cried. Everyone looked fit to faint.

'It's nothing to be ashamed of,' I said. 'I've tried it too.'

'So have I,' said Sturgeon calmly.

He needen't have come in like that. He just did it bravely, unostentatiously, to support me, to support her, to support everyone. And I would guess there was a lot of misery and disappointment in Ted's life, for all the affection he generated. Yet he remained kind, loving, giving. (The lady is improving by the way. We're still in touch. That's another story.)

If that does not strike you as a positive story, I'm sorry. I'm not knocking suicide, either. Everyone should try it at least once.

Ted was a real guy, not an idol, an effigy, as some try to paint him. He was brilliant, so he suffered. I know beyond doubt that he would be pleased to see me set down some of the bad times he had. He was not one to edit things out. Otherwise he would have been a less powerful writer.

There are troves of lovely Sturgeon tales (as in the collection labelled *E Pluribus Unicorn*), like 'Bianca's Hands,' which a new generation would delight in. He wrote well, if sometimes over-lushly. In many ways, Ted was the direct opposite of the big tech-nophile names of his generation, like Doc Smith, Poul Anderson, Robert Heinlein, et al. His gaze was more closely fixed on people. For that we honoured him, and still honour him. Good for him that he never ended up in that prick's junkyard where they pay you a million dollars advance for some crud that no sane man wants to read.

Ted died early in May in Oregon, of pneumonia and other complications. Now he consorts with Sophocles, Phil Dick, and the author of the *Kama Sutra*. He had returned from a holiday in Hawaii, taken in the hopes he might recover his health there. That holiday, incidentally, was paid for by another SF writer – one who often gets publicity for the wrong things. Thank God, there are still some good guys left. We are also duly grateful for the one just departed.

The Glass Forest

What do we seek in the glass forest? Our shadows, our souls. It is a place for soul-searching, where we find much else besides. We can draw a clear line at the point where life begins. The expulsion from the womb marks our entry into the world. Where a life-story begins is less clear. So mine will open with the Tea Vision. The Tea Vision marked a first awareness that I enjoyed an interior life apparently not communicable to others.

I was three years old. Our living room, high above our shop, had large windows and comfortable window seats, from which one could look out at the people coming and going in Norwich Street. Opposite was the grocers, Kingston & Hurn. In the upper windows, my 'Aunt' Nellie Hurn could be glimpsed occasionally, living out her life in velvets, playing patience behind her clicking bead curtains.

In the shop windows below, Nellie's husband installed an advert for Mazawattee Tea, based on *Alice in Wonderland* characters. There sat Alice, at the head of the table, pouring Mazawattee tea from a huge red pot into cups which the Mad Hatter and the March Hare were holding. Beaming with pleasure, they lifted the cups to their mouths to drink. When they lowered the cups, the cups were immediately refilled. No pause in the action was permitted.

In those days the design would be solidly made of three-ply and worked off the electric mains.

Passers-by in the street watched the advert for a moment, smiled and walked on. I was its captive. I could not stop observing from my window. The pleasures of the Mad Hatter and the March Hare never dimmed. Their smiles never grew less. The teapot never emptied. They never had too much Mazawattee Tea.

Only in the early morning, before Kingston's opened at 8:00, were they still, Alice with the teapot poised, the others smiling in anticipation.

I truly feared the Mazawattee Tea advert. It introduced me to metaphysical horror. I 'knew' these creatures could not have feelings. And yet – why not? They had movement, smiles, appetites, the appurtenances of feelings. *Who knew I had feelings?*

From such infantile questionings, much follows. I always wanted to find out, always wanted to know the truth.

Our shop – the shop known in bold lettering facing up Norwich Street as H. H. Aldiss – is gone. We left it long ago. Yet it is there that everything must begin. All the trails lead back to H.H. Aldiss.

When my Aunt Dorothy died in the late spring of 1984, she had delivered back much of my life to me. A life story cannot be said to start with birth or end with death. Mine is a jigsaw which might as well continue with Dorothy's modest funeral.

Dorothy Aldiss left her last wish in my wife's and my care. She wanted to be buried beside her husband, who had died back in 1937. No one could have been more devoted to a husband's memory than she; and through her I had come to love the tough old man.

Auntie lived near us in Oxford. The family grave lay across the country, in East Dereham, in the dull heart of Norfolk where I had been born. From long distance, Margaret and I arranged gravediggers, parsons, undertakers, and a firm of stonemasons to heave the marble cross off the mouldering remains of my grandfather and his first wife and to prepare for a new incumbent.

But my aunt was no blood relation. She was my grandfather's second wife. They married in 1930, when he was seventy and she some thirty years his junior. The family was furious; they saw their inheritance threatened.

The funeral was private. I said a few words of valediction. I had become the head of our small family. We then ate lunch in Dereham's one acceptable restaurant, after which we left the town forever – or forever as far as I was concerned.

Dorothy was ninety-five when she died. She had a dry sense of humour and never told a story twice. She remained compos mentis until the last fortnight of her life. She wished I was the son she never had.

The man Auntie married late in his life was Harry Hildyard Aldiss. He hailed from Hornchurch in Lincolnshire, where my father, Stanley Aldiss, was born. As a young man, H. H. went to Dereham and bought an ailing draper's business. He was a stocky man of great force of character. No one trifled with him, but he was just and had a quick wit. He was respected by his staff, which numbered nearly fifty as the firm prospered. His sons called him 'Guv'ner.'

H. H. became a big name in East Dereham, and a JP. He was a devout Congregationalist, so that Congregationalism became the creed we all followed. We had our own family pews in the William Cowper Memorial Church in the market square, and were not allowed to look at the stills outside the nearby cinema when we escaped from the church services. God was not in favour of Hollywood, or card-playing, or drink, though he made, in his mercy, an exception for elderberry wine.

My grandfather's success in business probably owed much to his teetotalism – not a noted characteristic in the Aldiss family. Indeed, one etymological dictionary derives Aldiss as a corruption of 'Alehouse,' which says much about our ancestors.

The Aldisses have been in Norfolk for many generations. When I was bookselling, I came across a slender pamphlet detailing the names of those who had contributed to the Defence of the Realm Against the Spanish Armada. One John Aldis, yeoman of East Anglia, had contributed a sheep and a farthing. For centuries, the family fortunes have scarcely varied, sandwiched between peasants and the squirearchy, neither dying out nor over-running the county, as rabbits did in my boyhood. Ours are the middle parts of fortune. Her privates we.

My grandfather was the son of a seventh son of a seventh son. All the earlier sons went to sea. One, I know, in the middle of last century, caught a fatal fever aboard ship, and was buried at sea off Newfoundland. My grandfather stayed on dry land. But every Christmas we gave him a book on his hero, Scott of the Antarctic, if a new study was to be found.

One day travelling home to Dereham on the train from Norwich, H. H. got into conversation with a man who was trying to sell his house. H. H. showed interest. The man described it. 'I know the place,' said H. H. 'How much do you want for it?' The man told him. 'Is there anything wrong with it?' 'No.' 'I'll buy it.' They shook hands there and then. The deal was done before they alighted at Dereham Station.

Thus 'Whitehall' passed into the family hands, a fine villa in the Italianate manner, with a tower, ground floor windows reaching almost to the soil, much stained glass, and excellent grounds. Now demolished. In 'Whitehall' H. H. lived with his wife, Elizabeth, and their servants, gardener, dog and cats.

Elizabeth lay abed when I knew her. It was a fashionable thing then to be a permanent invalid. She was placid, and fed visiting small boys on grapes. She died before I was five.

Three sons, as in a fairy tale, were born to H. H. – Nelson, Gordon and Stanley. Stanley arrived on 12 March 1896. Nelson died of a neglected appendix at his public school, Bishop Stortford, but that didn't stop H. H. despatching his other two sons there.

Stanley, my father, knuckled down under his father, as boys did in those days, and ran the men's outfitting department of the Aldiss shop. His brother ran the furnishing department.

When the First World War submerged Europe in 1914, my father joined the Royal Flying Corps. He saw action in Egypt, Mesopotamia, and Gallipoli, recorded on stacks of sepia photographs now in my care. When the war was over, he married a young lady from Peterborough, Elizabeth May Wilson, nicknamed Dot. I, their only son, was born on Tuesday, 18 August 1925, in an odd humour.

We lived in a spacious flat over the shop. My first memory is of the decorations on the walls. There were paintings of camels, framed certificates to show that father was twice mentioned in despatches, and a photograph of him looking jovial in pierrot outfit. He had a taste for fun in those days. Nor did he appear to take religion very seriously, despite all his good work for the church. 'Hail, smiling morn,' he would sing when he got up on rainy days. Many hymns were turned laughingly to subversive use.

Father was an athlete. We went to see him swim, run, and hurdle. Once he won a tortoiseshell clock for swimming. He was a handsome man. I admired him greatly. Hero-worshipped him, in fact, though it was the self-made HH who became my role-model.

What a paradise for a child was that conglomeration of Aldiss shops. Beyond description. Gormenghast was no more inexhaustible than the property of H. H. Aldiss. There were cottages, where staff had 'lived in' in the old style, now decaying and stuffed with inscrutable objects, brass bedheads wrapped in straw, wicker bath-chairs, dummies, wardrobes, the makings of wash-hand-stands, boxes of this, boxes of that. There was a factory, so-called, crammed with carpets and lino and coconut matting, very abrasive to a boy's bare knees. There were dark passages leading to fitting rooms or stores or cabinets full of empty boxes. There were two enormous underground stoke holes, where furnaces were fired which kept the whole organisation heated. There were also stables and attendant outhouses, including tack-rooms, presided over by a ferocious being, enemy of all living things under the age of ten, called Nelson Monument. The horses stomped out from the yard wearing black sables, for H. H. Aldiss also did funerals. The firm – like an ideal utopia – would see you safely from the cradle to the grave. In various nooks throughout this rambling territory, one stumbled on little bands of people doing whatever they did. Tailors sitting cross-legged, making up suits. Milliners, presided over by a hostile fat lady, making hats. Dressers, carpenters, removal men, dress-makers. Busy men, idle men with pencils tucked behind their ears, men with pins in their lapels. Each nook a world in itself, where one was greeted with various degrees of interest, affection, or derision. The perfect playground, until my father or grandfather appeared, wrathful, to larrup you round the legs with a yardstick for interrupting the great Congregationalist God of Work.

Upstairs in the hat department was a young lady with whom I was enchanted. How beautiful she was. I loved her desperately. She sat me on her knee and would tease me unbearably. Yet I endured it because sometimes she would hug and kiss me. The scent and warmth of her were enough to burst my heart with excitement.

In this environment, I thought myself the luckiest of boys. I could run wild. Nobody knew where I went. I used to rove at large beyond the shop, exploring the back alleys of the country town, sometimes being allowed into people's houses. I was always curious to see how others lived. Sometimes I could get our terrier, Gyp, dear faithful Gyp, to come with me; but his absences were noticed more easily than mine.

I was tremendously happy and yet desperately insecure.

My maternal grandparents, the Wilsons, had four children, three sons and then a daughter, who was to marry my father. The sons grew into cheerful men, my uncles Allen, Bert, and Ernest; I loved them all greatly, my Uncle Bert best of all. My mother shared in the family love of fun, but she had in addition a vein of melancholy which went deep and was reinforced by what befell her early in married life.

When we buried my Aunt Dorothy in East Dereham, I went to the council offices to pay for the gravedigger. I took the opportunity to enquire if there was any record of a daughter being born to my parents and dying soon after birth.

The clerk found nothing in the burial record. Unexpectedly, she wrote to me some months later, to say that she had found the information I required by accident, while looking through the old register of funeral fees. On 17 February 1920 my mother had given birth to a baby girl; since the child was stillborn, it was buried in unconsecrated ground without a funeral. The grave was unmarked. Such was the custom at the time. Thus, in 1984, a ghost was laid which had haunted me for over half a century.

One feature of the story is particularly poignant. When telling us about this dead daughter, my mother always insisted to my sister and me that the baby lived only six weeks, and that she was the prettiest little thing.

The record showed that the child had been born dead. That remission of six weeks remained my mother's consoling fantasy. 'I understood the child was deformed,' Aunt Dorothy said once, with a certain stately relish.

Hardly had I learned to understand speech before I was aware that my arrival in the world profoundly disappointed my mother. She was still mourning the daughter who had died five years earlier. There was no room in her heart for a boy.

'Your sister's with the angels.' Avenging angels, I thought.

My much adored father beat me regularly; I never questioned that I deserved what I got. Worse than being beaten was the way he made me shake hands with him afterwards to prove that we were still friends.

Such early experiences are always echoed in fiction, either consciously or unconsciously. It was with considerable interest that I read – many years after the death of my parents – what one perceptive critic, Joseph Milicia, wrote about my novel, *Hothouse*:

In an adventure tale without a home-world, the atmosphere of dream may be no less intense; in fact it may be intensified by the disturbing sense that there is no place to wake up to. This is the case in *Hothouse*, where home is an easily invaded village that must in any case be abandoned after childhood, and also in Aldiss' first novel, *Nonstop (Starship)*, where 'home' itself is a subject for questioning and exploring. In either situation, the comfort of home disappears and the sense of alienation, frighteningly felt as a waking nightmare, permeates the narrative.

It is a perceptive piece of criticism, which needs to be read all through.

Mother would say prayers with me, both of us kneeling, at bedtime. We prayed to our Congregationalist god that her next child would be a little girl. How we prayed! Mother grew larger; she took longer rests after lunch; she wept more. I got whooping cough.

There's the touch that transforms these mean anecdotes into history. Nowadays, whooping cough scarcely exists; in the early thirties, it was still a killer of young children. My attack was serious; I became a stumbling block in the path of the procreational process.

April 1931. The house was quiet. Our maid read a book to me. Doctor Duygan was closeted with mother. A wailing cry arose. Father came to me smiling. 'You have a baby sister.' So was my sister Betty born, in the middle of Chapter Two of *Alice in Wonderland*. I was taken to the bedroom door, where mother lay in bed cradling a red-faced infant in her arms. Then I was rushed from the house without ceremony, golliwog, cough and all.

Not my father but one of the men from the shop drove me the sixty miles to Grandma Wilson's house. There I was dumped.

That period in exile lasted for six weeks; it was my equivalent of Dickens's spell in the blacking factory. For many years I was far too ashamed to speak of it to anyone, anyone.

In the story of our century a number of people equivalent to twice the entire population of the US has died through war, genocide, various ingenious forms of extermination, plague, and famine. This is my trivial testament, the history of one mortal.

Nor have I cared to set my history within any kind of social-historical framework. For those who want such things, let me conjure up the kitchen table in our flat above the H. H. Aldiss shop. It was a table about which I was happy to linger as soon as I could toddle. There my mother worked companionably with our maid, Elizabeth – 'Diddy' to me. (How we wept when Diddy left to be married. Like Grandmother Wilson, she was a farmer's daughter, and I was sometimes allowed to ride in her father's spanking pony-and-trap down the leafy lanes to Gressenhall.)

Mother and Diddy prepared unlimited delicious meals on that table. The rabbit pies, apple pies, buns, cherry cakes, jam roly-polys, and so on would then be transferred to our oven, which was heated by three paraffin burners. The table would then be vigorously scrubbed down. Through usage, the texture of the wooden surface resembled the coat of a polar bear when it comes heavily out of the water. The two women were always happy and fulfilled when working together, chatting of this and that.

How often did I think of that scene when exiled at the Peterborough house. There seemed no end to the weeks until I was allowed home again, unprepared for change.

Thus my earliest years. They comprise a complete small life, choked with incident and emotion. I had escaped from my playpen to become a little wild character – a photograph shows me about to indulge in my passion for climbing trees, dressed in an Indian suit, with head-dress – I took the role of the persecuted, not the cowboy – the cucumber smell of a crushed elder stem still reminds me of those days – whose thought processes had a natural death with the birth of my sister. My second sister, perhaps I should say.

Those early years were transfused with a grief not mine. I call it grief now. Then it was life, since I knew no alternative.

Once I saw a steel engraving of an angelic child hovering over a boy walking on a hillside. My dead sister became the steel engraving angel, always hovering, always threatening by her absence.

My grandmother, Elizabeth Wilson, a member of an older generation, went into widow's weeds when my grandfather died in 1926 and never came out of them. I remember her in Peterborough dressed only in black, the dress adorned with black beads and a high white collar tight to the throat: the costume of an earlier age. My mother had no similar ritual on which to fall back. One must suppose that my father, being unable to comfort her, being unable adequately to enter into her feelings, introduced a note of estrangement which then became part of their marriage.

Meanwhile, there I was, caught helplessly in that early phase, without reassurance, feeling inadequate at the bottom of a wall of sorrow, not knowing where to find comfort.

Yet I was willing to comfort others (the great recourse of the uncomforted). In 1929 my father became so ill of a bronchial complaint that our doctor told him he must spend the winter in South Africa if he wished to live. Mother broke this news to me dolefully in her bedroom, one afternoon after she had been resting.

'Never mind, mummy,' said I, with all the assurance of four years. 'I'll look after you.'

Her response was to turn away and weep, her elbows resting on the chest-of-drawers.

When I came as an adult to study the life of Mary Shelley, I well understood her feelings of isolation caused by the death of her illustrious mother, Mary Wollstonecraft.

Nothing was the same when I was restored coughless from Peterborough to my home. The baby was the centre of attention and, two years later, when I was seven, my parents packed me off to boarding school, and at boarding schools I remained for ten years, until I was called up into the army in 1943.

In my second exile, all the family were involved. My grandfather, as I have said, married again, which caused divisions among relations who could accept the idea of a seventy-year-old man marrying again and relations who could not. My father, ever dependent on his father, was in the former class. The shock my grandfather gave everyone was enhanced by his brilliant stroke in marrying the attractive cashier with whom he had enjoyed a relationship for some while.

H. H. and Dorothy had only nine years together before the old boy died. According to the story, retold by my mother, my father begged H. H. on his deathbed to divide the business in two, or else there would be trouble. 'You must fight your own battles from now on, Stanley,' said H. H., and died as he had lived, never the most sympathetic of fathers.

Within a year, father had lost the battle and sold up his share of the business. We could not stay in East Dereham. What a disgrace! An Aldiss lopped off from the Aldiss business! The Congregational Church gave father a memorial Bible, suitably inscribed, as we disappeared to settle into a terrace house in Gorleston-on-Sea. I say 'we'; how it happened as far as I was concerned was that I left Dereham as usual at the onset of a new school term, and returned to a small house by the sea. Friends and familiar things gone. Nothing in my life seemed secure. This was in 1938 when war was on its way.

My one friend was my sister. Contrary to the doctrinal pronouncements of Dr Freud and Dr Spock, I loved my sister greatly; we were as close as we could be considering the five-year gap in our ages. Betty was terribly bright and funny, and more rebellious than I. We had a wonderful time together at Gorleston, and used to walk barefoot from our house to the promenade and beach, where we would spend all day. The Punch-and-Judy routines we had by heart, being proficient at all the comic voices. In the winter, huge waves provided a spectacle, breaking against the old Dutch pier which marked the mouth of the River Yare.

My father was at a loss without the shop and his cheerful assistants. I was secretly relieved by that loss. Even at twelve, I knew I had no interest whatever in outfitting, in measuring people, or indeed in clothes. I also knew that I would have obeyed my father's wishes like a dutiful son and have 'gone into the business' had we stayed in Dereham.

By then I had developed what were to be lifelong interests. My prep school was a Dotheboys establishment whose educational structure was founded on punishment, boredom, and semi-starvation; there I learned to enjoy the mercy of reading, and began myself to make books. To quell my homesickness – worst at night – I smuggled in a small kaleidoscope, which I viewed under the bedclothes with the aid of a torch; the tumbling patterns delighted me and encouraged a feeling for aesthetics. I was also allowed a microscope and a telescope, since those were not toys. (Still to need toys at eight!) From those instruments grew an interest in science, and the hidden world.

Before the war came – an event prayed against with fervour and no effect – my father put some black boot polish on his sideburns to hide encroaching greyness (he would then have been forty-three) and volunteered for the R.A.F. They turned him down as too old. This was a cruel blow. From then on, he became increasingly bitter.

He sold the house in Gorleston and took us to live in Devon – almost a foreign country to us. We could hardly understand the local accent. I was put into a public school on the fringes of Exmoor, West Buckland School. After some casting around, my father bought a poor little business outside Barnstaple, a combined general store and sub-post office. There he worked day and night without complaint, and mother worked beside him. She liked a laugh and company, and had a jollier time than he did. By this time, her melancholy had dispersed, and Betty and I were on good terms with her. We did a lot of laughing and singing.

One of our treats was to go to the cinema. Attached to our outside fence was a billboard on which the Regal, Barnstaple, advertised. As payment for this slot, the cinema allowed us two free tickets each week. Betty and I went to the cinema just as often as we could manage.

My tastes ran towards 'thrillers,' in particular those thrillers featuring Humphrey Bogart or Edward G. Robinson. I was mad about Eddie G., and wrote to him in Hollywood for a signed photograph, which duly arrived from Warner Brothers. I still have it.

Another Warner Brothers star was Ida Lupino, the beautiful loser. For me, she generated more emotional current than the synthetic Betty Grable – but rather less than the sumptuous Hedy Lamarr. Hedy was not merely gorgeous, she was foreign and had appeared on the screen in the nude, thus adding greatly to her attraction.

My reading tastes were slightly more sophisticated than my film tastes. Anxiety had converted me to insomnia at an early age – at least by nine – and this enabled me to devour many books during the hours of night. By the time we were expelled from East Dereham, that poisoned Eden, I had read a wide variety of novels, including *Jane Eyre*, *Wuthering Heights*, *John Halifax, Gentleman* (which I loathed for its false piety), some Dickens, several novels by Zola, and Murger's *Vie de Boheme*, which gave me a longing for the bohemian life never entirely assuaged or forgotten.

I was also reading all kinds of ephemeral rubbish with avidity. A friend called Harold Leeds started me on 'The Schoolboy's Own Library,' by giving me several of the fourpenny volumes he had finished with. So I met the lads of St. Jim's, the lads of Rookwood, and the lads of Greyfriars, those three great fictitious English public schools which, I suppose, most boys of my generation and before encountered. All were the invention of Frank Richards, a most prolific author who used different pen names for the different schools. The adventures of these lively characters appeared in two weekly magazines, *The Magnet* and *The Gem,* which flourished between the two world wars and embodied, rather like P. G. Wodehouse stories, a sort of sporting Edwardian view of the world, with stern codes of conduct cheek-by-jowl with horseplay. *The Gem* was my weekly reading for many years, although I was forbidden to read it at my loony prep school, on the grounds that it was subversive.

Eventually *Modern Boy* overtook *The Gem* in my affections. To

Modern Boy I owe a happy debt. It was full of the future and of exciting technical developments, like the building of the Channel Tunnel. It carried stories of all kinds of sports, including motor-racing. Sir Malcolm Campbell occasionally wrote for *Modern Boy*. So did Captain W. E. Johns, whose stories about Biggles, the flying ace, first appeared in those illustrious pages in serial form. So did Murray Roberts, whose hero – and mine – was Captain Justice.

Justice fought off menaces from the Sargasso, an interstellar gas which plunged the world into darkness, a hellish telepathic dictatorship arising in Africa, a runaway planet, gigantic robots, and many other science-fictional phenomena. It was all meat and drink in the pre-teens.

Out of sentiment, I still possess some of Captain Justice's adventures. They are totally unreadable now, alas. All cliché. The irrepressible Midge should have been repressed long ago.

When Britain declared war on Nazi Germany in September 1939, the Aldiss family was in a caravan on a wild stretch of the North Cornish coast near Tintagel. We stood looking blankly at the peaceful Atlantic as the news came over the radio. My father went to an estate agent and bought a nearby bungalow, then standing deserted on the cliffs.

We used to sit in the front room of that bungalow looking out at the sun as it sank into the bronze Atlantic. It was a season of stillness, of ominously calm weather. Sometimes a convoy would be outlined against the setting sun. We listened to the news. My father did not speak.

Similar calm prevailed in May 1940, when France fell, and Britain fought on alone. My father then took the smaller of his two shotguns from a corner and handed it to me; we expected to use them in earnest within a month or two.

By that period, we had moved into the house behind the general store. It was still possible to find science fiction here and there. In particular I had come across *Astounding* magazine and the works of H. G. Wells. Wells was my preference: three of his stories in particular caught my imagination, *The Time Machine*, imperishably one of the brilliant books associated with science fiction, 'The Country of the Blind,' and 'The Door in the Wall,' which I read over and over again, relishing its poignance, in which I felt something of my own situation. A door had closed for ever.

What I liked about *Astounding* was its sense of continuance, and the subjects under discussion, though in some mysterious way they lacked the metaphorical quality which is such an enrichment in Wells's best writing.

The correspondence columns of *Astounding* in the late thirties bandied about the name of Nietzsche in connection with the rejection of religion and the concept of a superman. I had no particular affection for supermen, but Nietzsche sounded interesting. None of his books could be found in Barnstaple. A friend recommended I join the local Atheneum, which had a good library. What this solemn club thought when a thirteen year old tried to enlist I have no idea; however, they allowed me to join, and there I sat in one of their stiff leather armchairs, reading *Thus Spake Zarathustra*. To my great benefit and confusion.

Thus developed a taste for exotic foreign names. In the Atheneum, I discovered Chinese poetry through Arthur Waley's translations. At school, I stumbled over Ouspensky, whom I was later to send up in *Barefoot in the Head*. A top grade lunatic.

Meanwhile, I wrote. At home, at school, I wrote.

West Buckland was a rough tough school. The freedom of wild Exmoor was much to be enjoyed. We even swam in some of the pools and corries up there, the water being crystal clear but freezing. When we were old enough to join the Home Guard, we were able to get into the little pubs at Stagshead and Brayford and become drunk on beer or cider.

Before leaving those prison years behind, I should say something about the twisted intellectual development which led to my becoming a writer. I believe that that ambition formed within me when I was eight or nine, although it may be hindsight which suggests this.

Certainly I was interested in writing at an early age. The study of Latin improved this faculty. I did nine years of Latin and became proficient enough almost to enjoy the language.

I also enjoyed English Grammar, a subject no longer taught in British schools, a sad deficiency. It is much more important for a writer to know the intricacies of the hard geological backbone of his medium than to understand how to operate a computer efficiently. The death or permanent displacement of the apostrophe is imminent.

As well as being interested in writing, I was interested in story-telling – the two things are separate. Story-telling became almost a source of salvation, certainly a source of pride when I had little to be proud of, at an early age.

The first public school to which I was sent (before West Buckland) was Framlingham College in Suffolk, a thriving hot house for bullies, toadies, and all creeping things. There my shyness and a propensity for making weird gadgets (especially light planes, board games, and cardboard things which jumped out of lockers) led to my being called The Professor. I acquired greater fame as a story-teller.

The Junior Dormitory was a horrendous place in which some twenty beds were ranged round the walls under long windows. Each bed had a locker beside it. There was no other furniture, no carpet or rug on the bare floor, no flicker of a curtain. Picture a workhouse in Dickens's time. Thus were young English gentlemen brought up.

At Lights Out, the rule was strictly No Talking. Nevertheless, a subversive tradition survived of telling tales. The wretched inmates had no campfires, but a Stone Age thirst for narrative remained intact. At the start of a new term, each infant in turn had to stand in the dark and tell a story. It was an ordeal. Most stories were greeted with derision. The most derided boys were silenced, often rather forcibly. The survivors lived to spout again. Gradually champions emerged. The two champions in my time were B. B. Gingell and I.

Gingell was a skilled and witty teller. His handicap was his subject-matter, which generally centred round some contemptible denizen of the animal kingdom, an otter (I think he once purveyed Henry Williamson's classic over the course of a spring term), a beaver, a deer, a wolf, or even a snake. Whereas I went for planets, wonders of the future, and the re-hashed adventures of Captain Justice. What's more, I did all the voices.

I would be in full blood-freezing spate when the door of the dormitory would be flung open. In would stride the housemaster, Mr Broughton, 'Bonzo,' in his gown. 'Who's talking?' My hand would rise into the air with memorable sloth. I would then be made to bend over and be given Six with the cane on my pyjamas. Six was particularly painful when the previous Six had not yet healed.

Such was my first reward for my art. After which, the astringent remarks of critics could hardly be expected to compare in cutting power. I have often wondered how many other writers had such a formidable christening in the line of duty. Very few.

At the much pleasanter West Buckland, there was no oral tradition. I wrote my stories down.

It proved a better way to fame. The stories were pungently primed with sex and violence and general schoolboy naughtiness.

These stories were hired out at a hypothetical penny a time. They changed hands rapidly. The danger with them was that they might fall into the hands of authority; I would then have been beaten and expelled.

The Sixth Form at West Buckland was a good one. We were a tight-knit community who had survived the arduous ascent through the school. A lot of wit and laughter enlivened our days. Without the moral support of my friends, I doubt if I would have had the nerve to keep producing.

The headmaster was not above conducting a desk-to-desk

search. One of the worst features of the public school system was the lack of privacy; the unscrupulous were set over us to teach us scruples.

At the end of each term, we held a solemn ceremony. My stories were sealed into a large Huntley & Palmer biscuit tin, which my friend Bowler and I then took and buried in a rabbit hole in a nearby wood, to await resurrection next term. Shortly afterwards, a new wave of myxamatosis swept England.

In my last term at West Buckland, I wrote and acted in our house concert. I co-directed with our housemaster, Harold Boyer, only a staunch friend ever since. Home was twelve miles from school, yet my parents did not attend my night of glory. Well, it was wartime.

But it was a relief to escape into the relative safety and comfort of the army. No military training came hard after public school.

All these years, I suffered the incommunicable pain of rejection. I read deeply in psychology and philosophy to try and heal myself.

The army proved a great healer, particularly when I was sent on a troopship to India, into a third exile. I forgot about my family situation and enjoyed the independence. To be abroad was wonderful – Betty and I had always longed to go abroad. How delighted we had been when a relation wrote to say that Grandma Wilson's maiden name, Ream, was explained by the fact that she came of Huguenot stock fleeing from Rheims. So we had a pint or two of French blood in us to dilute the boring English stuff. Anything exotic we loved. India and Burma were nothing if not exotic.

Life in the ranks of the British Army in the East in wartime was hard. Full of laughs, of course. The redeeming feature was that most of it was conducted outside, in the sun, the glorious sun. I never forget the beauty of some of the places we visited. Of my experiences in India and Burma, I wrote a novel, *A Soldier Erect*, because I wanted people to see how things were. As far as I know, nobody else who served in the ranks ever spoke out on that subject.

The war provided an initiation rite for young men. If you came through it intact, it gave you a sense of privilege. It made you – and of course in many ways it unmade you.

Even when riven by war, Burma was intensely seductive, a country of magic. Late in 1944, our division, the Second British Division, moved into action from the area of Kohima and rolled south, crossing the Manipur River into the Letha Range. As I reported in my novel, our commander addressed us before we went into action, finishing by quoting the famous speech Shakespeare gives to Henry V before Agincourt:

And gentlemen in England now abed
Shall think themselves accursed they were not here
And hold their manhoods cheap whiles any speaks
That fought with us upon St. Crispin's Day.

We were caught up in an enterprise which united us all, in which we could accept that an individual's life was of less importance than the survival and ultimate victory of his tribe. Our hardships – the fact that we saw no water at all for six weeks, for instance – were a source of pride. It is sad that human beings rarely achieve such unity in time of peace. We called ourselves 'The Forgotten Army'; so it was, and so it has remained ever since. There was almost no media coverage, as we would say nowadays; Assam and Burma were simply too difficult to get to, and all transport was stretched to its limits and beyond. Nor were there poets to speak for us, in the way that Sassoon and Wilfred Owen and many other tongues spoke for the war of the trenches. There was Alun Lewis, it is true, but his was a minor voice – and he shot himself before going into action. Nor have any novels come out of that campaign, except my own.

Before moving from Yazagyo to Kalewa, where we established a bridgehead on the River Chindwin, we crossed the Tropic of Cancer and, once over the Chindwin, were on the dry flat plains which lead to Mandalay, killing Japanese all the way. Soon Mandalay was again in British hands.

One of the awful features of being in action was the fear that you might be killed before you had really enjoyed a woman. It made dying terrible. I was no virgin; nor had I really experienced an intense affair. But even small children experience rending sexual passion, as I did for the girl in the hat department. In kindergarten, we were very wanton. When I once innocently came home, aged five, and told my mother how we played Cows and Milkmaids, with the boys being the cows, she phoned the school in a panic so great that it was a wonder that she did not ring the police and the Milk Marketing Board as well.

After Burma, with its decaying piles of Japanese bodies and its immense moons, back to India – or rather to Chittagong, now in Bangladesh. In Chittagong, we were so delighted to see water again after the Burmese dry season that we swam in the river there – practically an open sewer – and came to no harm. We were fit, hard, long-haired, lean, randy.

The Fourteenth Army, that raggle-taggle army of many races and tongues, was breaking up. I was posted on detachment to Bombay, to work a radio link connecting up various units then preparing as a task force to invade Singapore by sea, code name Operation Zipper. I lived in a rather grand private house near Breach Kandy, where I swam most days, and began to know and like Indians better.

Then to a purgatory sixty miles outside Bangalore, to a vicious bit of jungle to practise more jungle warfare. The monsoon was coming. We lived in straw bashas. Under every stone lurked enormous centipedes. Scorpions scuttled everywhere, ants of all dimensions abounded, frogs made the evening intolerable with their boastful cries. Snakes emerged from every bush. Little snakes worked their way down from overhanging trees and through the thatched roof, to fall on top of one's mosquito net; bigger ones slid through the doorways. We killed a monster cobra in the generator room. It was a horrible place. We were there when the atom bombs were dropped on Hiroshima and Nagasaki.

My friend Ted Monks came over to me and said, 'You know those bombs, Brian? They're the things they've been talking about in your science fiction magazines.'

The universe had shifted. What had been alarming fantasy had become reality. We rejoiced. It meant that we were not going to have to invade Singapore by sea, using leaky old landing craft left over from the Mediterranean theatre of war. The A-bomb, in bringing the war to a rapid conclusion, spared many lives.

As the years pass since that time, the dropping of those first atomic bombs – as we used to call nuclear weapons – become increasingly to be seen as a turning point in human history. So it is worth even a humble witness giving evidence on the matter.

Early in 1945, the Japanese war machine was showing no signs of yielding to intimations of defeat. The American Chiefs of Staff were planning two major operations for launch when the war against Hitler in Europe was over. In November 1945, there was to be Operation Olympic, involving 750,000 men; and in March 1946, Operation Coronet, involving an amazing 1.8 million men, landing in the Tokyo area. At the same time, the U.S. Air Forces were bombing the Japanese islands. On the night of 9 March alone, a raid on Tokyo killed 84,000 people and rendered a million homeless.

In my own forgotten theatre of war, Supremo Mountbatten's forces were being mustered for the dire Operation Zipper, to take place in September 1945. Between Penang and Singapore (all along the Malayan coastline, that is), 182,000 men were to be launched in seaborne landings. The Japanese at this time had over half a million troops in S. E. Asia.

In all these operations, which ran to a scale hitherto unknown, casualties would have been extremely high on both sides. It was clear that the Japanese under pressure would have killed – by gas or shooting or whatever means convenient – all the Allied and Chinese prisoners in their hands. No mercy would have been shown.

No one at the time doubted the evil of the Japanese regime. The Japanese themselves were regarded as both sub-human and superhuman. They seemed to respond to no moral code. Only the dropping of the two bombs could have ended protracted misery – not to the Allies alone, but to the indigenous populations of the Pacific area and S.E. Asia who had the ill fortune to fall under the Japanese yoke. Some 300,000 deaths can be attributed to the bombs on Hiroshima and Nagasaki. It was a small price to pay for the abrupt cessation of that barbarous war.

The Japanese surrender was greeted with universal joy. The British had come through six years of war. Their country had been broken economically and shattered physically. Moreover, the British troops sent to the East were never given a date for the expiry of their service abroad; it was not like the war in Vietnam, where terms of service were brief; we were out there for keeps, as far as we knew.

After the surrender, there was another messy job to be done. The Japanese invaders had somehow to be shovelled back into their homelands. That was the next item awaiting the victors.

I was posted to an Indian barracks in simmering Madras, and there became a member of the Twenty-Sixth Indian Division. We sailed eastwards, across the equator, to Padang in Sumatra, where our task was to disarm a Japanese army and send the invaders packing back to their distant homeland. More adventures!

Forty years after leaving West Buckland, I met a rather distinguished man who had prevailed upon his parents to remove him from the school, on the grounds of its sheer awfulness, cold, discomfort, and general misery. To my surprise, he remembered me as someone who had been kind and comforted him, and had lent him my long story – which he still remembered – about the adventures of a penny. My first audience was grateful to me, many years after the event!

The determination grew in me while in Sumatra to write as

truthful an account as possible of life in the East. I felt that the British were blind to its beauties. The evidence for this blindness was all around me; while I loved Sumatra, my army friends longed only to be home. They felt their lives were in a state of suspension, whereas mine was in full spate. The exotic was a state of fulfilment.

With some manoeuvring, I got myself in charge of the camp theatre, where we had shows, films, and dances. I became the unit draughtsman, and redecorated the theatre with paintings and caricatures. This gave me more leisure to write, edit a magazine, and generally enjoy tropical existence.

The eventual return to England marked my fourth exile. I had no particular wish to get back. The England I had known as a child had gone. A new harsh grey post-war world established itself. I could not even comprehend the monetary system, and confused florins and half-crowns. The behaviour of people was mysterious. The towns were filthy, with evidence of bomb damage everywhere, while rationing for some years became more stringent than it had been during the war. It was cold. The sun never reached zenith. Women were prudish and cautious. Another generation was coming along, rancid young Teds with something ugly to prove because they had missed the action.

During my demobilisation leave, I took a train up to Oxford and got a job in a bookshop. I told the bookseller that I was ready to set to work that day – which I did, later finding myself a room round the corner from the shop.

Oxford's a charming city – not free of blemishes, but its blem-ishes can become dear. I soon found friends, and began to enjoy life. My parents decided, rather to my surprise, to join me and buy a house in Oxford. Which was good for Betty, who went to the local Art School. For me, the advantages were less obvious; I had to go back under the parental roof.

It took me eight years before I had gained enough skill and confidence to leave the bookshop behind, to be independent as a writer. By then, two books had been published, *The Brightfount*

Diaries, a light-hearted account of work in a fictitious bookshop, and *Space, Time, and Nathaniel,* a collection of stories in the SF vein, known as STAN – my father's name.

It might appear that I have so far painted a rather negative portrait of my mother. When my sister and I were older, she was supportive, and entered into all we did with enthusiasm. No one was more pleased than she when I began to make a success with writing. In a letter to me from London in 1957, where she went to live after father died, she wrote:

> I have just been thinking how my great ambition was to publish a successful book, but am certain that could never have been as much of a thrill as my son doing so. God bless you, and all power to your pen.
>
> I can't go from the subject of your writing without mentioning your dedication in S.T.A.N. I thank you most sincerely for that, and can't tell you how touched I was (and shed a few tears over it) and longed for your dear Father to see it; almost (but not quite) made me feel I ought to stay at '548'...
>
> If this letter is more incoherent than usual, it is because I am really excited.

Just as one is hardly a real driver immediately one has passed the driving test – many miles of experience are still needed – it was several years before I felt able to call myself a writer. Or, for that matter, before I felt irrevocably a writer.

Yet I was always irrevocably a writer. The pressure to express something within me was the more intense for the emotional struggles through which I had to fight. I have written of sorrow; yet there were always within me moments of intense joy, just as beneath my conformity was a tough vein of wildness.

Even as a child, the rapid flow of reflections through my mind delighted me. Terror was there, but pleasure and astonishment also, and laughter. I still chuckle aloud at some surprising juxtaposition of thoughts, arriving unheralded. This is the creative vein, unfakeable.

Anything in nature – a bare twig against the sky – can lighten gloom. When in the army, I came on a metaphor for mind as I swam in the Irrawaddy near Mandalay. That great stream contains veins of icy and of warm water, veins intertwined but never mixing. A swimmer across the river cannot anticipate whether he is about to enter a stream originating from a local tributary or one coursing down from remote sources in the Himalayas. Yet all waters contribute equally to the life of the river, all will finally flood into the distant sea.

Much has been said about the art of writing; it is an inexhaustible subject. The written word, rather than the flint spear, has brought us such civilization as we now enjoy. It is the duty of the writer to fumble his way towards truth. The view, often expressed, that writers are paid liars, holds no appeal for me. At the same time, truth is elusive; if the future is fluid, so is the past, open – like the rest of the universe – to our interpretation of it.

Rejection slips never came my way at first. My early publishers, Faber & Faber, an illustrious imprint, approached me for my first book. I was happy with them for a long time. And when one went into their old terra-cotta buildings in Russell Square, one could encounter T. S Eliot on the stairs and exchange a few words with him. There also I met other Faber authors, including William Golding, a great science fiction reader and future recipient of the Nobel Prize for literature.

All my old inferiorities crowded in again once I was back in England. Eager though I was to see myself published again, to reinforce a budding reputation, I took the time to look at myself in the mirror of my typewriter and write an autobiography, *Twenty to Thirty*. There I anatomised all my qualities. I was disappointed by what I discovered. So much potential, so little achievement! 'By their fruits ye shall know them' seemed to me the bitterest apothegm in the Bible. I had borne no fruit, though I felt myself a great tree. Handicapped by my poor opinion of myself, I had yet to offer the world the diversity within me.

Once I had the picture clear, I proceeded to remould myself. Novels are messages, not only to the reader, but to the self.

Whatever emotional problems I suffered from – as do all young people, I imagine – I never had existential problems. Amorphous I might be – and that was the sort of question to be traded with girl friends in discussions that went on for all hours – but behind it all I was never plagued with doubts about the reality of myself planted firmly in the world. Part of the eagerness to write has always been eagerness to share experience and reflection.

But being a full-time writer, having no place of work to go but the front bedroom upstairs where I wrote, brought fresh challenges.

It broke up my marriage. I had married in 1948. By 1958, my wife and I had nothing much to say to each other, and only boredom to communicate.

What I could not stand was the silences. After a decade of trying to make things work, we began to come apart – no easy matter in those days. Yet how could I say the marriage was a failure, since from it were born my cherished children, Clive and Wendy?

To be away from them was another exile. I could not allow myself to let the pain go. All divorced parents must feel something of that remorse: each must suffer it alone. My writing abilities departed from me, to return only when I dressed the pain of the event in literary form, in the novel about a world where there are no children, *Greybeard*, dedicated to Clive and Wendy.

My father died during this period. A large number of marriages disintegrate after the death of a parent. My poor father suffered many heart attacks before giving in. He lived his last two years confined to house and garden, nursed devotedly by my mother, surviving attack after attack. The attacks were terrifying. Then he would recover to potter about the garden, which he kept fanatically neat. Every last twig on hedge and rose was trimmed. He liked to have small bonfires. Once he kept a tiny little fire going for two weeks, sheltering it under a bucket when rain fell. Every morning he would go and look at it, watching the thin spiral of smoke rise up.

He died on the first of June, 1956, on my mother's birthday, with a bunch of his roses by his bedside, and the evening sunlight filtering through the curtains. As his features relaxed in death, he began to look more and more like the Stanley Aldiss of old, the man who had been photographed in a pierrot suit, laughing and making others laugh.

At least he saw and held on his knee the first of my children.

Later, father appeared to me in a dream or vision, standing at the bottom of the stairs which led to the attic room where I slept. He half-raised a fist. His features were distorted in fury.

Such thoughts and more came back to mind as I stood by Aunt Dorothy's coffin in the town where I was born. My second wife, my children, my sister and her husband also stood there. The pain of the old drama was dead. So were all its actors, except for my sister and me.

Here is what I wrote about SF. If it has a familiar ring, my publishers liked it well enough to make it into a postcard for publicity purposes. 'I love SF for its surrealist verve, its loony non-reality, its piercing truths, its wit, its masked melancholy, its nose for damnation, its bunkum, its contempt for home comforts, its slewed astronomy, its xenophilia, its hip, its classlessness, its mysterious machines, its gaudy backdrops, its tragic insecurity.'

Science fiction has always seemed to me such a polyglot, an exotic mistress, a parasite, a kind of new language coined for the purpose of giving tongue to the demented twentieth century. I have noted an instance already of how it spoke of one decisive event of our century. Another of science fiction's most powerful themes found expression in the fifties and early sixties, the theme of the alien creature that can assume human form and move among human communities undetected, while it works their destruction.

No doubt this hideous idea derived from fears in the society at large. It is a cold war theme, and shows how effectively SF can hold a mirror up to our fears and aspirations.

Another popular SF theme was that of the world dictator, the iron man, who rules the globe or the galaxy. When Stalin died in 1953, the world seemed to begin to breathe again, like a corpse reviving among ice fields. Yet another tyranny was over. Slowly the deleterious effects of human misery caused by the Second World War began to drain away, in East and West.

The end of the Cold War has removed the threat of nuclear war and the rebirth of many nationalities. SF was my mode of expression. My worlds became watertight compartments, like my own life-experience. A new compartment opened when the death of my marriage caused me to lose my home and go to live alone in a rundown district of Oxford.

I rented one room in Paradise Square, soon to fall under the bulldozers. A multi-storey car park now stands where I lived for three years, at No. 12. I had a papier-maché suitcase containing my possessions. My wife had custody of the typewriter. In Woolworths I bought a knife, fork and spoon. No. 12 housed in its crumbling rooms one or two eccentric undergraduates, together with reporters or sub-editors from the local paper, *The Oxford Mail,* of which I was then Literary Editor.

It was of Len Aitken and the other denizen of No. 12, Derick Grigs, that I saw most. We were united in drink and desperation. Griggy was a dear chap, beloved by all on the *Mail* and *Times.* He was making a small collection of Japanese prints. Griggy remembered everything you said, and would quote it back to you, flatteringly, some years later. He was an amusing conversationalist, and any crisis would send him flying into a fit of calm. His sex life was a mystery to us. We had immense stamina at that time, staggering into bed in the early hours, rising zombie-like at eight. Len's room, by the look of it, had served as a set for a film of one of Gorki's or Dostoyevsky's more depressing ventures into the lower depths.

Dozens of milk bottles full of cheese or urine stood on the bare boards. We got through life in the hope of more booze and each other's company. Not unlike the British Army, come to think of it.

Other chaps with staunch drinking habits included the poet, Adrian Mitchell, and D.A. Nicholas Jones, both of whom wrote novels while on the *Mail*.

Among our friends was the remarkable Kyril Bonfiglioli, then living in Norham Gardens with his second wife. Before his marriage he lived in Jericho – a down-market sector of Oxford – with Anthony Harris. They had Griggy as their lodger, though his habit of grilling kippers over the electric fire did not endear him to them. Dim indeed would be the man, and perhaps more especially the woman, who did not remember Bon forever after one meeting. It's a small world: Bon bought Sanders of Oxford, the bookshop where I had first worked, and set himself up as a bookseller.

Bon knew everything, particularly the everythings that no one else knew. His conversations ran on into the night, although this was often because they did not begin until 2:00 a.m., at which time he would turn up on your doorstep with a bottle of Glenfiddich, already broached. It was Bon who spotted a Giorgione, which he knew to be worth a half-million, lurking in a seedy Reading junk shop. The dealer wanted sixty pounds for it ('I believe as it was painted by a gentleman called Brown, sir, lived over Wallingford way, sir'). Bon knocked him down to forty.

Like J. G. Ballard, I had my early stories published in two magazines called *New Worlds* and *Science Fantasy*. These magazines were edited by Ted Carnell – the renowned E. J. Carnell. Carnell was good to his writers. I stayed with him when my marriage finally collapsed and my wife carted the children off to live at the seaside. Carnell was honest down to the last half-penny, and brought his magazines out regularly. He had no literary taste. When I submitted to him one of my best early short stories, 'The Failed Men,' he wrote back saying, 'This will make you laugh. I hated your story and couldn't make sense of it but, since we were going to press and I was short by five thousand words, I shoved your effort in. Here's the cheque.' I didn't laugh. One wants appreciation as well as money. Particularly money on Carnell's minuscule scale.

The magazines slowly failed. Year by year, overheads mounted, sales slumped, Carnell himself became more locked into arthritis. He was always affable, with a good Cockney humour; everyone liked him. Eventually his parent firm sold the magazines. New editors were appointed by the new publisher. Much of this transaction took place in Oxford. It was arranged that Michael Moorcock, who had already made a name for himself, should edit *Science Fantasy*, and Bon *New Worlds;* however, owing to some misunderstanding, probably not unconnected with Glenfiddich, their roles were reversed. The magazines now went into new trajectories, *New Worlds* upwards, *Science Fantasy* downwards.

The agony of having to be separated from my children never quite left me –but somehow times improved. One omen of the happiness to come was the appearance of a female kitten I called Nicky, who arrived unbidden one evening at my house in Marston Street. She was a special and mysterious cat who lived with me for some thirteen years, and became to some extent an embodiment, an anima, of a new woman in my life, Margaret.

The sixties came in like a spring tide. Poor worried depressed England – for a few years at least – became an exciting and positive place in which to live. Harold Wilson's two terms as Prime Minister have since been marked down by Tories as a time of fraudulent economic practices. That may have been; I am no judge. But a longer view may regard that oddly classless man as exactly suited to preside over a time when, for many people, the bounds of life extended, horizons opened, new life-styles became possible. The Beatles' music, too, was classless, and a suitable accompaniment to a fresh way of looking at things.

In the other arts, too, there was what George Melly called a 'revolt into style.' We found a new way of interpreting science fiction to go with the times. Even as I was shaping the last adjective in *Greybeard*, I had in mind a newer sleeker model, which emerged as *The Dark Light Years*. Both novels were published in 1964. A growing reputation encouraged one to do mad things. Novels were easy to write in those days; they come more difficult as one's thought becomes more complex.

Bonfiglioli somewhat neglected his editing and possibly his bookselling. He had hit upon – with Bon one uses the verb instinctively – an absolutely irresistible lady, the veritable dark lady of the sonnets herself. Occasionally there are girls off whom it is impossible to keep one's hands; reason does not supply an answer to this fascinating conundrum. Probably the imponderable pressure of the pheromones has much to do with it.

Anyhow, I had also met my irresistible girl, a Scots lass called Margaret. Helen Shapiro, aged sixteen, was singing about 'Walking Back to Happiness,' unaware that the Beatles were about to doom her to tour Australia for ever. I took the song, innocent that I was, as an omen that I should allow myself to be happy with Margaret and cease the grieving for my children. I was very unforgiving with myself. Many years later, going to do a broadcast in London, I went into a studio and found them playing 'Walking Back to Happiness.' There was Helen Shapiro, still young and attractive. When I told her of my passionate fandom, she fell into my arms in gratitude. I gave her a copy of *Helliconia Spring* on the spot, but she never wrote.

With Margaret, life went on to the same sort of trajectory as *New Worlds*. Upwards. England appeared to be going the same way. Harold Wilson was Prime Minister. I actually believed in the white heat of Britain's technological revolution. I really liked Harold and his buddy George Brown. The latter I met later in the House of Lords, a bit ripe on the old Glenfiddich. He wasn't as pretty as Helen Shapiro, but just as much fun in his way.

Something had to be done about the stalemate in my life, otherwise Margaret was not going to wait. She had been secretary to Lord Harewood, and John Tooley at Covent Garden Opera House, and obviously had higher expectations than I ever did.

Flitting abroad seemed a good idea. The epoch was dawning when people did funny things to themselves with flowers, beads, dope and hair. Time to be off.

So I learnt to drive, bought a secondhand Land Rover, and took Margaret away – to Jugoslavia for six months. We did it all on about £120. Most of the time we camped, sometimes we stayed in a hotel to get a shower.

Jugoslavia in 1964 was still pulling itself out of the destruction which it had experienced in the war years. Many of its cities, from Maribor in the north to Prilep in the south, presented images of decrepitude.

Now as I write it is destroying itself all over again. Tragically, it is impossible to lose the past, one's individual past or the past of a country.

Our vehicle had painted on its doors OXFORD-OHRID in Roman and Cyrillic script. Ohrid, on Lake Ohrid, was our furthest point. You stand on the shore of this miniature Mediterranean and look across the water to the unforgiving mountains of Albania, which clothe their peaks in snow even in mid-summer. Many years later, Wendy and her husband Mark also made it to Ohrid. It is still an inaccessible. In Ohrid once, the tasty lake trout were caught, to be wrapped in moist leaves and carried alive by runners to the courts of Constantinople.

We lived a rather gipsy life, a bit like Burma sans bullets, often camping in the middle of nowhere or, even worse, on the perimeters of nowhere. Or we would camp in the grounds of a monastery, or by the Adriatic, rising for an early morning swim. We lived on the harsh bread of the country, with a chunk of salami, a bottle of rich local wine and maybe some chocolate (Kras orange chocolate from Zagreb preferred). Plus plenty of slivovic to keep the germs away. It was the diet of many Jugoslavs.

On the way home, at the port of Makarska, under the austere putty walls of the karst, Margaret and I met up with Harry and

Joan Harrison. They were living in Denmark. Since we had no address, there was no chance of two-way communication, but we had dropped them a line to Rungsted Kyst, asking them to meet us at twelve noon in Makarska camp site (the existence of which we hypothesized) on a certain day in July. We found the camp, rolled into it, and within five minutes the Harrisons also arrived in their Volkswagen camper. There was reason to celebrate.

Harry has somehow eluded me in this account so far. In life, it was different. We first met at a World Science Fiction Convention in London in 1957, and have been friends ever since. Harry had newly discovered the world; he had received a cheque from John W. Campbell on *Astounding* for his story 'The Stainless Steel Rat,' and had plonked the money down for a one-way ticket to Europe. Most SF authors buzz about the galaxy on paper, yet are afraid to venture into the world in real life. Harry went everywhere, spoke all languages, including Esperanto.

It was Harry who had first driven me into Jugoslavia, with Kingsley Amis and the girls, in 1963. There on a remote Croatian hillside, with the cicadas serenading somnolence, we had our taste of the south. It wasn't quite the Far East, but at least it had once been known as the Near East.

William Kinglake's wonderful book *Eothen* opens with him leaving wheel-borne Europe and crossing the Danube to the plague-bound fortress of Belgrade, then only recently liberated from Turkish rule. For the mid-century Victorians, the Near East began in what is now Jugoslavia. One can still see what they meant, though the minarets start a little farther south, in Prijedor and Sarajevo.

Back in England towards the end of 1964 we found that the first issue of Mike Moorcock's *New Worlds* was published. I settled in to write up my travel notes, to turn them into the book called *Cities and Stones* which Faber published in 1965, illustrated by Margaret's and my photographs. We planned other travel books.

Turkey was on our list. And Brazil. But it didn't quite work out that way.

The Jug trip left us with an abiding love of Jugoslavia, which remained even after my book was banned in Belgrade. Now all is forgiven, and a new generation regards my book as a truthful and, I hope, generous account of what their country was like at that time. Hardly a novel written since has not contained something of Jugland, as we affectionately call it. For instance the story of King JandalAnganol's child marriage in *Helliconia Summer* is based rather remotely on the story of King Milutin long ago in the medieval Serbian state.

With science fiction, there has always been a cause, a battle. It is not considered 'respectable' reading. Yet the subject matter of good science fiction is the subject matter of our time. Science fiction readers, banding together as fans, formed a strong support group for their writers, editors and publishers; many of them grew to fill those vital roles themselves. Science fiction fandom encompasses the most active and concerned readership one can meet. They collect, they catalogue, they throw tremendous parties and conventions. Lucky SF writers, to receive such support.

Lucky SF writers, too, to be invited abroad to meet foreign fans. One of the best such shindigs ever thrown was in Rio de Janeiro in 1969. The cast of thousands included Robert Heinlein, Poul Anderson, Damon Knight, A. E. van Vogt, and Robert Sheckley. Harry was also there, and Ballard and I flew in from England. Was it there I met Frederik Pohl for the first time? We became friends, decided we liked the jet-set life, and determined to meet somewhere else the following year.

Working at long distance, we persuaded a Japanese fan, Hiroya Endo, to arrange an SF symposium in Japan to coincide with Expo 70. Endo worked the Miracle. With Sakyo Kumatsu as chairman, we duly met. Fred took his wife Carol with him. Judith Merril, one of the great propagandists for Moorcock's New Wave, was also present, and Arthur C. Clarke. There we met some of our Russian equivalents, the doleful Dr Eremi Parnov, the genial and learned Julius Kagarlitski, and the forceful Vasili Zakharchenko, then a TV personality and editor of a popular science journal which sold two million copies every month. A great deal of international toasting went on.

We visited Tokyo, Toyota Motor City, and Kyoto, where we were taken to the extraordinary Expo 70. The futuristic parts of the Mitsubishi tower were designed by Komatsu. Even more impressive, we met our Japanese publishers, who had put out our work magnificently, in leather-bound editions. Well, mock-leather.

On the way home from Japan, I stopped for a week in Hong Kong, to see how it had fared since I knew it at the end of the war, when the Japanese had reduced it to a vast rubbish pile.

In 1979 I visited China under the aegis of the late Felix Greene. Felix was a saint, though many people thought him a deluded one. He had the difficult role of being 'Friend of China.' His position was, Your country right or wrong. By espousing China, Felix also espoused Mao Zedong. Judgement is a fine quality, but does not rank as high as devotion. Those of us who saw China through his eyes loved him. He died in 1985 of cancer in Mexico, with his wife Elena to look after him.

China puts its mark on everyone. Everything is seen anew. An old fence is not an old fence but a fence that has weathered many Chinese years. Everything is different – yet not alien, as may be the case in Japan. The sounds, the light, the smells ... well, they have their quality which is not easily conveyed, just as some wines do not travel.

Among our small party were Iris Murdoch, Michael Young – now Lord Young of Dartington – David Attenborough – now knighted – a n d Maysie Webb, deputy Director of the British Museum. We were granted audience with Chairman Deng Xao-Ping. At that time, China was a great novelty place, on everyone's lips, and we were favoured. Awaiting audience with the great man was much like awaiting audience with one of the Ming emperors. We kicked our heels and speculated and grumbled and sent messages, just as did travellers in earlier centuries. I made a side trip on my own to Shanghai to see American friends, Philip and Sue Smith, who were teaching English to the Chinese students via science fiction. My present for them was twenty-four copies of my Penguin *Science Fiction Omnibus*, which has been in print for over quarter of a century.

Life was hard for the Chinese people. 'Eat bitterness,' is what children are taught. We found they liked the English sense of humour. The Smiths' students were so poor they often sat in the evening to drink 'white tea,' as they called it – hot water to which no tea leaf has been added. Their attitudes to sex were very straitlaced. Whether this was provoked in part by the crowded condirions in the cities, one cannot determine. In 1991, as an ex-president of World SF, I returned to China, to Chenghu in Sichuan province, to find the Chinese as ever: warm-hearted, humorous, and besieged by problems.

China has always held a fascination for me since an early age. Nor was it a disappointment. I might say much the same about the United States. Most of the lively arts I enjoyed as a child came from the USA: the films, popular music, jazz, comic strips like Bill Holman's 'Smokey Stover,' and, of course, science fiction magazines. Margaret and I visited the States first in 1965, to collect a Nebula Award for my novella, *The Saliva Tree*. Since then I return regularly, and have many friends there, though there was a time when almost no one in SF wanted to know me. It means something to have a reputation there as well as in my own country.

The three books published on my writing have all appeared only in the States – though the most comprehensive one, *Apertures*, is by my English friend, David Wingrove.

For the last ten years I have attended the IAFA Conference of the Fantastic. I know and like many of the scholars of our across art, David Wingrove's my *Trillon Year Spree* has put me almost on an equal footing with them. They have now promoted me to Permanent Special Guest. I'm grateful.

My travels took me to Australia and I even went back to Sumatra to revisit old haunts and discover new ones – especially the amazing Lake Toba in the Highlands. That is a story in itself.

Wherever I have been, without exception, I have observed two things: the beauty of the smallest manifestations of nature, and the difficulty or downright wretchedness which still attends the lives of most people – though the 'quiet desperation' which Thoreau observed in men's lives appears to be endured with more fortitude in the East than in the West.

Harry, Fred Pohl and I, together with Peter Kuczka of Hungary and some others, got together to found World SF. Harry was its first president, then Fred, then I, then Sam Lundwall of Sweden. The objective of World SF is to link anyone in the world who has an interest in SF literature which transcends national boundaries. It is open to professionals only. Politics add to the difficulties in this sphere as in many others, but still we are a great success and have met in several different countries in our short existence, to communicate and bestow awards including China as mentioned.

There are advantages in having one's books translated into many languages, and to find that those same books are reprinted at home over and over again. Some of my short story collections have been in print for twenty-five years. Even my 'difficult' novels like *Report on Probability A* have been continuously reprinted – to my surprise, for many of my books had to be fought for on their first appearance.

My relationship with fandom was not always smooth. Given the freedom to write, one must be wild and free. Carnell's reception of 'The Failed Men' in no way discouraged me. I wrote whole novels he could not abide. And by then he had become my literary agent. He thought *Dark Light Years* disgusting and *Report on Probability A* incomprehensible. *Probability A* marked my commitment to bringing art and artistic concerns into SF. But fans heartily disliked the book. When *Probability A* was followed a little later by the Acid Head War stories, also in *New Worlds*, and when they appeared in novel form as *Barefoot in the Head*, fury broke out, and I was practically drummed out of the regiment. Fresh fury when my history of SF, *Billion Year Spree*, appeared; evidently I had not toed the party line. My history is civilised, intelligent, and entertaining. The comments I received were not.

Writing at that period had not devoured my life. For us, England was a sunny place. Hilary Rubinstein, Victor Gollancz's nephew, bought a partnership in the oldest literary agency, A.P. Watt, and I joined. Feeling that it was increasingly impossible to write SF, I turned to ordinary fiction and, over the seventies, wrote three novels about Horatio Stubbs, whose career parallels mine in some respects. They were *The Hand-Reared Boy*, *A Soldier Erect*, and *A Rude Awakening*. The first two topped the best-seller list, and I enjoyed my meed of fame. The third got nowhere. It was my Sumatra novel. At last I had written it, thirty years after leaving those steamy shores; perhaps the communiqué arrived a little late.

Margaret and I have lived in several houses. We enjoy the change of ambience. Jasmine House was a lovely thatched Tudor cottage, near Oxford but seemingly isolated. We have always resisted the lure of living in London, or the equally strong attraction of escaping swingeing British taxes by living abroad.

After Jasmine came our favourite house, Heath House at Southmoor, a darling place where all the top floor was my study. We were away from other houses and could have huge noisy summer parties outside in the courtyard. There were lots of friends around, some good, some bad. We were quite trendy; at one time, tiring of our first names, we attempted to persuade people to use our middle names, Chris and Wilson. Only my old friend Anthony Price, now also a successful writer, obliged for long.

First Timothy, at whose birth I was present through what was a long ordeal for Margaret. Clive was glad it was a boy; Wendy said,

'Please make the next one a girl for me.' Margaret obliged – to such an extent that Charlotte was born on the morning of Wendy's tenth birthday. Charlotte has her sister's sanguine temperament. When watching the TV weather chart with a promise of snow about, she cried (age six): 'Goodee – sleet!' She is now doing European Business Studies with French.

My mother fell ill when I was at a conference in Sicily. Fortunately Margaret was around. I returned on the Monday to find mother barely conscious; but the doctor was so optimistic that I was scarcely more than concerned. At the time, I was Chairman of the Committee of Management of the Society of Authors. I had turned the society into a mess. That afternoon, just as I was preparing to get on the platform with the AGM report, one of the Society women told me (against Margaret's instructions) that Margaret had phoned through to say my mother had died. It was a good moment to practise soldiering on.

By mother's bedside lay the last book I had bought her. She wanted a Dickens. I chose *Hard Times*, which she had not read. I regretted that I had not made a more cheerful choice. Inside the copy were sheets of paper with the last word games she had been playing to keep herself amused. I still have them.

Something of this event and this time I wrote into my non-SF novel, *Life in the West*. That book did well in Britain, and was chosen by Anthony Burgess as one of his '99 Best Novels since 1939.' This study of thought and feeling was published ten years later in the United Studies.

We moved outside Oxford again, to a lovely stone house, three centuries old, near Woodstock. In its garden was a marvellous heated swimming pool, our delight. Timothy and Charlotte spent a whole summer in the water. But disaster struck us at Orchard House. We had accrued massive tax debts, through the inefficiency of our accountants, which suddenly became due. The British economy was going down the drain yet again. There was no money. My name in the States, where it had once stood higher than in

England, was down to zero. We had to sell up and move back to a smaller house in North Oxford.

So it goes, as Vonnegut used to say. At least we were near to my Aunt Dorothy, who had shared her house with my mother. We could keep an eye on her. By constant work, we dug ourselves out of the financial hole we were in. Although I seem to have written a great deal, some of our happiest times have been while there is a novel 'up the go', as they put it. There is always pleasure in coming down in the morning to a new sheet of paper, new possibilities, new opportunities to surprise the world and oneself.

About this time, I contacted PVF's (Post Viral Fatigue Syndrome). Hethnaery, decline of libido. Loss of short-term memory are some of the symptoms of which the latter is by far the most scary. Like looking on the edge of a mist-filled abyss.

In the summer of 1984, when *Helliconia* was finished, we sold our North Oxford house and bought another mansion we could not, by any realistic accountancy, afford. But it was love at first sight with Woodlands. We are back outside Oxford, with trees round about and a copse at the bottom of the garden. There's space to breathe; architects and craftsmen cared about the building of the house back in 1907, before the First World War, when the world changed. We shall not always need such a large house, but at present we have the excuse.

My tortured interior life of long ago is remembered only when I sketch in a reconstruction here. I even got rid of God, that old spectre from East Dereham or what I think I believe. He has haunted my novels as he has me. But in *Helliconia* I worked my way through to what I really believe.

Much of that new-found belief is grounded in a complex response to nature, and the workings of the planet. The scientist Jim Lovelock, in his book *Gaia,* expresses beautifully the way in which living species form part of a self-regulating system which keeps Earth's biosphere habitable for its tremendous diversity of life. We all, before we are born, have to work our way up to

232

consciousness from molecular levels of being. After life, we shall sink back to them again.

Standing among the trees in our copse as dark comes on, I sense with my entire being the presence of Gaia. We are in kinship – in league with – all else that lives in nature, including the invisible microscopic life which in total far outweighs all visible living things. We are not eternal. Seventy-odd years and we are spent: consciousness is too delicate a balancing act to endure. But we are composed of things that are eternal. Part of us has never died.

For more of this kind of mysticism, you must consult the three volumes of *Helliconia* where the argument is better, because less briefly, deployed. To worry about death is useless. But by worrying about life, we can shape ourselves, at least for a while, into what we want and need to be.

The *New York Times* book critic, Gerald Jonas, concluded a full page of praise for *Helliconia* with the words, 'I would say that Mr Aldiss is now in competition with no one but himself.' Welcome praise. But aren't writers always in competition only with themselves?

Part of that competition has been to take my own reveue on the road. My inspired media agent Frank Hatherby, put *SF Blues* together from my writing poems that shines novels, all clearly dramatised. With my cherished fellow actors, Ken Campbell and Petronilla Whitfield, we have toured England.

My latest novel, *Remembrance Day*, will appear in 1992. I have hopes for it. Already it exists. As usual not all characters speak English. While I was writing it, a woman asked me what it was about. 'Mysterious', I told her, the subject of all novels. Our complaint to god for each other.

What do my books, what does my life amount to? I always wished to be someone. I felt myself less than the dust. My wish was to help, to reach out generously, to give generously. As I was impatient with East Dereham and the narrowness of its mores, later I became impatient with England. The impatience extends to my writing. Why is it not better, harsher?

Jules Verne ran away to sea, but was taken home by his father before the vessel sailed. He wrote novels of travel for the rest of his life.

It cannot be said that my fiction does not take large subjects. The truths it tells are generally symbolic ones. It is not literal, though it uses an abbreviated realism to convey its inferences. Its closeness – or its distance – from the events which inspired it is unimportant. It forms a kind of substitute reality, a gloss on real experience. It seeks to crystallise.

Perhaps for readers it works this way. It does for me. Only after I had completed *A Rude Awakening* was I able to return to Sumatra. Only after I had worked for many years on *Helliconia* was I able to walk on the ground which inspired the name, Mount Helicon, in Greece.

And for a writer, his writing has also a more direct, less mystical function.

My wish was always somehow to restore the scattered family – an impossible ambition. I am a rare writer. For many years, I have written what I chose, defying editors and fate, a poor man's intellectual, famous but only slightly famous, with nothing of my work filmed or televised. If no great sums of money have come my way, I have kept my family from starving.

Now I read about the Shelley circle. Margaret and I exchange Mary Shelley's collected letters, a life of Claire Clairmont, essays, Shelley's poems, Byron's letters. An intensely creative group of personalities, too soon destroyed by fate. Yet their interest lives on. That is something to leave behind.

Aware that I have survived in an age when so many millions of lives have been shattered by war, I must not emphasise either my difficulties or my successes. Exile means a loss of home. But I built my home in writing, and achieved security there, both for myself and my family, in 'the Republic of Letters and the Kingdom of Dreams.'

As to the durable qualities of those writings – they were built to last in these transitory times. Whether they will do so is not up to me to judge, but to the Twenty-First Century.

www.ingramcontent.com/pod-product-compliance
Ingram Content Group UK Ltd.
Pitfield, Milton Keynes, MK11 3LW, UK
UKHW022302180325
456436UK00003B/182